SOUR APPLES

A Novel For Those Who Hate to Read

Paul Jantzen

Black Rose Writing | Texas

ISBN: 978-1-68513-481-5
PUBLISHED BY BLACK ROSE WRITING
www.blackrosewriting.com

Printed in the United States of America
Suggested Retail Price (SRP) $19.95

Sour Apples is printed in Garamond Premier Pro

To My Mom

PRAISE FOR
SOUR APPLES

"Sour Apples is a delightful read that captures the essence of childhood with warmth and authenticity. Paul Jantzen's narrative invites readers to reminisce about their own youthful adventures and the timeless thrill of simple pleasures."
–The Literary Titan

"Sour Apples...It's captivating and nostalgic. Jantzen's brilliant storytelling, combined with rich and detailed depictions of scenes, takes your mind to the suspense and adventures that very often lead to hilarious situations."
–Alex Ndirangu, *Reader's Favorite*

Equal parts nostalgia, smooth prose, and good, old-fashioned story-telling! Author Paul Jantzen channels the mind of a ten-year-old boy, giving his adventures substance and emotional weight. A marvelous coming-of-age tale!
~Brian Kaufman, author of *A Persistent Echo.*

"This charming and nostalgic book, written simply with forthright prose and gems of observation, drips with youthful energy and boisterous high jinks."
–Gojan Nikolich author of *The Gopher King: A Dark Comedy*

"Hilarious coming-of-age tale with *A Christmas Story* vibe. Thoroughly enjoyable, it's a rollicking tale of the adventures and misadventures of an engaging boy perched precariously on the threshold of adolescence."
–Bill Sweitzer, author of *Doves In A Tempest*

"A Grand Slice of Americana. Paul Jantzen's *Sour Apples* is everything a boy's tale should be – adventurous, romantic, earthy, at times poignant, and relentlessly funny. Evocative and blessed with the spirit of Tom Sawyer, *Sour Apples* is a coming-of-age novel that is both a wonderful read and a rich evocation of an earlier, not-so-simple time."
–Michael Hartnett, author of *Windmill Bluff*

"Reminiscent of classic films such as *The Sandlot* and *The Goonies,* this series of entertaining coming-of-age stories offers a nostalgic must-read account of childhood. It encapsulates the essence of that bygone era, complete with the inevitable bruised shins, hearts, and egos that accompany the journey to adulthood."
–Troy Hollan, author of *Clucked*

"Perfect for middle-grade readers, *Sour Apple* serves up a slice of adventure and imagination."
–Lena Gibson, author of *The Train Hoppers* series and fifth-grade teacher

SOUR APPLES

CHAPTER ONE

-THE LIBRARY-

Jimmy lay with his back flat on the floor of his tree fort. His feet dangled dangerously over the edge some fifteen feet above the ground. He tossed a baseball straight up and caught it as it came back down. His new baseball glove was stiff and needed breaking in before the upcoming Little League baseball season. But, honestly, he was more worried he wouldn't be ready for the new season than he was about his glove being broken in. He wanted to be a great pitcher. Deep down, he knew he was not.

He tossed the ball up again, and it struck a branch above him, causing it to carom towards the edge of the fort on its way down. Jimmy lurched for it and caught the ball just in time—in time for the ball, not in time for Jimmy. His brief life flashed before his eyes as he rolled off and out of the tree fort, rapidly hurtling towards the ground.

Luckily, he pin-balled his way through three tree branches before catching himself. Maybe ten feet from the ground now, he held on for dear life. He couldn't look to see if his mother had seen him. But he figured if she had, he'd have heard her by now. Dangling by his pitching arm, he weighed his options. His arm, at that moment, was all that stood between him keeping his fort and his mother burning it to the ground. Gathering his courage, he dangled until he had the strength to pull himself up and hook his legs around the branch.

His heart racing, he pulled himself up branch by branch and back onto the fort floor. Glancing toward the house, he double-checked to make sure his mother hadn't seen. No curtains fluttered, no squawking that he could hear. He was safe for now.

Once he caught his breath, he tossed the ball up a few more times until he was bored with it. Sighing, he sat up and took in his surroundings. His fort was built around an old walnut tree, as if the tree was growing straight up through the middle of it. Next to the walnut tree was an old crabapple tree. The fort was a simple structure with a plywood floor and a handrail all the way around. His favorite part was the trap door used to enter and exit. A rope hung from underneath just next to the trapdoor.

Jimmy was ten years old and having such a place just for him was amazing. If not needing to be elsewhere, he could be found in his fort. This was not just some clubhouse. That meaning would be wasted on such a fantastic structure. His lair was a sanctuary. He spent many a day, even a few nights, out here navigating his world, solving his ten-year-old problems, and imagining worlds more brilliant than his own. Why would his mother want to take that away?

Jimmy felt a cool rush of air and a cloud sweep over him as he stared up at the sky. He felt an odd tug in his mind. The fort faded, and he found himself standing on the mound at Yankee stadium. How did he get there? He glanced around. There were 45,000 screaming fans. He thought it was a little odd that Yankee stadium had a roof now. He realized even more that the roof looked like the inside of a circus tent. Where exactly was he? Gazing down, he saw he was wearing pinstriped baseball pants. That would be a nightmare for any true Red Sox fan. But looking further, he noticed he was wearing large clown shoes. He was struggling but knew what he needed to do, so he concentrated on getting the sign. The catcher was calling for the fastball. But, wait, why was a giraffe standing in the batter's box? Was Jimmy pitching in the circus? Was he the circus? Or was he just a clown? He went into his windup...

"Jimmy," he heard the crowd yell, and then again. "Jimmy," but this time he found himself back in his fort. "Jimmy," his mother called.

Jimmy peered over the edge of his fort to see his mother staring up, seeming to be a little nervous that he was so close to the edge without a care.

"Hi, Mom," Jimmy said.

"Come on down, it's time to go to the library," she said.

"Okay," he said. He was not happy about the news, but it was no surprise. It was a Saturday ritual in Walnut Creek. Every child that ever grew up there was dragged, against their will, on a Saturday to the Main Street library. It might sound like another library existed somewhere in the town, but that was not the case. In fact, there was only one of everything there. Walnut Creek was home to one courthouse, one filling station, one greasy diner, one hardware store, one department store, one barbershop, and one Jimmy Hamilton. It was a small town.

Jimmy opened the trapdoor and, with ease and confidence, managed the labyrinth of rope and rungs to reach the ground. His mother's body seemed to relax slightly once his feet hit the ground, but it was obvious she was upset. He sidled up next to her as they walked to the car.

"Mom, why do we gotta go to the library every Saturday?" he whined. The look of bitter lemons across his face did not suit his mother.

"The library is a wonderful place to explore and expand your mind. So much is out there in this world for you, Jimmy. It's all waiting for you to find it, honey." She glanced back with slight disdain at the tree fort. "You won't find it hiding up in a tree."

"I don't even like reading," he said, folding his arms defiantly.

His mother fixed him with a stare, her hands on her hips, "Reading is good for you, Jimmy. It generates-"

Jimmy interrupted, "If reading is so great, then why are all the books at the library free?" and he nodded, smiling smugly because he knew he was right. Suddenly and without provocation, at least in Jimmy's mind, his mother snatched him from where he stood and shoved him into their car. Jimmy was so unhappy he failed to notice the moving van across the street.

"Look, Jimmy, someone's moving into the Randell's old house," his mother said with a smile in an apparent attempt to brighten her son's mood. But ten-year-old Jimmy was busy holding his breath in protest of being dragged to the library, yet again. He let out a gigantic sigh of air and snuck a glance at the moving van, trying not to let his mother see him. "Maybe they have a son your age you can play with."

"Just so long as it ain't no girls. We have enough of them around here," Jimmy said with a sour expression on his face as if he just bit into a crab apple. It was something Jimmy deeply believed at the time, but after that summer, he would never utter those words again.

Jimmy forgot he was supposed to be holding his breath and instead pressed his nose against the glass, watching the world go past. It was a short drive to town, but it allowed plenty of time to ponder why his life was so much like biting into a sour apple.

When they arrived at the library, Jimmy, like always, looked around for his friends, but he could see no other children. Was this library some sort of geological oddity? Did it have a secret labyrinth to sort the children to keep the high jinks to a minimum? Jimmy was sure there was something magical about the place, but not the desirable kind.

Jimmy thought of grabbing a stack of any old books from the shelves but remembered the last time he did that. He was pretty sure his mother was onto him when he showed her *World History Part III*. He tried to throw her a confident look, as if he had read the first two parts, but he wasn't fooling anyone. The second book was *Moby Dick*, a more reasonable pick, but Jimmy's mom challenged him to read the title out loud, and he burst into laughter. And finally, he had presented two romance novels, both clad with voluptuous women on the covers, neither of which was Jimmy's type. Thinking better of it, Jimmy slumped off to the children's section and found two detective books, an instructional book on how to pitch, and lastly, a book titled, *Make Your Fort Impenetrable From Your Enemy*.

He was so proud of himself. Jimmy knew his mother would be very impressed with his selections. She shuffled through the books he presented her, smiling at first, then said adamantly, "OH NO, I don't think so." And Jimmy left the library with three books.

Jimmy hunkered down in the backseat of their car and went back to staring out the window. As they passed the park, he saw what appeared to be a gnarly old tree except it had a human face and was lying on a park bench. That it was a person never even registered to Jimmy.

Instead, Jimmy went back to brooding about the uncertainty of his lair, his castle. He wished he had never seen that book about defending your fort because every time he reminded his mother of the fort; she seemed to get even more incensed. He should have known better. Why couldn't she understand? Did she not know what that fort meant to him?

Jimmy would do whatever it took to protect his fort, even if it meant battling the meanest monster or the fiercest dragon. At that thought, the backseat quickly transformed, and he was staring down the barrel of his walnut stock rifle. Jimmy was in a fort he did not recognize. Nor did he recognize the enemy. He would fight to his death to protect what was his, though. The enemy was in his sights. He didn't even need a scope at that distance. Inhaling calmly, then holding his breath, he cleared his mind and pulled the trigger.

Amid cheers, Jimmy laid his rifle against the fortress wall and surveyed the remains of the fierce, bloodthirsty dragon with its accompanying army strewn across the field of battle. They won the battle. The victory was his. He nodded to his comrades. But...but what about next time, or even the time after that? The thought made Jimmy pause. Shrugging, he did what most boys would do at that age. He decided he would worry about it another day. One battle at a time, he figured.

His friends scurried out of the fort to collect any weapons and valuables they could scavenge off their enemy as Jimmy contemplated another victory. That wasn't the first time they would have to go to those lengths to protect their lair. Jimmy may have only been 10 years old, but that was just one of many battles he fought to fend off his enemy from taking his citadel. Most of those encounters were of the imaginary kind and fought with stick guns and plastic swords. Then there were the real battles.

The year was 1975, and that summer would prove to be epic for Jimmy Hamilton, imaginary or not.

CHAPTER TWO

—KEVIN—

When Mrs. Hamilton pulled her station wagon back into the driveway of their house, she hastily ran inside with an armful of books.

"Mo'om?" Jimmy moaned as if that word, mom, was two syllables and a question.

"What is it, Jimmy?" she asked.

"Didn't you see the new neighbors as you pulled into the house?"

"I did," she said as she made her way to the powder room for a splash of make-up.

"Well, aren't you going to say hello?" Jimmy asked. He really hoped they had a boy his age to play catch with. He hastily grabbed his glove and ball just in case.

"Yes, dear, in a moment. Your mother needs to put her face on," she said.

Jimmy knit his brow. "You didn't have your face on when you went to the library?" His mother smiled at him adoringly.

"Of course I did. You wouldn't want me to scare all the library patrons, would you?"

"I wouldn't care." Then Jimmy imagined a faceless monster, his mother, running through the aisles of the library scaring children, mayhem and screaming ensuing. Then he remembered what his mother always said of the library. It was where marvels came to life, with a dancing sky of the most beautiful colors, ghosts that roamed the land, and trees that came alive. Jimmy paused in deep thought. "It might be cool." Maybe she was a monster.

Jimmy's mom reached out and patted his head. "Sometimes I wish you could stay young and innocent forever."

"What, Mom?"

"Oh, nothing," she said. "I'll be ready in a moment. Don't disappear on me."

On her way out of the house, she grabbed Jimmy and a plate of cookies. Jimmy wanted to meet the new neighbors as well, but by the way his mother was dragging him, one would have thought he was going back to the library.

"When did you make those, Mom?" Jimmy asked as they approached the woman in the driveway across the street. Jimmy's mom looked a bit embarrassed as she tried to hush her son without being detected.

"Hi, I'm Kathy Hamilton," Jimmy's mom said. "Welcome to the neighborhood."

"Hi, I'm Janet, Janet Spencer," the woman replied. Then she looked haphazardly around before beckoning for her child. Janet seemed to be in her thirties, just like Jimmy's mom, and they each owned at least one child. She might be a good friend for his mom, a fellow "housewife," as his mom called herself. But what about a baseball buddy for him? Jimmy tried hard not to cross his fingers.

"Honey, come meet the Hamiltons." Jimmy noticed a young, disheveled girl emerge from the garage.

"Ah man! They do have a girl," Jimmy moaned with a sour look on his face, much to the dismay of Janet Spencer.

"This is my *son*, Kevin," she announced peculiarly. Jimmy guessed it was because of his comment.

"Hi, Kevin," Jimmy's mom said kindly, "this is my son, Jimmy."

"Hi."

"Hi." When that was over, both boys withdrew their formal demeanor.

"You're not a girl," Jimmy informed Kevin.

"Neither are you," Kevin growled back at him. Jimmy stepped forward as if to challenge a fight, but his mother quickly intervened and swept her son to the side. Kathy shot Mrs. Spencer an apologetic look.

"Well, it looks like our boys will get along just fine," she said, raising her eyebrows. "Bye, Janet."

"Bye, maybe Jimmy would like to do something with Kevin later?" Janet said.

"Jimmy would like that," Mrs. Hamilton said on Jimmy's behalf.

"Kevin needs to go for a haircut before he does anything," Mrs. Spencer said while Mrs. Hamilton just smiled politely. Jimmy thought this meant one of two things. It was code for going to the library. After all, it was Saturday, or indeed Kevin was actually going for a haircut. Either way, it was cruel and unusual punishment for a child, and Jimmy quickly realized Mrs. Spencer would fit nicely in the neighborhood.

"The barbershop is right next to the library," Mrs. Hamilton told Janet.

Kevin immediately had Jimmy's sympathy. He was likely to get a double whammy.

"Good luck," Mrs. Hamilton said as she swept Jimmy toward home. "You were supposed to be nice," she said discreetly.

"I was," Jimmy cried in his defense. Jimmy's arm got an extra tug, and a wallop to his behind followed. Kevin's eyes widened from across the street. Jimmy didn't make a sound, not until he was in the house, anyway.

Once inside, he was sent to his room to read, a form of punishment in Jimmy's mind. He slunk to his room, knowing his mother was in no mood to watch over him. Jimmy occasionally dropped his baseball on the floor, but his mother appeared to ignore it. He shifted his focus and was quiet—until he wasn't.

"What was that? What are you doing? It sounded like an earthquake coming from this room!" Mrs. Hamilton yelled as she entered his room to find Jimmy laying on the floor with a baseball in one hand and his baseball glove on the other.

Jimmy sensed her anger and quickly showed her his book about pitching. "I was trying to learn," he said sheepishly, shrugging. Her face went from tight to accepting, and she smiled before leaving him alone again.

Jimmy periodically checked outside his bedroom window for any sign of Kevin. When he finally emerged, Kevin was riding his bike outside of his house. "Mo'om, can I go out and play with Kevin? I think he's home from his haircut," Jimmy said. At least the kid he saw didn't have long hair.

"All right, but you behave. I don't want to hear you've been fighting with him," Jimmy's mother said. Whether she was convinced, he agreed and was out the front door in a flash.

"Hey," Jimmy said as Kevin rounded on his driveway and came to a stop.

"Hey," he replied.

"Did you have to go to the library?" Jimmy asked sympathetically.

"No, but I'm sure my mom has it planned soon," Kevin said. That only confirmed Jimmy's suspicions of the adult world. Kevin wasn't even from around there, yet he too had been dragged to a library wherever he was from.

"Wanna play catch? I got a new glove I'm trying to break in," Jimmy said.

"Sure, I'll get my glove," Kevin said, and both boys darted back towards their houses. They returned shortly, gloves in hand. To Jimmy's astonishment and joy, Kevin was sporting a catcher's mitt, and Jimmy was in heaven.

"Are you a real catcher?" Jimmy beamed at this new possibility. His new friend was a real catcher, something every true great pitcher must have. Jimmy had only known of one person who owned a catcher's mitt before, and that was a coach. For a kid to have one was just simply unheard of. This was truly a great day for Jimmy Hamilton.

"No, not really. I want to be one though," Kevin said with the same aspiration Jimmy had of being a pitcher one day. Jimmy's enthusiasm waned slightly because of this news, but then he realized he wasn't a great pitcher yet either. They would become great together, Jimmy determined.

"You ready?" Jimmy asked.

"Sure," Kevin said, holding out his glove.

Jimmy began his windup with a very high and unusual leg kick, which sent him off balance, much like in his bedroom, starting a chain reaction. His other three limbs flailed about wildly as the ball left his hand. The ball screamed toward his new catcher in a blur. Jimmy was anticipating the pop of the ball against leather, but instead, it glanced off Kevin's mitt and caught him square in his eye. Kevin started screaming that high-pitched cry of pure pain as he turned and ran into his house. Jimmy, wary of his mother's reaction, slumped back and ran into his own house.

"I thought you went to play with Kevin," Jimmy's mom said.

"I did," Jimmy said.

When he dragged himself across the living room and plopped himself down in a chair, she followed him with her eyes.

"Did you get into a fight with that boy already?" she added.

"No, Mo'om," he cried in his defense. He sensed her anger growing and soon backed his bottom away from his mother's hand, but her eyes continued to bore holes in him.

"Then what happened?"

"We were playing catch, and the ball missed his mitt and hit him right in the eye," Jimmy said.

"Is he all right?" she said worriedly, jumping to her feet.

"He ran into his house," Jimmy said. His mother stared at him intently for a moment, apparently trying to decide whether she believed him. When his mother hiked him up by his one arm, like she had done so many times before, his free hand went to cover his bottom. Instead, she hauled him across the street and rang the bell.

"Hi, Janet, is Kevin okay?" Mrs. Hamilton asked. Jimmy looked guilty, even though he had done nothing wrong. Kevin appeared in the hallway behind his mother. He was sporting a huge ice pack on his face. The little of his face that was visible from behind the bag was red and puffy, as if he had been crying the whole time.

"Sorry, Kevin," Jimmy said as he pushed forward from behind his mother's leg. Kevin made his way to the doorway and faced Jimmy.

"That's okay, I shoulda caught that ball," Kevin said, slightly muffled from behind the big bag of ice. Jimmy was certain he should have caught it too, just not with his face.

"Thank you, Jimmy, for apologizing, but it wasn't your fault," Mrs. Spencer told him. "These things happen."

"Can I see your eye?" Jimmy said, a little too enthusiastically for his mother.

"Behave," his mother said. Kevin pulled the ice from his face and displayed the makings of a very nice black eye.

"Wow!" was all Jimmy could say. Kevin's mom returned the ice bag back up to his face. "You wanna do something?" Jimmy asked.

"No, Jimmy, I think you boys have done enough for now. Kevin needs to rest and keep that ice on his eye. You boys can play later," Mrs. Spencer answered.

"Okay, maybe he can come over, and we can play in my tree fort?" Jimmy suggested. His mother did not take kindly to her son's flippant attitude to his friend's injury, but she probably disliked hearing "my tree fort" come out of Jimmy's mouth more.

Once home, his mother suggested once again, "Why don't you go up and read?"

With no better options, Jimmy sat alone in his room, passing the time, mostly daydreaming. The baseball season would be there soon enough. He was going to be a champion. It just might take a while.

After enough time passed, he felt he was safe to venture back into the world without his mom saying anything. He checked one more time for his new friend out of his window. Not seeing anything, he headed to his backyard and to his tree fort.

Jimmy climbed up a makeshift ladder, which consisted merely of wooden planks nailed to the walnut tree. It was primitive but did the job, and that was all that really mattered to a ten-year-old boy. Halfway up the planks was a rope with knots tied at every foot and a half or so for grabbing while he climbed up the rope. The rope led to the trapdoor, which he had to open while dangling from the rope. It was not a simple task to overcome, but it was the fort's best defense, especially from girls.

Jimmy was slightly out of breath from climbing, so after he closed the trapdoor, he just laid on his back for a while, gazing at the sky. Jimmy was safe up in his citadel—a place with no girls, no mothers, no libraries or books, nope, nothing like that. All that was up there was Jimmy and his imagination, and sometimes his baseball glove.

Nestled up against the walnut tree, draped along the tree fort, was the old and gnarled crabapple tree. Jimmy had all the ammunition he needed from that tree to chase off any animals or, even worse, girls. Jimmy would never actually throw anything at a girl, but he had no problem using the neighbor's cat for a target or even a squirrel. Both animals proved difficult to mark, but it was fun for Jimmy to pretend, and it was always a moral victory to drive the enemy into retreat.

Sometimes, Jimmy just practiced his pitching using apples as baseballs and a tire swing, which hung from a nearby tree, as the strike zone. He couldn't hit that either, and it always left a pile of crab apples for his father to mow over. That was usually a sight Jimmy enjoyed watching from his tree fort. His father never passed on an opportunity to send a few apples from under the lawnmower at the neighbor's cat.

But that was fun for another day. For the time being, Jimmy just let his mind drift away until he found himself pitching in the major leagues. It was the bottom of the ninth and Jimmy stood tall but worn atop the mound at Fenway Park. There were two outs and two on with the Yankees' best hitter up to the plate. Jimmy's arm was sore, but his team did not pull the southpaw for a fresh arm. No, he was their man, and they went to the well one more time. Jimmy's face was expressionless as he got the sign from his catcher. The catcher wanted the heat, fastball on the outside corner. Jimmy nodded and then went into his stretch. He set himself.

"Jimmy," someone called out to him. He stepped off the mound and looked to his infielders. They stared blankly at him. They hadn't called his name. "Jimmy!" he heard again. Jimmy leapt to his feet in surprise. The voice came from under his tree fort.

"Uh oh, a girl," he said and prepared for a defensive assault.

"Jimmy, it's me, Kevin. What ya doing?" Jimmy peered over the rail that ran the entire edge of his fort.

"Oh, hey, Kevin, come on up," Jimmy said and then ducked out of sight. He opened the trap door and watched to see if Kevin was going to manage the passageway up to his haven. Kevin eyed the ascent and began climbing. He struggled as anyone new would and kissed the walnut tree twice, but was soon sitting next to Jimmy in his lair. Jimmy was so relieved. His mother was probably watching the whole time.

"Did you make this fort yourself?" Kevin asked, looking around, obviously impressed.

"No, I wish. It was here when we moved in," Jimmy confessed. Jimmy still took pride in the ownership, having a certain air about him, as Kevin admired every board and nail that made up his great fort.

"It's still real nice. I wish I had one," Kevin said with a slight, self-pitied tone. But then he went right back to admiring the fort.

"You can play in this one anytime you want," Jimmy told him.

"Really? Thanks, man." Jimmy played it off like it was no big deal.

"Unless, of course, I have a girl up here," Jimmy said slyly. Kevin just looked at him and Jimmy at Kevin.

"Eeeeewwww!" they said in unison, then fell back on the floor laughing.

"You ever kissed a girl before?" Kevin asked boldly. Jimmy appeared as if he was going to throw up.

"No," he said, and after a brief pause, he added, "You?"

"No… gross," Kevin said with a similar look. They went back to lying on the floor of the tree house and began staring at the sky.

"How's your eye?" Jimmy asked, thankful he had a way to change the subject.

"Feels okay. I see out it the same. How's it look?"

"Wicked, man." Jimmy said, leering at the black and blue stain. Kevin smiled. Getting a black eye as a ten-year-old was always cool. The stories and images that go with such an incident far exceed any truths spoken about it. And though it didn't seem to carry with it any legendary importance, catching a Jimmy Hamilton fastball in the eye and living to tell about it would one day immortalize him.

CHAPTER THREE
-A BLOODY LIP TO MATCH-

It was truly a great spring day for lying about lazily, with no better place to do it than the tree house. Jimmy and Kevin both wallowed the afternoon away. When the neighbor's cat made its way into Jimmy's backyard, the two boys took aim with crab apples and sent the cat scurrying for cover. When the cat made it to safer ground, the boys scouted for squirrels but came up empty. They must have gotten word from the cat to stay clear. That left the tire swing as the only seemingly worthy target.

"First one to get it through the middle wins," Jimmy suggested.

"Sure," Kevin said.

Jimmy threw first and was wide to the right, but only by a foot or so. Kevin hit the tree that the rope and tire hung from but was still six or seven feet off the mark.

After about eight attempts, Jimmy finally hit the tire, but the apple fell short of going through it. Kevin countered with his best shot yet, hitting the rope the tire was tied to, a feat both boys enjoyed immensely, but still no winner. A nice collection of apples had accumulated just beyond the swing by the time Jimmy finally hit his mark. The apple sailed through the black hole.

"Yes!" He threw both hands up into the air triumphantly.

"Wait, I still get a turn," Kevin insisted.

Jimmy looked at him, his joy momentarily cut short, but quickly realized it wouldn't matter. Kevin couldn't hit his mark with all the apples on the tree.

After a short while, when their arms were tired and their minds bored, they sat back, again thinking just how great that fort really was.

"So, what do ya do when it rains?" Kevin said, looking up at the sky.

"I go inside," Jimmy said, "and then my mom usually makes me read or something."

"We should build a roof," Kevin said.

"My dad wanted to, but my mom didn't," Jimmy said. "She hates this fort. She's always afraid I'm gonna fall out of it and get hurt."

"That would just stink," Kevin added.

"Shoot, I could easily jump from up here, so I'm not afraid of falling out," and Jimmy stood up and peered over the rail. When Kevin joined him, both boys seemed apprehensive. Neither boy was about to jump.

"I should get home," Kevin interrupted the silence. "I should, you know, check on my mom—the move and all."

Kevin waited for Jimmy to open the trapdoor and then began his descent. That first moment you abandon the surety of the wooden structure for an old, tattered rope can get your heart racing, but that was the fun in it. Kevin slid a little on the rope and that put him in a swinging motion. He managed to reach the bottom of the rope, but could not find his footing for the wooden slats. Still swinging slightly and leading with his head, he bounced off the walnut tree. Jimmy watched in horror.

Kevin dangled for what seemed like hours but was merely seconds before he let go of the rope and dropped to the ground. He moaned a little, got up, and ran off. Jimmy could hear Kevin's crying fade away until the front door of Kevin's house closed behind him. Then all was quiet.

"Crap! Not again," Jimmy swore. He made his way down the rope, then onto the wooden slats, where he finally jumped to the ground before heading into his own house.

"I'm going up to my room and read," Jimmy hollered on his way past his mother.

"Okay," she said cheerfully before she must have realized what he had said. "What? Wait a minute." And on that note, he started up the stairs. "Come back here, Jimmy."

"What's the matter?" he said, feigning innocence.

She glared at him for only a moment.

"Jimmy?"

"I swear it was an accident."

She sighed, but before she could reach him, he lifted his arm up for her to take. He knew the routine. He just wished she wouldn't pull so hard on his pitching arm. They were at the Spencer's front door in no time. The whole way over, Jimmy was sure his mother was going to cut down the tree fort, and if she couldn't cut it down herself, she'd burn it down, walnut tree and all.

"Hi, Janet," Mrs. Hamilton said with a look of exasperated concern. "Is Kevin all right?"

"Oh, he'll be fine. It's just a swollen lip," Janet said.

"Thank goodness—what are we going to do with these boys?" Mrs. Hamilton twisted her grimace into a smile, but to Jimmy, it looked more like his mom had gas. Jimmy and Kevin started giggling.

"Boys will be boys," Janet sighed.

"So what happened?" Mrs. Hamilton asked, "because this one is not saying."

Jimmy thought this was his cue to smile, and did just that, but it wasn't his cue, and he was met with an awful leer from his mother.

"Kevin says he fell from...," Janet started to say, but paused at the painful look growing on Jimmy's face. "The...," his look worsened, "tire swing." Jimmy looked up and let out a huge sigh of relief, realizing not only did Kevin protect the future of the tree fort, but he saved Jimmy's butt as well. Jimmy nodded to his new best friend.

CHAPTER FOUR

-INCORRIGIBLE-

The sun crept up to the horizon and, without hesitation, broke that fine line between night and day until a beam of sunshine blanketed the sleepy little town of Walnut Creek, starting a whole new day. The best thing about the day, at least to Jimmy Hamilton, was that the library was closed. He was, however, not overly enthusiastic about Sunday mornings, much like Saturday mornings, because of one thing.

"Go up and get dressed for church," Jimmy's mom said. Jimmy made a face and excused himself from the last of his pile of pancakes his mother had made and climbed the stairs to his room. Jimmy cared little for the things his mom did, things she encouraged or demanded of him. He hated church like he hated the library, and having to dress up for it didn't help. What was next, broccoli for dinner? Jimmy hated broccoli, too. He could have saved a lot of kids from going to bed without dessert if only he had been the one to first taste broccoli. Broccoli would have been deemed poisonous. Jimmy was that kind of hero.

"Pay attention," his mother said as mass at St. Anthony's Catholic Church was finally coming to an end. It was simply torture for Jimmy. That was certain.

Back home, he flew up the stairs, tearing out of his Sunday best for a pair of old tattered sweatpants and a t-shirt. He trampled back down the stairs with his baseball mitt in tow, wildly excited.

"Where's Dad?"

"In the backyard," his mother said. Jimmy tore off through the kitchen and out the back door in search of his father.

"Dad! —Dad!" he hollered. Finally, his dad appeared from around the corner of the house wielding a large woven bushel basket overflowing with crab apples. Each step he took, another apple would roll off the pile, causing him to jerk in response to save it, sending more apples cascading to the ground.

"What is it, son?" his father asked. Jimmy's dad was lean and muscular, quite the athlete in his time, and Jimmy thought the world of him.

"Whada ya doing?" Jimmy asked, having forgotten why he came rushing out in the yard. Jimmy's father continued walking as the pile of apples slowly got smaller.

"Just cleaning up the crab apples in the yard," his father replied.

"How come?"

"Your mother," his father sighed. "She wants the yard cleaned up a little better. I think she wants to have the neighbors over soon."

"What about the cat?"

"No, I don't think she wants to have the cat over," his father chuckled. Jimmy just loved his father's ribbing.

"No, you know what I mean," Jimmy said, "How can you launch crab apples at the cat if the crab apples are all gone?" It was a weekly game of cat and apple, which saw all parties involved willing to take part, even the cat, believe it or not.

"Yeah, —well your mother doesn't want us doing that anymore," he replied. "She says I'm incorrigible."

Jimmy smiled at this news, even though he didn't know what that meant. He was proud of everything his father was, and he was now incorrigible.

"You're incorrigible!" Jimmy said proudly with a slight laugh. His father smiled.

"Can you use these for your fort?" Jimmy's father asked.

"Yeah—sure, but they'll just end up all over the yard again," Jimmy explained.

"That's okay," his father replied with a twinkle in his eye, and they began hoisting up bushel after bushel of apples until Jimmy had an army's supply of ammo in his fort.

"Hey, Dad, can we play catch?" Jimmy lifted his glove for emphasis.

"How 'bout after I get this yard work done," his father said as he ruffled Jimmy's hair and smiled.

"You need some help?" Jimmy said, eagerly.

"No, helping with those apples was enough. Why don't you see if your new friend Kevin is home," his father suggested. "I'm always happy to have your help, but it would be a shame for a young boy to spend his weekend doing yardwork." And he rolled his eyes at Jimmy making it clear he certainly thought it was a shame that he himself had to do so.

Jimmy chuckled. "His mom took him over to sign up for baseball," Jimmy said.

"Oh, —good. Is he the same age as you?"

"Yeah, he's gonna be my catcher," Jimmy said with pride.

"That's great, son! Every great pitcher needs a great catcher."

Jimmy already knew this to be true, but it felt good hearing it from his father. If only his father knew just how bad a catcher Kevin was.

"You sure you don't need any help?" Jimmy was practically pleading now.

"I know what you can do, safeguard me from the neighbor's cat," he said. Jimmy's eyes lit up. He knew just what his father wanted. So, Jimmy climbed up his tree fort's passage and stood sentry against the evil nemesis, Mr. Whiskers. His father was incorrigible.

Quite a while passed before the cat made its way into the yard Jimmy was so carefully protecting. So long in fact, Jimmy had fallen asleep in his fort.

"Jimmy!" his father called. "It's Mr. Whiskers. He's on the near side of the house." Startling awake, Jimmy leapt to his feet and sent a barrage of apples at the wiry cat. When his father joined in, the ruckus was loud enough to draw out Jimmy's mother. That was not good. She rushed outside with her apron still attached to her thin frame and scolded both boys.

"I have a good mind to take that tree fort away," she said in a tone not to be challenged. Jimmy heard her words loud and clear. It would be the worst thing that could happen to him.

"Honey, it's ok, we were just having a little fun. Don't blame the boy," he insisted.

"You! —you are so incorrigible," she yelled waving a spindly finger in the air. Right then, Jimmy did the worst thing he could have possibly done. He laughed at his mother calling his father incorrigible. She turned on Jimmy so fast that before he knew it, he was in his room reading, with the future of the tree house in jeopardy.

Jimmy hadn't been in his room for five minutes when he began hearing mumbled voices through the walls. Those voices were of course his mother and father. His mother was not pleased, and his father, well, he seemed aloof to it all.

"That tree fort has been nothing but trouble for us," his mother said.

"But Kath," his father pleaded. "It's every boy's dream."

"Then he'll just have to dream then. I want it taken down," his mother sternly demanded. A knot formed in the pit of Jimmy's stomach. Then a silence swept through the house that left Jimmy feeling very alone. His father had not put up a good fight to save that fort. It was killing Jimmy inside, and he began to cry.

A knock on the door startled Jimmy, and he quickly dried his tears and opened the door. His mother walked in.

"Hi Mom," he whispered. It was obvious he had been crying.

"Jimmy, your father and I have been talking," his mother said.

"I know."

"Well, your behavior out there was detestable."

"It wasn't incorrigible?" he asked.

"What? Why...actually, yes, it was, but I realize your father put you up to it. Nevertheless, you know better."

"I—" He so wanted to boast that he too was incorrigible.

"Let me finish," she interrupted. "We have decided to give you one more chance with that tree fort. You know I've been against keeping that thing ever since we moved here." Jimmy thought about saying something but quickly decided against it. "There are to be no more incidents regarding the tree fort—no apple wars with the cat next door or with anyone for that matter. And I better not hear about anyone getting hurt because of that thing. Otherwise, the fort comes down. Is that clear?"

"Yes ma'am," he said sullenly but agreeably. Then, as if he had just started listening, he cheered up. His fort was saved. It was not coming down as he had thought. "Thanks Mom," and he beamed at her and gave her a hug. She seemed surprised by his reaction.

CHAPTER FIVE
—CHAD, DAVE, CINDY, AND THE TWINS—

Jimmy spent the rest of that afternoon and the entire evening feeling the same, relieved but worried his fort was in danger of being cut down. But he awoke the next morning feeling an unwavering dreadfulness, reminding him it was Monday—time to go to school. His tree fort woes would have to wait.

"Get up and get ready for school," his mother hollered up. He was still half asleep. Jimmy slowly made his way down to the breakfast table. He was shy one bowl of cereal from heading out to catch the school bus.

"Hey, son," his father said as he tussled Jimmy's hair. "Breakfast for champions, huh?" Jimmy stared down at a bowl of lumpy oatmeal, two orange slices, and a piece of toast.

"Wait until I'm a champion—breakfast will be a bowl of Froot Loops," he said. His father laughed and went back to his newspaper and his cup of coffee. Jimmy's mother shot them both a look of contempt.

"Just eat your breakfast." And Jimmy attempted to do just that. After pushing his oatmeal around, he finished arranging his bowl like some kind of artist. His wizardry was just that. He managed to push the oatmeal up the sides of the bowl, so it appeared he had dug an enormous hole in the mountain of oatmeal he was served. His father watched him carefully from behind the newspaper.

"Don't eat so fast, son," his father added. Had he been so good at his deception to fool even his father? Then Jimmy's dad winked at him.

"Your father is the all-time champion at doctoring up a plate of food to appear as if he has eaten more than he actually has, so I'm on to the both of you. Now eat!" His father hid further behind the newspaper. Jimmy had nowhere to hide.

"I don't feel so good," Jimmy moaned, hoping this would be enough to keep him from having to go to school. His mother had heard it all before, though.

"You know, Jimmy," she said with a sly smile, "it's Kevin's first day at a new school. It would be nice if his best friend was there to help him find his way around, get him used to the place."

"Yeah, you're right," Jimmy said, and a smile began to form on his face. Everything about what his mother just said made him feel important.

"And you can show him where the school library is," she added. His face dropped. Jimmy had a sneaky suspicion he had just been duped by his own mother.

"Gosh!" Jimmy moaned. Then he thought twice about saying another word.

"Get your books, you're going to be late," his mother said. "I better not hear that you were mean to Kevin, either."

Jimmy shot out the door with two loose-leaf notebooks, his math book, history book, and a brown lunch bag with a small grease stain already beginning to form on the bottom. He immediately saw Kevin moping about across the street.

"Hi, Kevin."

"Hey, Jimmy."

"Ready for school?" Jimmy asked, still rubbing the sleep from his eyes.

"Yeah, I guess. You mind showing me around today, where stuff is and all?" Kevin asked.

Jimmy was delighted. The tiredness drained from his body, and he began walking with a little more purpose. "Sure. The bus stop is this way. Hey, what's with the baseball cap?" Jimmy asked. Kevin looked up from the ground for the first time that morning and slid the cap off his head.

"What do you think," Kevin said.

"WHOA!" Jimmy gasped. Kevin had the blackest eye and fattest lip Jimmy had ever seen. Kevin looked back down and slid the cap back on his head.

"Does it look bad?"

"It looks wicked!" Jimmy declared. Kevin smiled, but it looked more like a grimace through the fat lip he was sporting. "Man, think of the stories people will tell," Jimmy added. This didn't help Kevin, in fact, he squirmed even more now.

"Please don't say anything," Kevin begged.

Right then Jimmy saw the anguish on Kevin's face. It made Jimmy feel bad for him. "I won't tell what happened. I promise. But let me make something up," Jimmy pleaded.

"No," Kevin said.

"You know the teachers won't let you wear that hat in class," Jimmy said.

"You're kidding! Man, I don't want to walk around the entire day parading this battered face."

"Sorry but it's not like the hat helps that much, anyway." Kevin glared at Jimmy but then he shrugged. The truth hurts sometimes. They finished the rest of their short walk to the school bus. When the bus pulled up, they piled on and found two seats near the rear and sat next to each other. Two other kids from that stop, a boy who was always picking his nose and a girl who never spoke but loved to stare at people, found vacant seats away from each other and slid their butts across to the window seat. Jimmy saw Kevin glare around at the few faces already on the bus. He was clearly shy and feeling nervous.

The next stop was only three blocks away. However, close to a dozen children were waiting—some miserable, some happy at the sight of the bus. As the bus neared, they meshed together, forming a crude line out of the clump they had been. Kevin peered out from under his cap.

"Hey, there's Chad and Dave. Chad's a little weird, but Dave is cool," Jimmy said looking for more faces to introduce to Kevin. "They're both in fifth grade, like we are. You're in fifth grade, right?"

"Yeah."

"Oh crap," and Jimmy slid down a little in his seat.

"What is it?"

"There's these two girls out there. I think they're twins. Their mother usually drives them to school. I think they are in love with me. All they do is bother me."

"Do you like them?" Kevin asked.

"No! Hey, Chad! Dave!" Two boys, both about Jimmy's age, were making their way to the rear of the bus.

"Hi, Jimmy," Chad said. Chad had a bewildered look to him, and his eyes were hard to see as they peered out from under a canopy of blond locks.

"Jimmy," Dave said, trying to be cool. Dave was a tough-looking kid.

"I bet no one messes with him," Kevin whispered to Jimmy.

Before Jimmy could respond, Dave gestured towards Kevin. "Who's your girlfriend?" Kevin looked up and balled his fists, but they were shaking, most likely in fear, Jimmy figured.

"Damn! What happened to your face, kid?"

"Nothing," Kevin sulked.

"This is Kevin," Jimmy said, intervening.

"Oh, hey, dude," Dave said.

"Hi, Kevin," Chad said as he sat in the row next to them. Chad did the slide to the window thing and Dave sat next to him.

"Hi," Kevin said to neither one in particular.

"So, what happened to your face there, dude?" Dave asked.

"My fastball went off the tip of his glove and caught him in the eye," Jimmy explained, but he was really bragging. Kevin looked at Jimmy for a moment like he wanted to tell him to shut up, but he didn't. So much for Jimmy keeping his word.

"Hi, Jimmy," two girls chorused, changing the mood altogether. Jimmy went pale as he looked up. Staring back at him were two very cute, identical-looking girls. They were in fact twins, identical twins. One was Jessica and the other Erica. They had long straight hair, pretty blue eyes, and smiles boys hated at that age. Dave and Chad stifled some laughter, making Kevin even laugh a little. But Jimmy was terrified. Just one of them was scary enough, but there were two, and they were absolutely the same.

"Hi," he peeped hoarsely but only because his mother taught him to be polite.

"Hi, Jimmy," chorused more voices. Then those same voices burst into a fit of laughter.

"Shut up, Dave! Shut up, Chad!" Jimmy demanded. Jimmy noticed the whole thing was a little too amusing to his friends. Kevin especially. He would fit in just fine.

When things quieted down some, a new girl with a dark brown ponytail walked right up to Jimmy. Jimmy froze in terror again. What was with these girls? Looking up, his mouth dropped open. Her eyes were made of chocolate. She smiled at him.

"Hi," she peeped shyly. Jimmy didn't want any more harassing from his friends, but he shot her a quick smile anyway because he just might like her. Jimmy was certain he didn't pull it off and just came across looking stupid.

If he had, that girl didn't mind. She continued smiling back, shrugged a little and turned and sat in the seat right in front of Jimmy. Her name was Cindy.

Jimmy's first instinct was to tug on that ponytail of hers, but Dave beat him to it. And when she whipped around with an accusatory glance at Jimmy, he pointed at Dave. The only thing was Dave seemed engrossed in conversation with Chad. She smiled at Jimmy again and turned back around. The hair pulling, the giggling, and the mocking eventually ended but not before it was time to get off the bus and go into the school.

"What homeroom are you in?" Jimmy asked Kevin.

"I don't know. I have to go to the main office first," Kevin said.

"Oh, okay. Go right in there," Jimmy said pointing.

"Thanks. I'll see ya later?"

"Yeah, see ya."

· · ·

Kevin's nervous feeling of being alone in a strange world crept right back in. It didn't turn out to be a very good morning for Kevin, either. He was teased constantly about his fat lip and black eye. In fact, it wasn't until Dave told some older kids that Kevin had been banned from his old school for always fighting did the teasing and ridicule stop. Dave told such a tale even Kevin started to believe it.

"Yeah, that's why he had to move here," Dave told two sixth-grade girls he was trying to impress. "The last fight he was in, where he got all busted up like he is, well it turns out the other guy got the worst of it." The two girls gasped and shrieked all in the same breath.

"Hi, Dave," Kevin said as he passed by the three of them in the hallway, having overheard the entire story.

"Hey, Kevin," Dave said giving him a nod and then quickly going back to acting cool in front of the girls. For some reason, Dave could talk to the girls, kind of like Dr. Doolittle could talk to the animals.

"You know him?" they both chirped in awe, as Kevin smiled behind their backs. "Oh yeah, we're friends," Dave said, playing it off as if it were no big deal. "Wow," they chirped again.

That was pretty much how the day rounded out for Kevin. The morning was awful with the afternoon getting better until...

"Kevin Spencer, please report to the principal's office," a voice rang over the P.A. system. A chorus of oohs filled the classroom he was sitting in. Then the oohs turned into whispers of unimaginable tales. None of which were close to the truth.

"The principal will be with you in a minute," a woman with horse teeth told Kevin as he stood in front of the office counter not knowing what to do next. She gestured a few times for him to take a seat behind him, but to Kevin, it looked more like a horse champing at its bit. So, he just smiled at her. Finally, the horse teeth spoke again. "Have a seat, please."

Kevin sat and then spent the next few moments looking around trying not to stare at her horse teeth. After a short while, she escorted Kevin into Principal Mack's office.

"Have a seat, please, Kevin. First, I'd like to welcome you to Walnut Creek Elementary School," Mr. Mack said. Mr. Mack was a throwback to 1955 with his thick black-framed eyeglasses, his greasy hair, and stale suit. He was not a man of strong presence or character. Kevin was still wondering why he had been called into the principal's office in the first place.

"Thank you," he said, a little confused still.

"Now, Kevin, I understand you moved here from Danton," he said. Danton was a town about two hundred miles north of Walnut Creek.

"Yes, sir," Kevin replied.

"And how was your situation there, Kevin?" he asked. Kevin didn't understand the question, so he just shrugged. "Did you get into a lot of trouble there, for... fighting or anything?" Kevin scrunched up his face in confusion, which apparently sent the wrong message to Mr. Mack. "Because, son," the principal continued, "we don't tolerate that kind of behavior here."

"What?" Kevin said.

"Don't play coy with me, son. We know about your past troubles, and we know why you had to move here."

"What?"

"The fighting," he added.

"Sir, I didn't get into any fights in my last town," Kevin tried to explain.

"Then where did you get that black eye and swollen lip?" Mr. Mack asked.

"It happened here, it was my first day here," Kevin added hoping this might make things easier on him.

"You got that here?" Mr. Mack looked even more concerned.

"Yeah, Jimmy Hamil..."

Mr. Mack did not let him finish. "Jimmy Hamilton did that to you?" The principle was incensed. Thinking right about now that he had said too much, Kevin tried to right the situation, but Mr. Mack was not listening and wouldn't have any of it either. This recent evidence had severe consequences, and Mr. Mack apparently had a new agenda.

•   •   •

When Jimmy Hamilton was called to the principal's office later that afternoon, his mother was already there waiting to meet him. It took some convincing before Mr. Mack would even consider Jimmy's explanation, but his story was corroborated by his mother, which was also confirmed by

Kevin when he was again called to the office. Walnut Creek Elementary had never seen the likes of this kind of trouble before.

Kevin had quickly become somewhat of a legend on his very first day. Mr. Mack seemed genuinely embarrassed and was quite apologetic when the truth had finally been unfolded, but Mr. Mack's callous and reckless accusations had put Mrs. Hamilton off. "Again, Mrs. Hamilton, I am truly sorry," Mr. Mack groveled pathetically. "If you would like, it is just about time to release the kids for the buses. You may take Jimmy home, if you like." Jimmy's mom looked at Jimmy. She seemed put off still.

"Can we walk home, mom?" Jimmy begged.

"No," she replied. "Take the bus home. I need to run some errands." She then escorted both Jimmy and Kevin out of the office towards the doors that led out to the buses. "Boy, that woman had some big teeth," she said. Behind her, a chorus of giggles came from her son and his friend, followed by a loud horse noise. Spinning around, Mrs. Hamilton caught Jimmy as the sound died from his lips. "Behave," was all she said.

"Sorry if I got you in any trouble," Kevin told Jimmy as they sat on the school bus, heading home.

"You didn't do anything. That Mr. Mack-ass," and they both started laughing, "has it in for me."

"Sorry anyway."

"Don't be. My mom's cool with it. At first, she was mad."

"Mack-ass," Kevin repeated, and several kids started laughing.

"Mack-ass," Jimmy blurted out for the same response. Then everyone joined in, and the only thing heard on the bus was "Mack-ass" and kids laughing. Even the bus driver repeated it.

CHAPTER SIX

-JIMMY'S BIRTHDAY-

By Thursday of that same week, Jimmy could barely contain his excitement. His birthday was just two days away. The invitations were out, the presents bought. Jimmy even noticed the pantry was filled with lots of party snacks and cake ingredients. This was going to be a grand celebration. He could feel it.

He also knew what he wanted for his birthday. His father had already given him that new baseball glove. He received it early, so he had a chance to break the glove in before the start of the new baseball season. What Jimmy wanted now was a baseball bat. He had been eyeing the same Louisville Slugger at the sporting goods store for about a month, each time looking at it in awe as if he was seeing it for the first time.

On Saturday, Jimmy woke early, too excited to sleep any longer. His mother kept him busy helping right up until the start of his party.

"Answer the door, Jimmy," his mother said as she scrambled to prepare platters of treats for the guests. He did as she asked, then shrieked.

"Mo'om," Jimmy said coming into the kitchen. "You invited the twins?" Jimmy moaned. He stood in shock. He was not happy. However, he knew the deal. The more guests invited, the more presents. But the twins? Well, it did mean he'd be getting two presents.

"Jessica and Erica are the sweetest little angels. Where are they?" his mother asked, peering out of the kitchen and into the hallway. "You left them standing outside?"

"I'm so sorry, girls, please come in," she told them, holding the screen door open for them to enter. "He's just acting like this to show off for you," she added. Within earshot, Jimmy winced. But it sent the girls into a fit of giggles. The sound they made was excruciating.

"Stop it," he said under his breath.

"There's the birthday boy," his mother sang in an almost more annoying tone. The girls continued their giggling.

"Happy birthday, Jimmy," the two girls chorused. They smiled at him. Each girl had on the same dress, with the same ribbon in her hair, and the same shoes on. They even had the same size gift, wrapped in the same paper, with the same bow on the box. Man, it was creepy. His mother, standing behind both the girls, shot Jimmy a look that kept him in line and better behaved than if he was left to himself.

"Jimmy?" his mother said gesturing for a response from her son.

"Thanks," he moaned insincerely. After an awkward pause, the doorbell rang, and Jimmy jumped into action. "I'll get it," he insisted and tore off out of the room. He returned to the family room shortly, tailed by yet another girl. It was Cindy. She was dressed tom boyishly, but she still had the look of an adorable little girl. It was like she could play first baseman in a pickup baseball game and still pull off having tea with the twins.

"Oh good, everyone appears to be here," Jimmy's mother teased. Jimmy went pale. He was so gullible.

"What?" he cried looking around. "Where are all my friends?" All four girls in the room started giggling. Jimmy was furious. What irritated him the most was hearing his mother giggle in just the same manner as the other three, so innocently and yet so devilishly.

"Mo'om," Jimmy moaned. The girls all giggled some more. Cindy smiled at Jimmy when she wasn't giggling. To his relief, the doorbell rang. Jimmy tore out and was gone. When he returned, he had the terminal nose picker tailing him and a sour look on his face.

"Hi, Chris," Jimmy's mother said. "Don't you just look dashing," she added and took the present he held under his arm.

"Thank you," the timid little boy replied.

The doorbell rang at least six more times. Kevin, Chad, and Dave made up two of those rings as they all slowly gathered. It was an awkward grouping of children with the boys to one side and girls to the other and the overwhelming sense of cooties seemed to linger, working as some sort of force field keeping them separated.

When all the children had finally arrived, they were released back into the wild, which was just the backyard. Kids scurried in every direction. Chad, Dave, and Kevin followed Jimmy to the tree fort.

Jimmy glanced back to see the twins had intercepted Cindy. He didn't much care because she wouldn't be allowed in the fort, not with his friends around, anyway.

"Cindy, would you like to have tea with us in the tea parlor?" asked Erica. It was such a prissy little invite. She accepted the offer reluctantly, but every time Jimmy glanced her way, she had her eye on Jimmy and the tree fort passage.

With little effort, Jimmy was first up the ladder and rope and into the tree fort. Dave followed with the same ease, as he had made the climb several times before. Kevin needed a boost, once again, but made it up safely. Chad, on the other hand, was heavy-footed and labored, as usual. He had been up to the top before, but each time seemed an odyssey. It was painful to watch as he torqued about in a desperate attempt to keep from falling.

All Jimmy could think about was the consequences of Chad falling. No one else knew of the plight of the tree fort. That added pressure might be too much for Chad at that point. But surely his mother wouldn't take the fort away on his birthday.

A small crowd of children began to gather, all watching Chad twist about madly. Jimmy was certain the extra commotion would draw his mother's attention, but she was way too busy preparing treats for the party. Hopefully, she would stay in the kitchen until Chad could gather himself.

Then, as if some force intervened, Chad managed to work his hands up the rope.

"Whoa!" the crowd moaned as one. Actually, Chad had two moves in his arsenal, climb or fall. He climbed which sent him side long into the trunk of the tree. He grimaced, but then righted himself until Dave and Kevin reached down and grasped his arms. Pulling with everything they had, Chad was hauled into the fort. He had made it. The kids on the ground slowly dispersed, disappointed they didn't get to see any carnage.

Jimmy knew the rules of the fort had changed, but as far as Dave, Chad, and Kevin knew, anything still went. Jimmy didn't want to be a bore with the new restrictions from his mother, but on the other hand, he didn't want anything to jeopardize his fort. Torn, he chose to worry.

Jimmy wasn't too worried about Chad doing anything wrong. If anybody were to be a problem, it would be Dave. Jimmy spied Chad in the far corner. He had picked a fresh crab apple and began biting into it. Jimmy grimaced slightly. The apples were edible, but they weren't much for eating. Then Jimmy caught Dave in the corner of his eye sending an apple over the bow. It was traveling right at the nose picker. Jimmy gasped. Kevin looked on in delight. The nose picker suddenly tripped over his own shoelaces as the apple screamed past him, completely oblivious to his luck. His knees were stained with grass, and the apple came to rest innocently in the middle of the yard.

"Hey, check it out," Chad gleefully expressed. He held his half-eaten apple out for the other three to see.

"What's that?" Kevin asked. Dave and Jimmy knew right away and shuddered.

"Dude!" Dave moaned amusingly.

"Is that a worm?" Chad spat.

"That's half of him," Dave tried to explain. Chad seemed to clue in on his misfortune. He quickly realized the other half of the worm was in his mouth, and his face paled. He slowly stopped chewing. His face became scrunched, and his cheeks began to bulge, as he was ready to blow. The next thing anybody saw was bits of apple and what may or may not have been the other half of that worm flying at them. Everybody but Chad started laughing as they picked pieces of apple and worm from their faces.

When his nausea subsided, Chad joined his friends laughing about it. As he smiled, tiny bits of worm could be seen in his teeth. His friends grimaced even more.

"Wha-aat?" Chad asked. No one said a word. Chad finally dropped the apple that housed half of that worm, and it rolled with a lopsided jaunt until it teetered to a stop near the edge of the tree fort floor. The worm slowly made its way out of the half-eaten apple. No boy knew whether the worm was backing his way out to see what happened to his ass or whether the worm was inching along blindly without a head, but they all looked on, curious as ever. A lesson was to be learned here—if only they knew what it was. Puzzling over it, they continued watching the worm's predicament.

That's when Chad felt the desire for a little retribution. He stepped back and reared up before charging the half-eaten orb. "Say goodbye, Mr. Worm!" His friends cheered him on.

A split second later, he planted his left foot, or so he wished. Instead, his foot slipped on a small piece of apple. The foot he was going to kick with hit the apple just as both feet slid out from underneath him. Chad reached out his arm in a desperate lunge for the railing that wrapped the fort, but he missed the post and slid right off the tree fort floor. Chad was gone.

A dull thud echoed when Chad's body hit the ground. Then three heads peered out over the edge of the fort and down at Chad. His body lay twisted, still and quiet. The other children from the party all rushed over and formed a circle around the body.

"Is he dead?" Kevin wondered.

"Don't know. Chad, you dead?" Dave hollered. Jimmy went ghostly white. Surely Chad would be fine. But what about his fort? All Jimmy was concerned about at that second was his fort and how he would surely lose the fort for something like this.

"Get up, Chad," Jimmy wished, a little more than to himself. His friends looked at him curiously. "Get up before my mother comes out here."

"Should we see if he's okay?" Kevin asked.

"Chad!" Dave yelled. Chad began to squirm like a live frog thawing out from a very cold winter.

"Cool, he's alive," Jimmy said. "Let's climb down and get him up."

Getting down from the tree fort was much easier than climbing up. They could have taken Chad's alternative route, but it didn't appear anyone wanted to go that way. So, they all shimmied down the rope, one after the other. And instead of using the ladder rungs nailed to the tree, when they reached the end of the rope, they just let go, dropping to the ground. It wasn't any more than a six or seven foot drop, but it was pretty cool watching them drop from the sky like some sort of fire jumpers or something. When they were all on the ground, they pushed their way to the forefront and stood over Chad's writhing body. Jimmy heard the screen door open and knew it was now or never for Chad to get up. Jimmy grabbed his arm. Chad moaned in protest, but it was too late. Jimmy's mother, along with Mrs. Spencer, were making their way through the small crowd.

"What happened?" Jimmy's mom cried.

"He fell," one of the onlookers said. Jimmy's heart sank. His mother looked directly up to see where Chad had fallen from. Jimmy followed her gaze. It was obvious.

"Chad, are you all right?" she asked him.

"Oh, hi, Mrs. Hamilton. You smell nice," he said as if he was unaware of the situation. Everyone giggled, everyone except Jimmy, of course. Mrs. Hamilton blushed and then went back to tending to Chad, making sure he wasn't seriously injured. He was not. In fact, the only thing different about Chad was his now incredibly acute olfactory senses. It was weird, but from that moment on, Chad had a superhero-like sense of smell.

Chad sat up a bit dazed and a bit confused but otherwise okay. He had a curdled look to his face, as if he could smell the town dump to the west, which he now could, all because of that fall to the ground. Jimmy thought there was a chance his fort was safe, but it was not. It happened right after Chad was up and about playing with his friends again.

In the middle of the party, Mr. Hamilton, under the direction of Mrs. Hamilton, made his way to the tree trunk underneath the fort. He had a hammer in one hand and a small crowbar in the other.

"Sorry Jimmy," he said in passing. Jimmy moaned in protest, but it was to no avail. Mr. Hamilton proceeded in taking down all the wooden planks that made up the gateway to the harrowing ascent to the top of the tree fort.

There, dangling from the underbelly of the fort was the rope, knotted and ready for climbing but unreachable without those planks.

"Damn it!" Jimmy said. All four boys just stood underneath the rope looking up.

"That sucks," Dave said, never changing his gaze upward.

They soon dispersed back among the other children who seemed to be enjoying themselves on Jimmy's special day. Really special, Jimmy thought.

Every aspect of the party was now overshadowed by the loss of the tree fort. The cake was disappointing, even though it was Jimmy's favorite. The presents got little or no rousing reaction, almost as if all the presents were clothes from his Aunt Sylvia. They were not though. Jimmy got some really nice presents, including the Louisville Slugger bat he wanted. He just couldn't appreciate anything right then.

After the presents were opened and the cake was served, each kid having cake somewhere on their body other than their mouth, they made their way back out into the yard. Most of them were either participating or spectating in what looked like a game of dodgeball. It may have been kickball, probably was, but Jimmy didn't care enough to pay attention either way.

When Dave creamed the nose picker in the side of the head with the ball, and the kid went to the edge of the playing area, it definitely appeared more like dodge ball.

No matter what they were playing, Jimmy was not in the mood for it. That was quite uncharacteristic of Jimmy, given his competitive nature. Whack! Chad was out and went to stand next to nose picker. Jimmy took that opportunity to sneak away from the other kids so he could be alone.

Keeping a sharp lookout for his mother, Jimmy made his way to the far end of the crabapple tree. He looked up and studied the gnarled limbs and twisted branches before he began to climb. From there, the two trees completely shielded him from the view of the house and the other kids. He took to the crabapple tree as if there was a path already etched for his ascent. The path took him to the edge of the tree house floor where he lifted his leg up over the lip, and he was in. That was easier than he had thought. He had never climbed up the tree before now to get to his fort. He was gleaming with a new pride, but he couldn't tell anyone. It would have to be kept a secret, for if his mother was ever to find out, both trees would be cut to the ground. That secret lasted two seconds.

"Huh?" Jimmy muttered, as he stared at Cindy sitting comfortably in the middle of the tree fort floor. She was hidden pretty well from plain view, especially since Jimmy hadn't detected her until then, and he'd been eyeing this fort ever since Chad fell out of it.

"Hi, Jimmy," Cindy said.

"How?" was all that came from Jimmy's mouth. She sat calmly on the floor and smiled at him.

"Same way you just did," she said. She was even cuter now.

"Girls aren't allowed to be up here," he stated with wavering conviction.

"Why not?" she asked. Jimmy, suddenly, wasn't sure. He stared at her without an answer. He thought her hair looked nice let down to dangle around her shoulders. She didn't look like a typical girl, at least not right then and not from where Jimmy was standing. Was it because she just climbed a tangle of limbs to get up to his sanctuary? Was it those deep chocolate eyes?

"You have pretty eyes," he blurted. It was the eyes, and probably a little of her tom boyishness, too. It could have been her hair that was also like chocolate. Did he have a sweet tooth?

"Thank you." She giggled. Jimmy didn't care too much for the giggling, but he liked making her smile. Jimmy wasn't sure what had gotten into him. Suddenly, he was acting much older than eleven.

Finally, they settled down next to each other, sitting on the far side of the tree fort floor with their legs hanging off the edge. Where they sat, they were completely hidden from the house by the tree fort and the mess of gnarled limbs from both trees. An unmistaken awkwardness lingered between them when Cindy leaned in and kissed him.

He closed his eyes and felt a tingling on his lips. Even after Cindy leaned back, the tingling remained. Jimmy opened his eyes but not in sync with Cindy at all. She giggled. This time it didn't bother Jimmy one bit. He just sat there. Two minutes before, he hated girls, but then it seemed he didn't. He felt his lips with his hand as the tingling still lingered.

Cindy got up abruptly and stepped from the tree fort onto a thick branch of the walnut tree and began climbing down. "I gotta go. Happy birthday, Jimmy," she said before dropping out of sight.

Jimmy sat up in the tree fort for quite some time before he even thought about climbing back down to the ground. While he pondered all that had just happened, Jimmy swore to himself that before the summer was over, he would kiss that girl again, and he would somehow reclaim this fort or build a new one.

CHAPTER SEVEN
—THE WORN PATCHES MADE A DIAMOND—

When Jimmy had finally climbed back down from his tree fort, he noticed a group of kids had gathered just beyond his backyard. Most of the kids appeared to be from Jimmy's party. The few odd ones out were older boys all toting baseball gear. They came looking for a game if there was one to have, and this was the place to look.

Just beyond the Hamilton's backyard, past the tire swing and tree fort, was a large open field. That field was flat and extended far enough past everyone's backyards to house several ball fields if they wanted. At the far end of the field, there were thick woods and just beyond that was a farm. The field was a communal area of sorts, mostly for the neighborhood kids to play on. No one rightly knew who owned the property. Many thought it belonged to the farmer beyond the woods.

The field had been so often used for baseball that a diamond had been worn away in the grass. Bare patches existed for every base, the pitcher's mound, and even home plate. Surrounding home plate were two more bare patches so deep they collected water when it rained. Those patches made up the batter's boxes. The field butted up against the Miller's stockade fence. That fence made up the backstop, something Mr. Miller was fine with.

Mr. Peterson had mowed the grass on the field to a playable depth. They believed Mr. Peterson was the farmer.

Jimmy had his glove in hand and was at the front of the pack before either of the captains had picked a player.

"Pick me, pick me, pick me—" continued through Jimmy's head as he led with his ego.

"Tommy," the first captain said.

"Jason," the second boy picked.

"Maybe they can't see me," Jimmy wondered and pushed even closer with an overly eager expression.

"Chuck," called the first captain.

"Damn," Jimmy thought, and the captains continued rounding out their teams. Jimmy was picked ninth overall and three picks before the only girl playing, Cindy. Jimmy wasn't so sure a girl should be playing this boy's sport, but he wasn't so sure she shouldn't either. Cindy smiled at Jimmy as she walked past him to join her teammates. Jimmy turned to join his teammates and walked right into his captain. The captain gave him a shove.

"We're home team," Jimmy's captain called out.

"All right," the second captain yelled back.

"Hey, can I pitch?" Jimmy asked his captain. Derrick was the boy's name, and he turned to reply to Jimmy's request.

"Ya any good kid?" Derrick asked.

"I've heard stories," Jimmy lied of himself. Cindy giggled.

"All right, kid, take the mound. Let's see what ya got," Derrick said. Jimmy took to the "mound" which in their case was just another bald patch. While Jimmy warmed up, a few kids ran off to collect their baseball gloves from home. Jimmy's first warm-up pitch sailed past the catcher, nearly hitting Chad as he stood off to the side, and then broke two slats of the wooden fence behind them. Jimmy had an "excuse me" look on his face as he held out his glove, requesting the ball back for another chance.

"Nice velocity, kid. Can you get it over the plate?" his captain asked.

"If I need to," Jimmy answered. He let loose his second warm-up pitch, and it popped the catcher's mitt with a crack similar to when he hit Kevin in the eye.

"Nice," some of the older boys responded. Jimmy threw six more pitches to warm up, hitting the fence with three of those six pitches. He was ready, and the fence was battered.

The opposing captain thought it might mess with Jimmy's head some if he sent out the girl to bat first, so he did just that. Cindy pulled her hair back in a ponytail and jammed the batting helmet over it. She grabbed the smaller of the two bats they had and walked to the plate. The captain was correct. Jimmy's mind was reeling. He now knew why girls shouldn't play a boy's sport. What was he supposed to do? He mulled over his options.

If she got a hit off him, he would never hear the end of it. If he struck her out, big deal, she's a girl. He could walk Cindy. No, again, he would be razzed. He could hit her with the pitch. Jimmy couldn't do that; he had just kissed her. Well, he couldn't kiss her again, not here anyway. So, he closed his eyes, wound up, and pitched the ball. He heard the crack of the bat. Fear of humiliation rushed over him. And before he could open his eyes back up, the ball whizzed past him, nearly taking off his head. When the dust settled, Cindy stood smiling at first base.

The razzing never came. It was as if everyone was just impressed. And the look on Jimmy's face said it all as he stood there daring anyone to say anything. If they had, they may have found the ball in their ear on the next pitch. Chad walked to the plate. Four pitches later, he walked to first base. Jimmy bore down and then proceeded to walk the next two batters. He was furious, but two very nice defensive plays by one of the older kids got him out of trouble and out of the inning.

Jimmy had impressed Derrick enough that he let Jimmy pitch another inning. He faired a little better, too. He walked the first three batters, but then he struck out the next three to end the inning without giving up a run. Cindy was one of the walks though, something Jimmy was okay with.

Most of the game went without incident. An occasional argument erupted over a safe or out call, and the usual bickering over balls and strikes wafted the field, but what pickup baseball game would be complete without a little competitive squabbling?

When the game was over, all four boys—Jimmy, Dave, Chad, and Kevin—were pleased with their play. Enough so that they were excited about the upcoming Little League season. Chad had a couple of nice hits, Dave caught everything hit at him, and Kevin did a good job as catcher, especially it being his first time.

Cindy, of course, walked off the field and back to what was left of the birthday party by herself. She should have been in very good spirits, having had three hits and two nice defensive plays, but she was the odd girl out, and that was apparent. Jimmy just watched her walk off. His friends were whooping it up a little too much for him to get away and check on her.

The party for Jimmy was quickly coming to an end as most of the kids returned from the game searching for shelter from the hot sun. They all grouped together on the Hamilton's back porch with its canopy that shaded them comfortably. The boys were all sweaty and dirty and looking exhausted, which pretty much sucked the remaining life out of the party. The twins left, but not before tormenting Jimmy one last time. They were just being friendly, in their creepy little way, but it was all torture for Jimmy.

•   •   •

Cindy made her way quietly over to Mrs. Hamilton, now that she knew she would not be part of the gang that just finished playing baseball. That was a shame too, since she played better than any of the boys who were there, lying about lazily rehashing the game. She was sweaty and dirty too, but still had a girlish glow about her.

"Thank you, Mrs. Hamilton, for inviting me," Cindy said.

"Oh, you're such a little dear." Mrs. Hamilton beamed at her, making her feel a little better. Cindy returned the smile. "Did you have a nice time?" Mrs. Hamilton added.

"Yes, I did, thank you," Cindy answered politely as sweat dripped from her face.

Apparently noticing this, Mrs. Hamilton asked, "Were you out there playing baseball with those boys?"

"Yes, I was," Cindy admitted, hoping this admission was reason enough to wipe the sweat from her face.

"Oh my, you are a brave soul," she said, shaking her head. She glanced around to see where her son was. "Did you bat against Jimmy?"

"Yep," she peeped with a grin.

"You be careful out there. He gets pretty wild, ya know?" Mrs. Hamilton said.

"Yeah, I know," and they both giggled.

"Did Jimmy say goodbye to you, dear?" Mrs. Hamilton asked.

"No, he looks busy," Cindy said.

"Jimmy, come and say goodbye to your guests," his mother hollered.

"Bye," Jimmy yelled, not even looking up to see whom he was saying goodbye to.

"Jimmy," and this time the tone was sharp enough for Jimmy to get to his feet and meet Cindy on her way out.

As he walked Cindy out, the other boys began a cry of coos and howls. Cindy felt bad that she had put that on Jimmy, but was pleased all the same to get a chance to say goodbye.

"Sorry," she said.

"I'll see ya around," Jimmy said.

"Sure," she said and managed a shy smile at the newfound Jimmy. He was clearly trying to act cool but was pulling off awkward instead. She kind of liked it.

"You played good out there," Jimmy told her.

"Thanks, it was fun," Cindy said, pleased with herself.

"Maybe you could come see me play in Little League," he suggested, and this lit her smile the rest of the way. Jimmy gave her a half-bent smile himself.

"Happy Birthday, Jimmy," she said and was gone before he could say another word.

•　　•　　•

As Jimmy watched her go, he smiled to himself. He thought he'd handled himself just fine. He knew every time his father seemed cool, he never said much. Jimmy thought he'd pulled it off—he had been cool.

The cooing started up again once Jimmy was in sight of the boys. He turned a deep crimson. A few '*Oh, Jimmys*' were heard, followed by bouts of laughter and a lot of giggling, not too different from when girls did it.

Jimmy came back to the herd and punched Kevin in the arm for making fun of him. He could have punched any one of them, or all of them for that matter, but Kevin was the recipient. It was something Jimmy quickly took a liking to, and from that day on, it became a regular thing for Jimmy to punch Kevin every time Kevin, or anybody, had it coming.

"I smell ice cream," Chad said with a bewildered look on his face. Everyone just looked at him weirdly. Dave took the opportunity to punch Chad, much like Jimmy had just punched Kevin. "Ow!" But there it was two seconds later, Jimmy's mother followed by Kevin's mother, and both had several servings of ice cream on a tray and were headed straight for the boys.

"Here you go, boys," Mrs. Hamilton said cheerfully. New life came to those tired and dirty boys as each one took a serving and dug in.

Dave looked at Chad and started to ask, "How?" but he never finished.

CHAPTER EIGHT
−A BOY'S BRIEF MOMENT−

The fate of the tree fort weighed heavily on Jimmy's mind. It wasn't enough to ruin what was a particularly good day for Jimmy, but it was close. He had a nice birthday with acceptable gifts. The prettiest girl he knew kissed him, and he liked it. He escaped going to the library on a Saturday, and that was a big deal in itself. And Jimmy got to play baseball, and he played well at that. As it stood now, the fort was still up, so its demise was not yet final. He still had hope, and he still felt good about everything else.

"Breakfast," his mother's voice reached Jimmy. He made his way down to the kitchen, knowing he still had to go to church, but it wasn't like his mother could stop by the library on the way. The library was closed. He would do his time at St. Anthony's Catholic Church and then get out, leaving the rest of the day for whatever. Jimmy smelled pancakes and couldn't wait.

"Wha..." Jimmy said, staring in disbelief at an enormous stack of library books in his place at the kitchen table.

"Good morning, dear," his mother said, greeting him with a little pinch of his cheek. "You noticed the books, good." How could he not, they sat like a big stack of pancakes and right where he expected to find a big stack of pancakes. His father never came out from behind his morning newspaper.

"Hey, champ."

"Hi, Dad," Jimmy said.

"We were so busy yesterday with the party and all, you know, so I thought you might like, well... I picked up some books from the library for you," his mother explained.

"Damn!" Jimmy uttered. His mother's eyes got big immediately. "Sorry."

"Sit and eat your pancakes," she said, moving the books to the counter. When the stack of books became a stack of pancakes, Jimmy dove in.

"Did you have a nice birthday, son?" his father asked, finally peering over his newspapers like fathers often do.

"Yeah," came a voice muffled by pancakes. Jimmy tried to block the tiny bits of flying pancake from his mouth.

"Don't talk with your mouth full," his mother said.

"Sorry," came from another mouthful. Jimmy snorted, and then his father joined him just before they were both in trouble.

"Eat!" his mother said, her eyes glaring at both of them.

"These are good, dear," Jimmy's father quickly said.

"Don't you even," his mother snapped back. Jimmy snorted some more.

"After church, we are going to go shopping for new clothes for you," she added.

"Aah—do I gotta?" Jimmy moaned. His mother came back to the table and dropped two more pancakes onto Jimmy's plate.

"Well, if you don't want new baseball pants, I guess we don't have to," she reasoned.

"No, I want to go," he said with new enthusiasm.

"And new underwear." Jimmy was duped again. That woman was sneaky.

"Looks like she got ya again, son," his father said quietly, just not quietly enough as he was met in the back of his head with a hard wooden spoon.

"And I invited Kevin and his mother to come along," Jimmy's mom added. She smiled as if that would be good news to Jimmy. It wasn't. He was sure nothing good could come of the situation. Then he wondered if he and Kevin were running into an ambush of sorts where they would have the library open just for them until he remembered the stack of books next to his pancakes.

"Okay," he said suspiciously.

"I was thinking we could go up to that new mall they built," she said.

"Okay," he replied, planning his escape just in case it was a hornswoggle.

•   •   •

When church was over, the shopping trip took them out of town considerably, and that was always exciting for a young boy. His mother forged a path north towards the mall, taking the most direct route of two winding country roads. Jimmy stared into the dense forest that lined both sides of the road. Their path was dark, as the canopy above shaded most of the road. Jimmy let his imagination run as to what might lurk in those woods—the same woods where he might one day need to rebuild the tree fort. He would build that one with a mighty barrier to fend off any evil that lurked. He wasn't certain he'd even need a "no girls" sign for those woods. Then, without warning, the canopy was gone, and the sun splashed down almost blindingly. When their eyes adjusted to the new light, they saw the magnificent structure towering over the flat and barren landscape. There, in the middle of a vast emptiness, was the mall.

"Wow," Jimmy said. Kevin looked impressed as well. Jimmy's mother drove to the entrance and made her way to the main parking lot. She parked just about as far away from the building as she could, which perplexed everyone.

"Are we gonna take a bus from here?" Jimmy asked. He snorted. Jimmy's mom shot him a look. They all began to walk. When they finally reached the mall entrance, both Jimmy and Kevin were very much out of breath, having sprinted most of the journey in a race. The two boy's mothers had a good "let's shop" pace going themselves and were not far behind when Jimmy and Kevin finally entered the building.

Once inside, Jimmy and Kevin took to the first thing that caught their attention, and their faces were soon pressed against the glass of the window front to Friedman's Lingerie. Two plastic blondes with crooked hair and perfect skin stared back at them with blank expressions.

"Dude, I think I'm in love," Jimmy confessed, gazing at the blonde goddess with bronze-like skin. His particular mannequin was wearing a pink see-thru teddy with a garter wrapped around her left thigh. She was dreamy. Jimmy looked for Kevin, but Kevin had vanished. When Jimmy returned his gaze to his coppertone bunny in the window, she was being fondled by Kevin. He had snuck into the store and somehow managed to climb into the window display without being seen. Jimmy collapsed on the floor, laughing. Kevin ran his hand up and down the silken leg of blonde number one.

A minor commotion ensued as a store employee spotted Kevin and snatched him from the display window, but not before Kevin copped himself a good feel of her leg. As Kevin resisted the store employee, he grabbed at the mannequin's arm and managed to get hold of her hand as the employee tugged on Kevin's other arm. Jimmy watched in horror as the arm of his statuesque beauty twisted clean away from her body. The shoulder strap of the teddy she was wearing fell to her side and out came her breast. It was smooth and tan and perfect. Jimmy shrieked.

This got the attention of the two mothers, who immediately came running over, leaving the giant shoe sale behind. Both boys were dragged away in that one arm high in their mother's hand, one arm rubbing a freshly walloped bottom maneuver both boys were accustomed to.

Despite their response, it seemed neither mother was really all that upset over the matter and couldn't help but laugh a little at their son's mischief. The display of being dragged away with bottoms spanked was more for show than anything, Jimmy realized. Once they had turned the corner and were out of sight of the store, both mothers released their holds on their boys.

"Now you two behave," they both told Jimmy and Kevin and then giggled. The two boys gazed around at all the delightful sights and began running from store front to store front, absorbing all the marvels. It was too much for their little minds, but they tried anyway.

When they got to Hank's Sporting Goods, neither Jimmy nor Kevin could contain themselves. The two boys shot down the aisle and into the baseball department, which consisted of about two aisles of space, about a third of the store. They tried on gloves, swung a few bats, and even knocked over a basket of baseballs in their attempt to retrieve one from it. They chased baseballs halfway across that store before they collected them all. Finally, they got to the baseball pants.

"How 'bout these?" Jimmy's mom said, holding up a pair of white pants lined with pinstripes.

"Pinstripes, no way!" Jimmy said. No true Red Sox fan, eleven years old or ninety years old, would ever willingly wear pinstripes. Why his mother did not understand this as common knowledge, he did not know. They both left the store with white baseball pants, no pinstripes.

Two shoe stores later, the four of them walked to the far end of the mall and entered Finley's Department Store. The fancy lighted sign at the entrance was nearly blinding. The two mothers were glowing back at it, while Jimmy and Kevin walked with indifference.

As they entered the store, the boys were given an odd task, at least to them it seemed odd. Their mothers had instructed them to go to the boys clothing department and find a package of underwear, a boy's size small. Neither boy was sure what to think of that. They had never been asked to pick out clothes before, not seriously, anyway. So off they went in search of the boys department.

"This could be a trap," Jimmy said cautiously. Kevin looked at him oddly.

"What kind of trap?"

"I've heard stories that would make your skin crawl." Jimmy replied. Kevin became very interested. They quickly ducked down, as the simple task of retrieving a pack of underwear became a covert operation with the possibility of grave consequences.

"Under here," Kevin shouted.

"No, underwear," Jimmy said. They both darted under a clothes rack of woman's skirts and dresses. Poking their heads out, Kevin stared out at the back end of an enormous woman. Jimmy looked over and then withdrew. Giggles emanated from the clothes rack. They darted to the next rack. Three screams came from inside the rack of clothes, and Jimmy and Kevin quickly darted back and under the next closest rack.

"Who was that?" Kevin asked.

"I don't know, may have been nose picker. We should split up. They can't take us both hostage," Jimmy said.

"Okay," Kevin agreed.

"Go down three racks, and we'll meet back together at that coat rack." Jimmy said, peering out and pointing to their next destination. The plan was to dart out the sides of the clothes rack, a slightly different path than they just tried to take.

Jimmy immediately got tangled up somehow and slammed into a pair of large buttocks, possibly the same backside Kevin had stared at earlier. Jimmy fell back under the clothes rack.

Kevin, on the other hand, seemed to make it out, but quickly became tangled inside one of the skirts. A woman screamed. Then Kevin bumped into a gnarly looking bearded midget wearing a mask. A muffled scream pierced the air, and Kevin scrambled back under the clothes rack with Jimmy. Out of breath and considerably frayed, Kevin looked at Jimmy. Jimmy, who had seen the whole thing, couldn't stop laughing.

"Did you hear that woman scream?" Jimmy said.

"What?" Kevin grunted.

"Dude, do you even know what just happened?" Jimmy asked.

"What?" Kevin repeated, still shell-shocked. A commotion stirred just outside the clothes rack. Jimmy tried to listen.

"Quiet," he demanded. "I can't tell what's going on."

"I think the place is being robbed by a bearded midget wearing a stocking mask," Kevin explained. Jimmy grunted. They both just looked at each other, when all of a sudden, an arm reached into the clothing rack and snatched Kevin from his spot. Kevin came out looking alarmed.

"I think you're being robbed," he said, staring directly at one of the store clerks. The clerk's eyes got big as he let go of Kevin.

"Robbed," the young man repeated and scurried off in a panic. Kevin ducked back into the clothing rack, and Jimmy jumped back slightly.

"Let's get out of here," Kevin said, and both boys scampered off on their hands and knees until it seemed safe, coming to rest against the far wall of the store.

"That was close," Jimmy said, still laughing a little. "On to the boys department?"

"Yeah," Kevin replied. They got up and gave the area a once over, looking for their mothers before proceeding. Not knowing if they were in the mens department or the boys, Jimmy grabbed a shirt from a nearby rack and held it up to his body to see if it would fit. They pressed on when they saw the shirt went to the floor on him.

"There," Jimmy pointed. A large sign hanging from the ceiling read Boys. They walked up and down several aisles of shelves until they found the underwear. That seemed pretty easy, or so they thought.

They rummaged through several packs of underwear until Jimmy held up what he thought was the ticket.

"Here we go," he said, examining the goods. "Size small," he added encouragingly. Kevin gave the package a good going over.

"Three boys briefs," Kevin said, reading the packaging.

"What?"

"Right there, in the upper left-hand corner, three boys briefs," Kevin said, pointing out the markings on the plastic.

"Damn, there's only two of us," Jimmy said. Kevin picked up another package and examined it.

"They all say three boys briefs," Kevin said, and then picked up another. "Three boys briefs."

Jimmy examined another package for himself. "Three boys briefs," he said. They searched the rest of the packages in front of them, then moved down the aisle. All the packages said three boys briefs.

"Wait a minute, six boys briefs," Kevin shouted.

"Six," Jimmy hailed, "that's absurd. Even with all my best friends, I would still be two boys short." They rummaged through the remaining packages of underwear.

"Nope, nothin' but sixes and threes," Kevin pointed out.

"Damn, what are we gonna do?" Jimmy wondered.

"I don't know," Kevin replied.

"Do you think our mothers already knew they didn't come in packs for one boy?" Jimmy asked.

"What?" He was still as confused as Jimmy.

"I think this mission was set up to fail from the very beginning," Jimmy explained.

"So, it was a trap," Kevin said. Jimmy nodded. "What should we do now?" Kevin added. Jimmy took a moment to think.

"I know," he said and grabbed two packs of six boys briefs. "We take these and give them to our mothers." Kevin looked confused.

"Six," Kevin said.

"Yeah, six. They'll have to notice something is wrong if we bring them five more pairs of underwear than we have boys," Jimmy thought cleverly.

"Then what?" Kevin wondered.

"Well, if they notice we brought enough underwear for six kids each and they don't say anything, then I'm gonna guess they are up to something," Jimmy explained.

"I see," Kevin said.

The boys were growing even more suspicious of what though, Jimmy wasn't exactly sure. What he was sure of was that underwear came in odd packaging and his mother, along with Kevin's mother, may or may not be up to something. Thank goodness he had Kevin on his side.

Jimmy and Kevin eventually headed back to where they originally left their mothers. The mothers had migrated a bit and were now over by the purses.

The department was ladies accessories. Jimmy and Kevin nonchalantly tossed the underwear into the shopping cart, turned and began acting suspiciously interested in ladies accessories. Jimmy's mother made her way to the cart, and after inspecting the two packages, she seemed pleased and went back to what she was doing. The two boys looked wide-eyed at each other, then quickly turned away, so as not to draw any attention to themselves. Jimmy was right—it was a trap.

When they finished shopping at Finley's, they made their way to the food court and enjoyed oversized slices of greasy mall pizza, the kind of pizza that drips grease with every bite. A single slice was nearly too much for each of them, but Jimmy and Kevin made a contest out of finishing them, a contest that almost ended in them needing a mop and maybe a shovel.

"Can you two do anything without getting in trouble?" Jimmy's mother cried.

"Nope," Jimmy yelped through the last mouthful of pizza. Kevin began laughing at Jimmy, sending soda clear up and out of his nose. Then Jimmy started laughing as Kevin choked on the carbonation rippling through his nostrils.

"Behave!" Jimmy's mother said.

When lunch was over, they all made their way back out into the sea of chain store merchants, stopping briefly here and there for shoe sales and toys mainly. Up ahead was another lingerie store! The mall apparently was a little promiscuous—it had two lingerie stores, but only one of everything else. Then something caught Jimmy's eye. After nudging Kevin with his elbow, the two boys tore off in its direction. Noticing the lingerie window, the two mothers made a face at each other and hurried after them.

"Uh oh," Jimmy's mother cried. In the path ahead stood a scantily dressed, plastic brunette who could turn any man's head. The women both sighed when their boys blew right past that window, though Jimmy did do a double take on that brunette. They stopped at a clapping toy monkey at the doorway of Slappy's Gags and Gifts. They were enthralled by the stupid-looking primate. So much so, they began playing a game of chicken with the monkey. It didn't take long for the monkey to slam closed on Kevin's finger. Kevin's reaction sent the monkey flying across the walkway, coming to rest at Mrs. Hamilton's feet.

"Can we go in, Mom? Can we?" Kevin asked. Both mothers were reluctant, but when Jimmy's eyes wandered to that raven-haired temptress next door again, they quickly agreed and hustled them inside.

Jimmy stepped forward into the enchanted world of magical spheres, black lights, and fake dog doo doo. Kevin was soon wearing a hat that had a straw for drinking from.

"Don't put that in your mouth," Kevin's mother said, but it was too late.

Jimmy found a drinking glass with a picture of a girl in a bikini on it. When he tipped the glass to drink, the girl's bikini disappeared. He was in heaven.

Their mothers quickly discovered it would be nearly impossible to corral their boy's exposure to this world of gifts and gags and were soon off themselves eying a calendar with muscle bound beefcakes wearing tight little bathing suits and holding a fire hose.

"Chad," Jimmy hollered. Chad, holding some sort of elephant trunk underwear, turned towards them and was pelted with a rubber replica of dog poo. The dog poo bounced off his shoulder, then slid down the aisle. His face told the story. He loved it!

"Ah cool!" he said, chasing the feces down. When he bent down to pick it up, another replica whizzed by his head and struck Kevin, who was closing in from the other side.

"Ow!" Kevin screamed as it left a red welt on his face.

"Sorry, Kevin," Jimmy hollered.

"Hey, guys," Chad said.

"This place is wicked, am I right?" Jimmy said.

Chad held out the model, examining its every nuance. "That had to be one large dog," Chad said, and he pulled it in close and smelled it. He made a face as he pulled his olfactory senses away in a hurry.

"Really?" Kevin took a whiff of it himself. "It doesn't smell," he said.

"Really?" Jimmy said and punched him on the arm. Chad started laughing. "Why would you smell that?"

"I don't know, because..." Kevin said.

"Awe, check it out, fake vomit," Chad interrupted. That set the boys off into a frenzy of violent but fake retching noises.

When the boys had tired, the entire aisle was completely littered with Slappy's very own gags. Somehow, the incident went without notice, probably because their mothers were all giggling up a storm over the elephant trunk underwear they too had discovered.

With the essential shopping out of the way, the two boys and their mothers finally made their way to the exit and then began the long walk back to the car. Just outside of the mall was a woman. She was dressed to catch one's eye, and she caught both boys' for one reason and their mothers' for another.

"Siren," Jimmy's mother whispered to Mrs. Spencer. Mrs. Spencer nodded. Jimmy gazed around. He didn't hear a thing.

CHAPTER NINE

-THE KILLING TREE-

The ride home was quiet. Everyone was tired from shopping, vomiting, and pooping. Well, the boys were tired anyway. Fake vomiting can be grueling, Jimmy and Kevin would attest to that. Jimmy's quietness could also have been attributed to the sullenness he felt having to leave behind his plastic sweetheart, and Kevin having fallen asleep. It didn't seem to take long before Jimmy's mother was pulling into their driveway.

"Wake up," Jimmy shouted as he gave Kevin a shove. Kevin took a moment to rouse, then climbed out of the car after Jimmy. Jimmy looked around, noticing something was different.

Jimmy started for the side of the house and quickly noticed that the stack of firewood along the side of the house had been cleaned up. It no longer looked neglected. The wood was now stacked, and the grass around the pile was trimmed back. Jimmy also noticed that the stack was considerably taller than before with what appeared to be freshly chopped wood.

"That's odd," he mumbled to himself. "It's summer. Why would we be getting new firewood?" He inspected the pile. Kevin followed lazily.

"What?" Kevin muttered in confusion.

"The new firewood," he said, trying to point out the obvious to Kevin. "Unless..."

Jimmy's eyes got wide. Then, like a bolt of lightning, he tore off for the backyard.

An eerie silence greeted him. Jimmy's mother shot his father a look as he appeared from the garage. Jimmy stopped dead in his tracks. The tree that housed his tree fort was gone! Next to the gnarled old crabapple tree was a stump. He couldn't believe his eyes. His tree fort was gone. He was madder than he had ever been. He turned in disgust, only to see his parents staring at him.

"I hate you!" he screamed through a downpour of tears.

"Jimmy," his mother called. He ignored her and ran to the garage for his baseball glove.

"Jimmy." This time, it was his father. Jimmy took off past them once more with his glove clenched in his hand. He headed for the woods behind his house. He had a long walk ahead of him before he would ever reach the trees.

Kevin looked at his mother, and she nodded. Kevin took off in pursuit of Jimmy. Both boys tired before they ever made it to the woods, but by the time they finally stopped, they were quickly absorbed into the thicket of dense brush and disappeared.

·   ·   ·

"Oh, by the way. We owe Mrs. Wilshire a new cat," Jimmy's father told his wife. She looked perplexed but not overly concerned that her eleven-year-old son just ran off.

"What?" she barked.

"Mrs. Wilshire's cat," he said, motioning something that looked like licking cat paws. "That um...Mr. Whiskers, he didn't make it."

"What?" she said.

"When the tree fell, it kind of...well, it fell on Mr. Whiskers," Jimmy's father finished explaining.

"You killed her cat?" Jimmy's mother cried out.

"You're the one who wanted the tree fort gone," Jimmy's father said in his defense. She glared at her husband. He never saw a set of eyes stare him down the way hers just did.

"What are we gonna do about Jimmy?" she said, now looking even less concerned that Mrs. Wilshire's cat was dead.

"He'll be back before supper," Jimmy's father assured her. And sure enough, he was. He wasn't happy and had nothing to say, but he made it home in time to eat.

•   •   •

Jimmy was surly at best for several days. He wouldn't say a word to his mother, and he couldn't look his father in his eye. The hardest thing to cope with was that Jimmy no longer had a place to escape, no place to brood when he had a problem. A few times, he was seen just sitting on the stump, kicking around the sawdust and wood chips left on the ground from the chainsaw. It didn't help any. He needed somewhere better to lose himself.

Baseball was about the only thing that could distract Jimmy from the loss of his fort. It couldn't have come at a better time, either. After their first practice, Jimmy had already made a good impression with his new coach. Jimmy still frequented the tree stump, but not nearly as often the next couple of weeks. In fact, he tried to avoid going out to it just because it brought back that sour taste.

Instead, Jimmy became possessed with being the team's best pitcher. He worked extra after practice with the coach and threw almost every evening with his father. The tree fort seemed almost a thing of the past.

"Hey, son, tomorrow's the big day," Jimmy's father said. "It's opening day!" Jimmy smiled nervously. He was excited, but a good barf wasn't out of the question. His stomach was turning with anxiety.

"Ugh," Jimmy moaned.

"Honey, Jimmy doesn't look too good," his father pointed out to his mother. Jimmy looked up at his mother for the first time in weeks, and with a look that said, "Mom, I need you," Jimmy started to cry.

"Oh, I think I have exactly what he needs," she said and walked her son to the kitchen. She gently touched his shoulder. He could tell she wanted to coddle him but knew enough that he wanted to be treated as if he was tough, with or without the tears. She made a cup of tea she said would calm his nerves and make him pitch better, if there ever was such a thing. He drank it with great comfort.

The next morning, he woke with that same nervous wrench in his stomach. He slid out of bed, ruffled his hair, and made his way down the stairs for breakfast and possibly another shot of that magic tea.

"Good morning, dear," his mother said, flipping a stack of pancakes onto a plate.

"Good morning," Jimmy replied sleepily.

"Whada ya say there, ace?" his father said doing his best radio announcer impersonation. He peered over the sports page at his sickly looking son.

"Hey, Dad," Jimmy said. Jimmy took two bites of his pancakes, then spent the rest of the time just playing with his food.

"Opening day jitters, boy, you'll be fine," his father told him. Jimmy looked at him, hoping he was right.

"Can I go get ready for the game?" Jimmy said.

"Oh, don't be silly. The game is not until later. We're going to the library."

"Mo'om," Jimmy moaned. The last drop of energy drained with each syllable. Jimmy looked to his father for help.

"Um, dear, whada ya say we give Jimmy here a day off from the library since it's opening day and all."

"Oh, now you're being silly. You know, there are more important things in life than baseball. It's just a game, for heaven's sake." Jimmy's mother sighed. Were all mothers completely insane? It was opening day. It was the biggest day of the year for Walnut Creek besides the county fair. Jimmy looked as if he was about to say something he would undoubtedly regret. His father caught him just in time.

"Dear, why don't I take him down to the park early so he can enjoy all the festivities and run around with his friends before the game, and I'll go to the library and get him some books." Both Jimmy and his father froze waiting for a response. The plan was genius. She would have to go for it.

"All right," she agreed, "but I better not come to find he is reading *MOBY DICK*," she added sternly. Both boys began to giggle. Absolutely incorrigible, her face said.

Jimmy went upstairs to get ready and took what seemed like forever to prepare for the game. Everything had to be perfect. His baseball sleeves had to hang out from under his jersey the same distance. His stirrup socks had to be the same height and his pants had to come down over them the same distance. It was quite a task, but he managed it, and soon he looked sharp.

"Oh, don't you just look darling," his mother said, beaming. She moved in to pinch his cheeks, but thankfully, thought better of it when Jimmy flashed her his game face.

"Mo'om," he said. Jimmy straightened his hat. "Are you gonna come to my game, Mom?" Jimmy asked.

"Of course. Unless you don't want me to," she said.

"No, I want you there. You have to go," Jimmy said.

"What time does the game start?" she asked, as if she didn't already know.

"It's at one," Jimmy's father told her.

"I'll be there."

Jimmy set out the front door with his glove in tow and his new Louisville Slugger slung over his shoulder. He looked like a real ballplayer.

When Jimmy and his father arrived at the town center, it was already bustling with just about everybody from town. A parade was making its way down Main Street, town officials were waving to the crowd, and every shop and building along the route was closed, including the library. Jimmy's father pointed it out to Jimmy with a wink. "I'll have to show your mother. There's no way she'll believe either one of us."

"Right, Dad," he said, returning the wink. "Hey, there are my friends." And he took off towards Kevin, Chad, and Dave near the ball field, leaving his father behind.

"Have a good game, son." His dad called after him.

"Thanks, see ya, Dad," Jimmy said.

The field was adorned with so many banners and flags it looked like the fourth of July, and the smell of freshly cut grass was the telltale sign it was baseball season. The excitement was epic. Jimmy found the rest of his team warming up along the left field foul line, and after putting his bat in the dugout; he and his friends went out to join them. There was about as much celebrating and organizing as there was baseball. When the vendor stands were up and running, all anyone could smell was hot dogs. It was opening day.

"Play Ball!" boomed from the umpire. The town buzzed with excitement as the Walnut Creek Wildcats took the field against their next town over rivals, the Mitchellville Mud Hens. Jimmy walked to the mound, still in shock that he got the nod as the starting pitcher for the Wildcats. Kevin was behind the plate, catching. Dave was in center field with Chad in right.

Jimmy scratched at the mound with his spikes, as he had seen so many pro ball players do before. He was a natural at it. When he was finished moving the hilly earth beneath his feet to his liking, he stood poised atop the rubber, ready to pitch. Jimmy threw several warm-up pitches, none of which were anywhere near the plate.

"Balls in, coming down!" the umpire shouted. Kevin repeated that message and threw the ball from the last warm-up pitch somewhere in the vicinity of second base. "Play ball!" the ump shouted again, and he donned his mask before crouching down behind Kevin.

"Let's go, Wildcats," came a cheer from some of the spectators.

"Let it rip, Jimmy," came another. Jimmy went into his windup and let the first pitch of the new season fly.

"Strike!" the umpire called. Jimmy felt a rush of adrenaline and let the second pitch go. "Strike two!" The batter was frozen. Jimmy was firing bullets. "Strike three!" The crowd erupted. His teammates were cheering as well.

Jimmy struck the next batter out with three more pitches, and Walnut Creek was going crazy.

"Come on, Jimmy baby!" shouted a woman with a deafening bark. "Come on, Jimmy baby!"

Jimmy was in rare form. He had never pitched this well in his life. He knew he was this good, but never once had he been able to prove it. "Strike three!" and Jimmy struck out the side. His teammates practically mobbed him on their way in from the field. He basked in every bit of the glory.

With their adrenaline still pumping, the Wildcats managed to score three runs in their half of the inning. Jimmy had a double, which scored two runs, and two errors later, the third run pushed across home plate. Jimmy again was at the center of the celebration. He cherished every minute of it.

When Kevin flied out to center field for the third out, the Wildcats then retook the field. Jimmy again scratched at the earth until it was just so and began his warm-ups. He was still riding the adrenaline from the last inning and his warm-up pitches looked sharp.

"Balls in," Jimmy would have giggled, but he was in a zone. The Mud Hen's number four batter walked to the plate. He was huge. He looked fifteen years old. Jimmy was slowly losing the confidence that got him there. The kid took a practice swing, giving Jimmy too much time to think. He tried to tell himself that this kid couldn't hit his fastball, just challenge him. So, that was the plan.

Crack! Jimmy plunked the boy right in the helmet. The boy went down to the ground, writhing in pain. Mud Hen coaches attended to the boy, and after a few minutes, the boy jogged down to first base, seemingly okay. The crowd went into a polite, "he's okay" applause. Jimmy didn't seem flustered, but he walked the next batter on four straight pitches. Then he walked the next and then the next. Jimmy's coach called time and went out to visit Jimmy on the mound. Jimmy looked up and waited for some words of wisdom, some enlightenment.

"You okay?" the coach asked. Jimmy nodded. "Let's throw strikes." And his coach walked off the field as if that was that. Jimmy thought for sure his coach would have said something more, something brilliant, something that would have helped, but that hadn't come.

Jimmy walked the next two batters, then an onslaught of hits and errors and more walks brought eleven runs across the plate. The cheering that Jimmy had enjoyed turned to moans and gripes. Finally, the coach came out and took the ball from Jimmy and replaced him with Kyle, the Wildcat's shortstop. Jimmy made the long walk back to the dugout with his head hung low and tears streaming down his face. No one clapped or said a word as he disappeared into the dugout. How quickly they forgot.

The Wildcats never got back on their feet from that inning and ended up losing the game 26-3. No one played particularly well that game, but Jimmy took it the worst. He was quiet the entire way home in the car, and when he got out of the car, he went straight to the stump to brood.

•   •   •

"He looks so sad out there," his mother said as she watched her son from inside the kitchen window. "You should talk to him," she told her husband.

"He'll be fine. He just needs time to himself," he said. She gave him a disappointing pout. He sighed and left the kitchen.

"There must be something we can do?" she said, following him.

"We already did," he said. "Remember?" and Jimmy's dad pantomimed a tree being cut down and crashing to the ground.

"Are you on the fort thing again?" she said. Her voice was stern. "What is it about a boy and his tree fort?"

"A tree fort is like a boy's castle, his sanctuary. It's where he can get away from his problems for a while and hash out what is bothering him. It's a place where he can feel important. You know, kind of like you are in the kitchen," his father said. The room got quiet in a hurry. Jimmy's mother glared at her husband. His face was askew, waiting for retribution.

"Oh really," she said pausing for just the right words. "Like you are in the bathroom?"

"I'll go talk to him," he said, wounded.

"Just leave him," she said, growing increasingly exasperated with the whole ordeal.

"You sure?"

"As long as he comes in by suppertime," she said. Jimmy's mom returned to watching him from the window. She was feeling sympathetic towards her child, but it was still her idea and persistence that brought that tree fort down. She couldn't back down now. Even if she did, it was too late to gain anything from it.

"He'll be fine," her husband reassured her.

"What if..." she said but hesitated.

"What if what?"

"Can you build him a clubhouse that's safer, something on the ground maybe?" He looked surprised.

"Yeah," he said. "He'll be just delighted to hear you say that."

"No, I don't think he should know I had anything to do with it," she said. Jimmy's dad wasn't sure what she meant.

"He'll figure out something when you don't burn it to the ground," he said sarcastically. She did not appreciate his humor.

"Go build it in the woods somewhere. Somewhere close, where he'll be safe, and make sure it's on the ground and not up in a tree," she said. She looked at him genuinely and pouted slightly. She may have been seeking vindication, but for now, she would settle with just not feeling horrible.

"I know the perfect spot," he informed her.

"I don't want to know about it," she said. He nodded.

•　　•　　•

Jimmy had to be called in for supper, but first he had to be awakened. The heat of the day, the spent energy brooding, and the out-and-out boredom of sitting out there had taken its toll. He was sound asleep with his face buried in the sawdust.

"Wake up there, boy," his father roused him. Jimmy barely stirred. Then he mumbled something, possibly from an encounter with Morpheus. Jimmy's father took his foot and pushed Jimmy's shoulder. That rolled Jimmy's body just enough that when he awoke, he came up with a snout full of sawdust.

"Wha...," he moaned incoherently.

"Wake up, it's time for supper," his father said. Jimmy sat up.

"I wasn't sleeping," Jimmy said.

"Yeah, okay," his dad said. "Look, before we go inside, I want to talk to you about this tree fort thing."

Jimmy looked surly. "I don't-," Jimmy started to say but was quickly cut off.

"Just listen. Me and some of the guys over at Jake's Lumber got to talkin' about this situation, and we all realize you boys need a clubhouse or fort to call your own, so we got to plannin', and this is what we decided." Jimmy looked less surly and more excited now.

"What are we doing?"

"We're gonna build you a new fort," his father said.

"What about Mom?"

"She doesn't have to know about it," his father said, checking his periphery for the monster. Jimmy, realizing the need for stealth, leaned closer to his father. Then he realized it wouldn't work.

"You don't think she's gonna notice it once we start hammering away. She's gonna burn it to the ground before we're even finish building it," Jimmy moaned.

"We're gonna build it in the woods so she doesn't find out about it," the father explained.

"Where in the woods?"

"I was thinking out by the old Cattank Furnace site," his father replied and gestured out past the open field in their backyard.

"That's just over the hill there, past them trees," Jimmy said.

"How's that sound?" his father asked.

"I love it. Mom won't find out?"

"Let's hope not," his father said.

"Let's hide her matches, just in case," Jimmy thought.

"Good idea."

"Will it be the same as I had," Jimmy asked.

"Better," his father said.

"Ah, this is gonna be awesome." With a new sense of elation, Jimmy could imagine his new fort in all its glory. His baseball woes were behind him.

"I think it will be best if we build it on the ground, though, and not in a tree."

"How come?"

"We don't want you falling out of it," his father said.

Jimmy took a moment. "Who's we?"

"Huh, what?" His father said. He had a nervous panic to his face. "Me and the guys," he snorted. Then he added, "Let's go have supper." And they walked back to the house, closer than ever.

CHAPTER TEN

−PIG IRON AND PICKLE−

On Tuesday evening, the Walnut Creek Wildcats took the field against the Dembrill Tigers in their first night game. That meant one thing. They would play under the lights. Dembrill was a small town much like Walnut Creek, and their ball field didn't have quite the appeal as Walnut Creek's home field, but with the lights on and the cornfield silhouetted against the outfield fence, it had its own allure. It was baseball in its purest form. The magic of the game filled the bleachers, the dugouts, even the outfield. The bugs glistened in the light, enticed by the huge glow of the flood lamps high above the field. That glow could be seen for miles along the flat earth sown with crops.

Only the second-year players had ever played under the lights before, but every kid stood dumbstruck, gazing at the magnificent glow that lit only the field. Everything around it was dark except for the crescent of the moon. It was beautiful. The Bermuda grass was crisp under their spikes, and the red clay that lined the base paths seemed just right, making ground balls a little truer and maybe easier to field.

Truer or not, neither the Tigers nor the Wildcats seemed to be able to field much of anything. The game would be decided by offense. Jimmy didn't think he would have time to pitch that game, especially after his last outing, but his coach had gone through every available pitcher, except for

Jimmy, by the fifth inning. With the score Wildcats 17, Tigers 15, Jimmy's coach had little option but to use Jimmy in that sixth and final inning.

Jimmy made his way out to the mound in the bottom half and scratched his markings in the dirt then took his warm-up pitches. He felt good. This could be the night. The game was on the line, and his coach called on him to finish it out. His confidence was high. Thunk!

Jimmy nailed the first batter in the side. The noise echoed into the darkness and then disappeared. Jimmy went into his stretch. Four pitches later and the tying run was on base. Kevin slid the catcher's mask from his face, called time, and went out to talk to Jimmy.

"You all right?" he asked Jimmy.

"Yeah," Jimmy nodded. Kevin kicked a little of the dirt around then looked back to Jimmy.

"Forget there's a batter, and just throw to my glove, or better yet, throw it at my face. That would be a strike," Kevin said. Jimmy smiled at Kevin's remark. He then reworked the ground back how he had had it. Kevin donned the mask once again and made his way back behind the plate.

"Stee-rike!" the umpire called. The umpire had a funny way about calling strikes. Jimmy didn't care for it much but wanted to hear it again. He heard it only once more before the Tigers tied the score. Jimmy was pissed he gave up the lead. He had let his team down. He had let himself down. He was beginning to think he wasn't the great pitcher he wanted to be. They managed to get out of the inning without giving up any more runs, and the game went into extra innings.

Jimmy stormed to the plate to lead off the seventh inning. He doubled. Kyle tried to bunt him over to third but missed twice, and ended up striking out. Dave walked to the plate with a mission, to get that lead back. He swung so hard at the first pitch that it hurt to watch his body twist and writhe until he fell over.

"Stee-rike one!" called the umpire. Dave got up, took the bat, knocked the dirt out from his spikes, and reloaded his stance to hit the ball. The pitcher let loose the next pitch and sent the ball right at Dave's head. Dave flung himself to the ground. "Ball," the umpired burped. Dave got to his feet and stared down the pitcher. Kicking the dirt out once more, he stepped back into the batter's box.

"Put it right here with everything you got," he challenged the pitcher. The catcher may have been able to hear him, but certainly not anyone else.

"Stee-rike," said the umpire. Dave froze. He took a hard practice swing, trying to shake it off. The next pitch was hurled to the plate. Dave never even heard the ball hit the bat, but his teammates went wild as they all watched the ball arc out and over the outfield fence. The ball was swallowed by the cornfield and disappeared into the darkness. With that home run, the Wildcats took a two-run lead. He and Jimmy were mobbed as they both crossed home plate. Dave had saved the day.

That turned out to be all the scoring the Wildcats needed, as Jimmy pitched a perfect inning by striking out all three batters for the win. The Wildcats celebrated in good fashion, right up until they turned out the lights on everybody.

Dembrill's field maintenance chief must have seen enough. The entire field went black as parents and players scrambled for their cars in the darkness. The game was over, as was any celebration. Jimmy's coach had to use the light from all the car's headlights to finish putting away the equipment. After everyone and everything was accounted for, they settled in for the long ride home.

When the energy from the game petered out, the ride home got quiet. Jimmy, Dave, Chad, and Kevin all stared out into the darkness as the Spencer's drove them back to Walnut Creek. The only light source other than the headlights was the hundreds of fireflies dashing about along their path. They were hypnotized by the sight until the bugs started hitting the windshield and bits of their illumination stuck to the glass. It was a fourth of July celebration, but only in green.

Mr. Spencer sent the wiper blades into action, only to smear the green glow across their sight. The boys sat quietly and enjoyed the light show. Mr. Spencer eventually dropped off all the boys and had Kevin and Jimmy home by ten thirty. Late for a school night, but since the next day was the last day of school before the summer break, no one really seemed to mind.

• • •

The last day of school passed without incident. No one really said goodbye or anything since they all knew each other and would see each other over the summer. That was one nuance of small towns. So, they just went about the day like it was any other.

When the bell rang and school let out, everybody got on the bus and headed home. Dave and Chad didn't get off the bus at their normal stop. Instead, they got off the bus with Jimmy and Kevin, and all four met out behind Jimmy's house at the tree stump.

"So, what's so important that we had to meet out here," Dave asked. Chad and Kevin nodded. Jimmy eyed the adjacent backyards and then leaned in.

"The new fort," he said in stealth. Dave, Chad, and Kevin leaned in too.

"Go ahead," Dave said.

"My dad and some of the guys at your grandfather's sawmill are going to build us a new one," Jimmy said, referring to Dave's grandfather.

"What do ya mean us," Chad asked.

"I guess it's gonna be all of ours," Jimmy said. Dave nodded with a thoughtful grin.

"Cool," Kevin and Chad said.

"My mom can't find out about it, though" Jimmy said. Chad rolled his eyes, and he nodded, his blond locks bouncing slightly even after he stopped nodding.

"She'd burn it to the ground, she would," Chad said. They all nodded.

"Like I said, she can't find out about it."

"Where are they planning on building it?" Kevin asked.

"Cattank," Jimmy said.

"Cool," Chad said.

"Where?" Kevin asked. They all looked at him oddly having forgotten he was still relatively new to Walnut Creek.

"Cattank Furnace, it's some old historic site where they made pig iron," Jimmy explained. "My dad said it's cool if we build near it but just not on it. I don't know why."

"So what's pig iron?" Kevin asked.

"I don't know," Dave said. "They also made cannonballs and things like that there, a long time ago."

"That's really cool," Kevin said. They all agreed. "Maybe we can find some old cannonballs out there."

"Doubt it, they've got to be all gone by now," Chad added.

"So, nobody knows what this pig iron is?" Kevin asked again.

"Hey," Jimmy said. "Can we get back to the matter at hand?"

"Yes," Dave said. "It's about time we talked about your pitching."

Jimmy's eyes flew open. "What?"

Dave chuckled and gave Jimmy a push. It was enough that his bum slipped off the stump, landing Jimmy hard on the ground.

"Oh shit, sorry, dude," Dave said, reaching for Jimmy. "I didn't mean to."

Jimmy pushed away any offer for help and got up on his own. He dusted the sawdust off his backside and sat back down.

"You guys want to talk about the new fort or baseball?" Jimmy sighed.

"Baseball."

"Baseball."

"Baseball."

"How 'bout a game of pickle then?" Dave said. Jimmy sighed again but agreed.

Kevin and Jimmy disappeared to fetch their gloves. When they returned, Dave took an old weathered-looking box top and made a base out of it. An old rag made up the other. And so, the four boys played the condensed version of baseball in Jimmy's backyard until Jimmy's mother called him in for dinner. She also informed the other boys that their mothers were wishing them home as well.

"Hey remember, tomorrow we go out to the old Cattank Furnace and check things out," Jimmy shouted. Dave, Chad and Kevin gave a stealthily nod in front of Mrs. Hamilton and walked off.

"See ya, Jimmy."

CHAPTER ELEVEN

—THE THREE-LEGGED FROG—

The sun ambled slowly through the green of the trees beyond Jimmy's backyard as it broke the horizon and started the day. Jimmy was already awake and had a small knapsack packed for his journey to the furnace. The anticipation for yet another adventure-filled summer had Jimmy excited. He was downstairs eating breakfast earlier than if it was a school day.

His mother had packed some sandwiches and cookies for his trip. She'd supplied enough for all four boys, so when Dave, Chad, and Kevin arrived, everyone was ready to set out.

"See ya, Mom," Jimmy said.

"Bye, Mrs. Hamilton," the three other boys said, and on their way they went.

"Bye, dears, be good now," she called after them. They all nodded, looking slightly guilty about something. Once outside, they made a beeline for the woods behind Jimmy's house. In no time at all, they reach the wood's edge, and they disappeared into the thicket.

They hiked with a purpose. There was little time for adventures. Jimmy led the way as if he was on a pilgrimage. After all, this new site would be for his new castle. They had to blaze their own trail, as the woods weren't well travelled. In fact, most people from those parts stayed clear of the woods unless they had good reason. The woods were downright creepy when they wanted to be, but Jimmy and his friends had good reason.

Chad's new olfactory compass came in handy. Jimmy referred to it several times. Chad stretched his neck out like a meerkat and took a deep breath. He used the town dump in the same way one would use due north on a real compass. They kept the dump to their left until they hit a cornfield. They walked along the wood's edge until they hit a small rise and back into the woods they went.

That was the sketchiest part of the forest. The trees were very tall and very old and nothing grew underneath them. It was as if death took its toll there. Jimmy felt the temperature dip with each step, but it was merely that the sun couldn't reach the forest floor.

Jimmy remembered his father talking of the death that lingered in those woods. He called it juglone. It had something to do with the walnut trees and a poison they emitted. His mother would have probably described it as the magical forest that comes alive. But in reality, it was the opposite of alive.

Jimmy marched on trying not to let the macabre set in, but it affected all four boys. Kevin seemed to keep close tabs on his friends while trekking through the strange woods. That would not be the place to get lost.

"How much farther?" Kevin asked.

"Not far," Jimmy said.

Chad stretched his neck for an olfactory reading, but again, death was the strongest thing in the air. He motioned they were headed in the right direction, so they pressed on.

"You guys still good?" Dave asked, a wobble in his voice. They motioned as if they were, but they needed to get out of this section of the forest. "Not much farther, guys."

Up ahead, light trickled down through the trees and began lighting the forest floor again. Their pace hastened. Their moods lifted. They began sprinting as if something was chasing them, but nothing was behind them, only the grim. Out of breath and out of the grip of death that was those woods, the boys reached a coppice where newer growth trees lived among the rotted out old growth forest. The older trees were once most likely used to fuel the furnace.

Jimmy couldn't make this stuff up in a book. It was library material, only in real life it just seemed better. They could make out a brick structure up ahead.

"The furnace," Jimmy pointed out, and he headed straight to it. They each scoured the area as they made their way towards the building. It was battered and barely had three good walls left to it. The roof only sheltered part of the flooring inside.

"Whoa! This is cool," Kevin said as he peeked inside.

"Oh, check it out," Chad said enthusiastically.

"What is it, Chad?" Dave said running over.

"It's some kind of ball," Chad said, poking at the wall.

"Let me see," Jimmy said as he leaned in for a closer look. It was a cannonball lodged in the brick wall as if it belonged there.

"That is so cool," Kevin said. It was cool too, so much so, that the four boys made a mock re-creation of the battle that brought that cannonball to its existence in the wall. Of course, whoever shot that cannonball wasn't likely up against machine guns—not until the boys' battle.

"Incoming," Jimmy hollered, and they all hunkered down to a nice rendition of a flying cannonball courtesy of Dave.

"We have to take out that cannon," Dave shouted. Jimmy gestured for Dave and Chad to flank the cannon to the east, as he and Kevin would cover them. Then it would be their job to advance their position to the west side.

"Ah, I'm hit," Chad shouted and fell to the ground. The other boys stopped the game.

"You're not that bad, get up." Dave said.

"Can you make it to that tank?" Jimmy asked.

"Cannon," Kevin said.

"Yeah, whatever," Jimmy said.

"Sorry," Kevin said. Their energy for the fight was waning. Then like a dog who just sniffed his butt, ate a bug, then found a squirrel to chase, the boy's attention moved to a black snake slithering across the fortress' dirt floor.

"Get him," Jimmy shouted. Dave picked up a stick and began poking at the serpent. It writhed and hissed then backed itself into a corner. Dave moved in closer but the snake headed for Chad and easily got past him as Chad yelped, much like a girl, then jumped away. Jimmy found a forked stick and broke off the leaves.

Kevin made a stick similar to Jimmy's and went in after the snake. He was fearless and managed to pin the snake just behind its head, where his neck would be if he had one. The snake coiled up the stick as if it was trying to pull it off its neck. Then it uncoiled, writhed some more and recoiled again.

"Hold its head," Chad said.

"I got him," Kevin insisted. Chad reached in with his hand and grabbed the snake's tail.

"Waaaa!" and he let it go.

"What are you doing?" Dave moaned.

"You grab him if you're so tough," Chad said.

"All right," and Dave did. "Waaaa!" The snake writhed but Dave never let go and Jimmy took his fork-like stick and pinned the snake's tail to the ground. It tried to writhe out of the hold the boys now had on it, but it was useless. The snake was disabled.

"Check it out, he has a lump in his belly," Jimmy pointed out. Kevin poked the lump with his finger.

"Eewe!" The snake bucked slightly as if its belly was sensitive.

"Whada ya think that is?" Chad asked.

"It's either babies or his lunch," Jimmy said.

"You mean her lunch," Chad said.

"What?" Jimmy said.

"What if it has a swarm of baby snakes inside it," Kevin said.

"Oh, that would be cool," Jimmy said.

"Let's cut it open," Dave said. They were all game for a little biology.

"Yeah, let's," Jimmy said. "Here, take this," and Chad grabbed the stick Jimmy had been holding. Jimmy went to his pack and pulled out a small pocketknife. This was something his mother would not approve of him having, but his father thought it was okay.

"What if it is babies, and they squirm out all over the place, and even start attacking us?" Chad said, fueled by boyish imagination.

"That would be so cool," Dave said.

"Yeah, that would be," Jimmy agreed. He then took the knife to the lump.

"Don't miss!" Kevin shouted alarmingly. Jimmy flinched and nearly cut his own finger.

"What the hell's wrong with you?" Jimmy asked.

"Sorry, I thought it was funny," Kevin replied.

"It kind of was," Jimmy said. Jimmy drew the knife even closer.

"Do it," chorused the group of boys watching Jimmy about to dissect his first living thing. Four faces squinched as the cold steel blade of the knife indented the skin before it actually cut into the snake. The blade dipped into the snake's skin sending its body into a crazed frenzy between the forked holds.

"Eewe," cried the lot. Then Chad got a waft of the bile of intestines as the lump oozed out of the snake.

"Oh my god, what is that?" Whatever it was, it was covered in slime and had a dark hue to it. Jimmy poked at it with his knife. It stunk. It resembled a frog, and indeed it was a frog.

"Hey, it's only got three legs," Chad said. Jimmy poked around some more and discovered that indeed, the frog was short one leg.

"That's wild," Dave declared.

"That's probably why he got eaten," Jimmy concluded and poked about it some more. Kevin and Chad let up some on their forks to discover that the snake was no longer resisting. It was dead. They continued their examination of the body parts in front of them.

"Should we cut open the frog?" Dave suggested. A morbid curiosity came over each boy. Jimmy poked its skin with his knife. When he withdrew the blade, a string of slime followed it.

"Eewe," they chimed. Jimmy pulled the knife away swiftly and wiped the blade off on the ground.

"That was so unbelievable," Jimmy said. Each boy agreed and thought it was a lot of fun too.

"I wonder what the hunt was like for either of 'em," Chad said.

"The frog probably just hopped around in big circles," Jimmy replied. They all laughed as they pictured the frog having a terrible time trying to go straight because of its three legs.

"Oh yeah, like that cripple with just the one arm who sits in his wheelchair out in front of the grocery store all the time," Dave said. Then he mimicked trying to wheel around in a wheelchair while using only one arm. He bumped into Chad as he came around in his small circle.

"My daddy says he's a vet," Jimmy said, not laughing with the others.

"No wonder the frog only had three legs," Chad said.

"What?"

"The vet, he's only got one arm, how the hell is he gonna sew on the frog's leg with just one arm."

"I think he's a different kind of vet," Jimmy said. "Who wants a sandwich?" he added. But while they ate, they thought about the three-legged frog. He would live long in the stories they would tell, his lore just beginning. The idea that only the strong survive would seep into their minds, teaching them all an invaluable lesson.

After lunch, they made their way out into the clearing for bits of further exploration, but Chad wasn't watching where he was going and stepped on the frog. It squished under his foot like he was wearing a wet tennis sneaker. Then it stuck to the bottom of his shoe. He tried to shake the half-digested amphibian from his tread only to make a mess of the situation before he took a stick and jabbed his sneaker clean of its hitchhiker.

"Chad, don't smell that," Dave said. Chad put his foot down. Apparently, Chad's newfound super power also gave him the propensity to smell things no matter how unpleasant. They walked on as they scouted the area for the most advantageous position for their clubhouse. Still in sight of the furnace building, the boys came to settle on a clearing. The land was flat, positioned well for spying, and protected from the rear by the maleficent old growth forest.

"This looks good," Jimmy declared as he stood where he believed the fort's front wall would stand. "We'll put the gun turrets here and here," he added excitedly. The others just looked at him, egging his imagination on. A new and wonderful feeling grew inside Jimmy. He was happy.

"Let's look for other stuff to cut up," Chad said. They all agreed and began a new trek for victims. Each boy slogged through the tall grass and brush but never came upon anything worth cutting open. They walked to the edge of the gnarled old trees from the old growth forest but never entered. Instead, they trudged along the brink of the sinister woodland.

"Hey, what's that path there?" Kevin asked. He stood looking down a clearing about as wide as a car. The path had two worn tracks, and overgrown grass and weeds filled in the rest.

"That," Jimmy said, "is the old Cattank Road."

"Let's take it. Where's it go?"

"It takes us back to the neighborhood," Jimmy said.

"Why didn't we take that road to get here?" Kevin asked.

"Because we didn't have to," Dave said. Kevin looked down the path one more time as though he was wondering if there was some other reason, maybe one that made sense.

"There's no thrill in taking the beaten path," Jimmy said.

CHAPTER TWELVE

-THE UGLY BOXSCORE-

When the boys finally had enough, they walked down Cattank Road, as they had a thousand times before, except for Kevin. They kept an eye on the woods, but their own imagination was as tired as their bodies.

"Oh man, what's that?" Kevin said. He stopped several yards ahead at a large tan object lying at the side of the road. Jimmy, Dave, and Chad made their way up to where Kevin stopped and looked down. It was a deer carcass, fully intact and dead as dead gets. Its legs were stiff and oddly erect as rigor mortis had set in.

"Why's his legs all stiff like that," Chad asked. No one knew.

"Who cares, let's stand him up," Jimmy said, and he started tugging at the deer's leg. Dave got hold of the deer's head, while Chad and Kevin pulled his other legs until the deer was lying on the road.

"Wait, we need something to keep him from sliding," Dave said. Kevin quickly moved to the other side.

They pushed, and when they got it nearly to its feet, they eased up. It was just enough to keep the deer's body balanced on its four legs. The boys stepped back and admired the hoofed mammal. It stood slightly eschew, but it stood all the same. Jimmy looked deep into its big brown eyes. He sensed pain and fear at some point from the poor beast.

Then from out of nowhere, like a piñata, the stomach of the deer blew out and dumped itself onto the ground. They looked on in horror. The remains of the belly crawled about the earth as hundreds, maybe thousands of maggots swarmed about trying to regroup themselves.

"Aaaah!!!" screamed four voices, and they were gone. They ran so fast down the dirt road that a small trail of dust kicked up in their wake. They never looked back.

When they reached the neighborhood, Kevin finally got a sense as to just how close the Cattank Furnace was to his house. Their journey to the furnace through the woods had left a completely different perception of its proximity. Kevin felt a little more at ease when he realized he would not have to trek those horrible woods every time he wanted to play out there.

"You guys up for anything?" Jimmy asked as they approached his house. Two shrugs and a mumble later, they all knew the day's journey had come to an end. Dave and Chad walked on as Kevin turned for his house.

"What an adventure," Jimmy told the world as he walked up his driveway. That had only been the first day of their summer break, and what a day it was. He knew it was going to be a summer to remember.

•   •   •

Baseball practice that evening was particularly grueling as Jimmy's team geared up for their third contest against a team that was one of the best that year, the undefeated Clarksburg Ravens. It would prove to be one of the toughest challenges all season, but after the hard work they put in, they were up for the battle. Saturday seemed too far away.

"How was practice dear?" Jimmy's mother asked, embarrassing the lot of boys in the back seat.

"Good," Jimmy said. The remaining ride home was quiet. The boys were exhausted from practice, not to mention their earlier adventures.

•   •   •

Saturday morning broke with cloudy skies but not a drop of rain. Jimmy was excited about the game but wary of a possible rainout. About an hour before game time, much to his relief, the clouds broke up and burned off.

To his surprise, Jimmy took the mound for the start of the game. He went through his pre-game ritual of adjusting everything once then putting it back. This started with his socks and usually ended with the dirt around the mound.

"Play ball!" the umpire bellowed from deep inside his large protruding belly. He was a stout man with an enormous head and equipment that didn't quite fit. His melon size head was squeezed into his face mask and his chest protector jutted out, following the slope of his stomach.

"Strike!" rang out. Jimmy was off to a good start. He felt good, too. "Ball." Well, maybe not that good.

"Say there, shooter," said a voice from the crowd. Jimmy was pumped with adrenaline. He was the shooter. It wasn't his nickname, just baseball jargon.

"Strike," called the fat man in the mask. Jimmy was in a zone. He hurled the next pitch for strike three. The umpire rang the batter up for the first out.

"Way to fire, Jimmy," Dave said from his spot at shortstop. Then more words of encouragement traveled the diamond in Jimmy's direction. Jimmy looked into the stands and glimpsed his mother and father sitting on the bleachers, cheering loudly and looking proud.

Then a sight caught Jimmy's eyes, and he forgot where he was. It was Cindy. She was sitting quietly by herself on the end of a row of the bleachers. She was watching Jimmy. Those beautiful brown eyes of hers followed his every move. Her precious smile beamed at him. Her brown hair whirled about in the wind as if trying to get his attention. And it did.

He gulped, but because of the size of the next batter, not because of Cindy. If he was the number two batter, Jimmy was pretty sure he didn't want to know who batted third and fourth. After walking that batter and then the next, he was going to find out soon enough who was batting fourth. He checked on Cindy. She was so beautiful. She sat there quietly with the same expression, the same beautiful smile, and the same warm eyes. Jimmy was in deep.

"I got to concentrate," he mumbled to himself but then found himself looking at his friend again. She was there to watch Jimmy play, and he knew it, and now he wanted to impress her. Then the cleanup hitter trudged to the plate. He was a barrel of a boy, perhaps the umpire's kid.

"Ball!" croaked the fat man. Jimmy thought he should have had that call. The next pitch Jimmy let fly, and so did the barrel shaped boy. It was a deep fly ball to left center. It skipped once and hit the outfield fence. Jimmy sighed and threw a quick tantrum as if he thought the centerfielder should have caught the ball. Then he stood and watched the rest of the play.

"Backup the throw," yelled his coach, but Jimmy was too busy being a spectator. The centerfielder got to it okay and hurled it back into the infield. Dave caught the ball on the fly, but when he turned to throw it to third, the third baseman wasn't paying attention. Dave tried to hold up on his throw, but in doing so, he sailed the ball over third and into the dugout. Then and only then did Jimmy realize he was supposed to back up the throw. The barrel shaped boy trotted home on the error.

The box score for Jimmy's outing went something like this, one third of an inning pitched, seven hits, eleven runs given up, six walks, two hit batters and at least one tantrum. It wasn't pretty, and Jimmy did not take the thrashing well. He stormed off the field, throwing his glove from the foul line all the way into the dugout. His hat followed. Then he kicked at the dirt the rest of the way to the dugout as if the dirt had wronged him. Cindy watched the episode without the slightest bit of reaction. She still had eyes on Jimmy the whole way.

The final score was 14-7, and the Ravens left Walnut Creek still undefeated. Jimmy sat on the bench the rest of the game, most likely because of his little tirade. The coach seemed furious and wouldn't even look at Jimmy. Jimmy started to wonder if he'd ever get to play again.

CHAPTER THIRTEEN

-THE WISH THAT CAME TRUE-

Jimmy was so dispirited by his performance that he didn't put up the slightest bit of resistance to having to go to the library later that day. In fact, he was more than happy to return one of his books, *The Art of Being a Pitcher*. A total farce as far as he was concerned. He left the library with the usual—a couple of kid detective stories; a baseball how-to book, but this one by a different author; a book about animals; and a sour look on his face.

"Hey, what's Dad up to?" Jimmy asked as his mother drove home from the library. He'd noticed his dad took off right after the game, and Jimmy hadn't seen him since.

"He said he had some business with Jake Warrell today," Jimmy's mother said, a slight smile on her face.

Jimmy sat up and the color of life came back to his cheeks. "Did he say when he'd be home?" Jimmy asked.

"No," was all she said.

The car barely came to a stop before Jimmy jumped out and ran into the house. Jimmy's mother hollered after him, but Jimmy had disappeared through the front door.

"Da'ad!" Jimmy yelled. That word also had two syllables when it was necessary. His father was not home.

"Honey!" Jimmy's mother called out.

"Yeah?" Jimmy said. She smiled.

"I was calling for your father, sweetie," she said. She pulled Jimmy's library books from her bag and held them out. His face dropped, and he took the books and moped up to his room. "You can come down when your father gets home," she finished.

"You can come down when your father gets home," he mimicked with an accentuated slam of his feet on each step all the way up to his room. The door slammed. Jimmy would have been proud to know, she whispered, "Incorrigible," to his back as he walked away.

•   •   •

When the back door creaked open and then closed again, Jimmy was down the stairs and in his father's way before he even had a chance to settle himself. Something in Jimmy's room was still crashing to the ground from him slamming open his door. His mother sighed and went to the refrigerator. His father shot him a secretive look then rolled his eyes toward Jimmy's mother. Jimmy got it right away.

"Right," he agreed like a cool gangster from an old movie.

"How about we have chicken tonight for dinner?" his mother said as she pulled a partially thawed bird from the icebox.

"Sounds great dear," Jimmy's father said.

"Well, there we go," she said showing everyone the plump fowl and plopping it onto the counter. "How would you like it?" she asked as her audience disappeared into the family room.

"So, Dad, how's the fort coming along?" Jimmy asked with great expectation. He was on the edge of his seat.

"It looks like it's coming along really nicely. We have a good bit of the framing already done."

"Is it at the old Cattank?"

"It's right where you marked it. That spot will be fine," his father assured him. Jimmy was beaming.

"What's it built out of?" he asked.

"Quarter sawn oak." Jimmy beamed even more. Quarter sawn oak sounded impressive. "Jake Warrell had stacks of the stuff at his mill. He cut a bunch of old trees down at Papi's old farm."

"Papi Whitaker?" Jimmy asked.

His father nodded. "Yep."

"Can I come out and help ya?" Jimmy pleaded. His father nodded and put a finger to his lips as he glanced over his shoulder for a peek at his wife.

"Yeah, Maybe," and he glanced over his shoulder again. Jimmy began rocking excitedly. He wanted this fort so badly. He was so excited, in fact, he never even asked his father to play catch, which was something they almost always did on Saturday.

When they finished dinner that night, a settling calm came over the table. Jimmy's tummy was full and his mind abuzz with fort plans. Outside, the cricket's chirp cut through the darkness.

"Who wants to break the wishbone?" Jimmy's mother asked.

"I want to," Jimmy declared with a childish innocence.

"Me too," said his father, the grown child.

They each took an end. "Now, both of you make a wish," she said.

At the same time, they pulled. Snap!

"Yeah!" Jimmy shouted.

"Damn it," his father bellowed in frustration. He slunk back down and into his chair. "Whada ya wish for?"

"He can't tell you or it won't come tru..."

But before she could finish, Jimmy blurted out, "I wished I won the wishbone." He smiled and sat back triumphantly.

Chuckling, his mother said, "Well, good for you," and patted him adoringly on the top of his head.

"Damn it," his father repeated, feeling slightly duped.

She patted him on the head in a similar fashion and said, "There, there, dear."

"That wasn't fair. Nobody could win against that wish," Jimmy's father complained.

"It just goes to show you, dreams do come true," she said and began clearing away the dishes. Jimmy waved the wishbone in his face.

"You should have used the wish on the fort," his father whispered.

"I don't need to, Dad, that already came true."

"Hey," Jimmy's father said, "tomorrow we'll be down at the Cattank. You and your friends should show up." He winked at Jimmy, who could hardly contain his excitement.

But Jimmy was worried about his mother. Gazing at her, she didn't seem to react at all. Maybe the coast was clear. He thought about tomorrow. He knew he would be in church first thing. Then, barring some kind of reprieve from the governor to open the library on Sundays, he would make his way down to the Cattank Furnace with Dave, Chad, and Kevin.

Church the next morning was sheer torture. Jimmy never sat still for one second. How could he? He was going to get a firsthand look at his new fort, and he'd probably get right in there and help too. That was so cool.

When Jimmy and his friends arrived at the building site, quite a few men were already hard at work. Jimmy recognized most of them from the sawmill and said hello to everyone as he made his way around. Jimmy ogled the structure in complete awe. He and his friends were absolutely overwhelmed by the sight of their new fort. It was huge, and it was solid. All the walls were framed in, and the adults were making quick work of the trusses, which made up the roof. Jimmy figured they were probably close to being finished. He hoped anyway.

As the day went on, the boys were more in the way than they were help, so it came as some relief when they discovered a rabbit hole, or maybe it was an opossum's den off in the distance. The boys stared at it for some time before deciding the hole needed to be jabbed at with sticks then filled with rocks. They did everything they could to torment whatever it was living in that burrow, but nothing ever showed itself. That was a little disappointing to the boys. Little did they know, the animal that resided there had merely left through its other entrance and watched quietly from a thicket not too far away.

The men broke for lunch when the final truss was up and in place. The building was beginning to really take shape. It was only a single room shelter, but it was a fine one at that. Jimmy and his friends joined the men for lunch.

Jimmy thought for sure he was about to sit down and eat with real men and eat real men food.

"Pass those cookies here," bellowed one man sitting on a tree stump. He was the same age as Jimmy's father but a bit gruffer.

"Aaah, get your own," barked an older man in overalls and a flannel shirt. Some of the other men joined in with jeers and cackles of their own. Jimmy found a peanut butter and jelly sandwich thrust in his face. He took it with surprise, having no idea that all this time he had been eating a man's meal—peanut butter and jelly, milk, and some cookies for dessert. He was starting to feel gruff himself.

Dave, Chad, and Kevin, with lunches in hand, sat down near Jimmy, but he was too busy watching his father to notice. The men were passing around a bottle that Jimmy thought must have fire in it from the way they were reacting when it touched their tongues.

"Whoa!" whistled Barry Spencer, Kevin's father. The other men exploded into laughter.

"Your buddy there ain't used to that, is he, Tommy?" a gravelly old man said to Jimmy's father.

"No, I guess not," Jimmy's father replied. Then Jimmy's father punched Barry right in the shoulder, much like Jimmy would punch Kevin.

Then Dave punched Jimmy's arm. "Hey whada ya think of the new fort, Jimmy?" Jimmy was so eager to answer he spit his peanut butter and jelly sandwich all over Chad.

"It's wicked," he blurted out through bits of his sandwich. His friends very much agreed.

"We should put a secret door in, that only we know about," Kevin said.

"Great idea," Jimmy said.

"How 'bout a tunnel?" Chad added.

Dave grinned. "Ooh, thada be cool."

"How we gonna dig a tunnel?" Jimmy asked skeptically. The boys all looked at each other oddly, hoping someone else had an answer.

"A really long shovel?" Kevin said.

"That's ridiculous," Jimmy said. "How ya gonna get it down in the hole?" Kevin shrugged.

"How 'bout a really big drill," Dave said. That drew some thought, but it didn't seem feasible.

"Where we gonna get a drill from, and how would we run it out here? There ain't no electricity," Jimmy said.

"You guys are thinkin' too hard." They turned their heads to see who had spoken. It was a thin man who Jimmy couldn't place.

"What?"

"You need a hole, right?" said the man. He looked familiar but was kind of freaking the boys out. Jimmy was sure he worked at the sawmill. "Who digs a really good hole?"

"My mom says my dad digs himself a pretty good hole," Jimmy replied. That would be easy. He would get his dad to dig the hole.

"No, not your dad, boy," said the old man.

"A guy with a really big shovel?" Kevin said.

"No, not a guy."

"A girl?" Jimmy hoped that wasn't what he was getting at.

"No." They paused, thinking hard.

"An animal?" Chad asked.

"Yep, now you got it," said the wise old man.

"I know, a groundhog," and Jimmy smiled.

"A groundhog's a mighty fine digger, son," replied the man. Jimmy was proud of his answer. "And remember this, boys, the bigger the groundhog, the bigger the hole he'll dig for ya," and the old man walked away.

"How do we catch a groundhog?" Kevin asked after the man left to join the other men, who were seriously inebriated by that point.

"We could always dig a groundhog hole and wait for him to fall in it," Chad said. The rest of them thought hard about this. How would they dig that hole?

When the firewater was gone, lunch was over. So, the men all resumed work on the fort. Twenty minutes into the afternoon shift, three men were down. One fell from a truss, and the second struck his hand pretty good with a hammer. For the other guy, well let's just say Kevin's dad couldn't handle his rotgut.

Excited about how close they were to finishing, it bitterly disappointed Jimmy when the men left without finishing the boy's citadel. Jimmy, Dave, Chad, and Kevin remained behind, though, and got a head start on their imaginary crusades.

•   •   •

Most of the men climbed into the bed of Clive's pickup truck. Clive worked for Jake Warrell at the mill. He was known to be the best damn saw operator in those parts, even after he lopped off part of his right hand. And down the dirt road they drove.

"Watch out for that deer!" A man hollered.

Clive saw it and swerved. The deer was frozen. It didn't move. Clive tried to keep his truck under control, but it skidded in the loose dirt of the road. He over-corrected as the tail of his truck full of drunken men fishtailed out from behind him. The men in the truck slid around like a loose bag of groceries. They held on the best they could until Clive sent the truck straight into the ditch across the road from the deer.

"Get off me," moaned the oldest and most ornery man there. No one could really hear what else he moaned over the loud moaning from the others. They had all suddenly sobered up.

"What the heck you doin', Cly," snarled Jake. By then, all the men had climbed out of the truck.

"You ain't seen that deer?" he said. They all looked back down the road about twenty yards. The deer still stood there, not moving. They grew silent then slowly moved towards the animal. Not rightly knowing why, they were cautious as they drew closer—either scared of it somehow or not wanting to frighten it and have it run off. Little did they know it wasn't going anywhere. If the truck hadn't scared it off, nothing would have. Apparently, sober men hadn't noticed it on the way in.

"He ain't moved yet," Jake said, and the men moved closer, exchanging puzzled looks. They were nearly next to the deer, and it hadn't so much as turned its head.

"I think it's dead," said Cly.

Jake was right up on it. He slowly reached out his hand. Everyone watched with trepidation. Jake's fingertips quivered from old age. Then suddenly, as if he was snatching something from the air, Jake grabbed an antler. A roar of congratulations erupted. Then the head of the deer tore away from its body, just as the stomach had when the boys were standing it upright. Jake held onto the antler the best he could, but the weight and awkwardness of the attached head was too much, not to mention the startling effect it had on him. He let go, and the head kissed the ground.

"Aaaaah!" the men screamed in unison. Without a second's hesitation, they turned and ran. Within minutes, they had pushed Cly's truck from the ditch, jumped in, and sped off, never once looking back until the dust was so thick they couldn't see behind them. In utter silence, they stared into the billowing air in fear of that creature following them; no head just a stunted torso dripping with maggots.

The boys watched the entire scene unfold from a distance. No one said a word. But it was obvious, after watching that, Jimmy couldn't have been more proud of himself for having stood that dead deer upright. What a hoot.

CHAPTER FOURTEEN

-A COOKIE IN HIS MOUTH-

About twenty-six miles out on highway 41 was the small town of Beaver Creek. Three cars carrying all twelve Wildcats along with two coaches, a team mom, and somebody's sister headed down the long stretch of country road. Of course, Jimmy, Dave, Chad, and Kevin were all riding in the coach's car.

They all liked their coach and always tried to manage carpooling in his car. The coach was a wiry sort of fella, tough as nails with a nasty scar over one eye. Some kids on the team thought he was a goof. Those four boys thought differently, and thought their coach was cool.

They knew they were entering Beaver Creek when the ripe waft of alley apples overtook them. Chad knew five minutes before anyone else. Jimmy didn't know why anybody gave cow poop a cute name but someone had.

"Eewe!" clamored the boys. The coach grumbled slightly, exhaled vocally, then leaned up and off one butt cheek, indicating only one thing.

"Sorry, guys," he said putting his butt cheek down again and his fist to his mouth, pretending to belch a little. "Chilly dogs," was all he added.

The boys moaned then laughed as the foul smell permeated the car. Chad held his glove over his nose, but his eyes were still watering. He had it the worst.

"We're almost there, boys," said the coach.

"Yeah, we can tell," Jimmy said through the inside of his elbow and shirtsleeve. It would seem that the malodorous distinction would prove to be a home team advantage, but it was not. It just stank like cow poop. That was all.

The Beaver Creek Braves seemed less affected by the smell than did the Wildcats when they took the field. The Wildcats looked sharp, but many kept their glove up to their face as an odorous shield.

As the game progressed, the stench seemed to lessen considerably, but probably because they got used to it. The place still smelled like poop.

Jimmy wasn't sure he wanted to get a chance to pitch that night, in fear of stinking up the place even more, but he did, pitch that is. He fared well in his first inning and battled through a rough patch in the fifth inning, his second. When he was done, the place only smelled as bad as it did before he took to the hill. The Wildcats left Beaver Creek with a 3-2 victory and the lasting memory of cow pie etched slightly in their nose hairs.

The same three cars left the town with twelve Wildcats, two coaches, the team mom, and as they found out later, Carl's sister. Carl played outfield for the Wildcats.

"Boy, it sure gets late earlier out here," their coach said as they drove down that same old country road they traveled in on. The coach was a huge Yogi Berra fan and loved his malapropisms. He noticed the bewildered looks on the boys' faces. "Yogi Berra?" There was a pause. "Nobody?" More befuddled looks eyed the coach. "So, who here fancies Carl's sister?" Apparently nobody did, or they weren't admitting to it. Give those boys two years and the answer would be yes for all four boys.

The rest of the trip was quiet, as the tired boys struggled not to nod off. Their record was now two wins and two losses, and they felt pretty good about the rest of the season and their chance of making it to the playoffs. They just needed to string together a few wins and build some momentum.

Jimmy's pitching was coming around, or at least he thought it was. In fact, his box score for the season was mixed, two good outings and two dismal ones. Jimmy had wanted to work more on his pitching, but he found a lot of his time being dedicated to the fort. His father put that same amount of attention to the fort as well.

To top it off, practice during the week for the Wildcats was cut short because of rain, so they went into the following Saturday's contest against the Rockville Nine not as prepared as they had hoped.

It could have been written up as a great pitcher's duel since every pitcher on both teams threw that Saturday. The final score was 28-23, with the Wildcats taking home the victory. Jimmy pitched that game, and when he was done, one might have thought he was in Beaver Creek. He stunk the place up pretty good, but so did just about every young man that took to that hill that day.

When the game was over, Jimmy collected his gear and made his way around the bleachers towards the parking area. Cindy startled him. Jimmy didn't mind the surprise. He got swept right into a sea of flowing chocolate. He was in heaven. His lips tingled again and were wet.

He drew back slightly and opened his eyes and there stood his Venus. Cindy smiled. In the background, his teammates were still running around on the field. Some had stopped to spectate.

"Bye," Cindy said softly, and whisked herself away. Jimmy watched Cindy bounce away. That was their second kiss.

Jimmy had to admit he was on top of his world. His tree fort was soon to be rebuilt, and he had kissed Cindy again before the summer had ended, both things he had set out to do. And to think, the summer had just started.

"Get off me," Jimmy shouted at Dave. Jimmy's friends were all swooning for Jimmy. The teasing continued for a short while before everyone left the baseball field. When the crowd was finally out of the park, an old man scurried out from nowhere and pulled closed the fence gate before locking it up with a chain and padlock. That had never happened before. Jimmy noticed it, as did the others.

"Good day, thank you," said the old man as he turned to leave. Jimmy tried the lock to convince himself it wasn't real. It was. His heart sunk. Dave tried the lock with the same result. They all looked up at the height of the fence that was now their obstacle. It seemed awfully high for a boy of their size.

"What's going on?" Jimmy shouted before the man could duck away.

"The field is only for organized leagues and games now," he said.

"How come?" Jimmy said.

"Keep vandals off the field," the old man said. "We had a bunch of teenagers driving all over the field a couple times now."

"But we like to play kickball here," Jimmy said.

"Not anymore. Sorry, boys," the old man said.

"That's not fair," Dave protested, but the old man was gone. The park was now locked off and only accessible during scheduled games and practices.

"There's always the diamond in your backyard," Kevin said. It was not the same. A terrible injustice was upon them.

Despite the incident with the locked field, Jimmy thought about Cindy the entire ride home from the game, which only lasted about two minutes, but it was two glorious minutes for Jimmy. But Dave, Chad, and Kevin kept distracting him, going on and on about the chain-link fence and the new lock on the gate.

"What are we gonna do?" moaned Dave. Jimmy thought about it for a short while and assured his friends that the locked fence issue would be addressed.

"Just give me a couple of days to figure something out. I think I got an idea," Jimmy said. He was obviously pondering bigger fish and had that problem under control.

Jimmy's mind started wandering from his many dilemmas. He had to sort this all out somehow. In the early afternoon, he and his father went out for a game of catch in the backyard. Jimmy worked on his pitching while his father drank a beer between pitches. Jimmy was in rare form. It was so much easier to pitch without a batter standing there.

"Hey, Dad, what do you think about when you kiss Mom?" Jimmy asked. This question came out of the blue and certainly caught Mr. Hamilton off guard. He thought for a moment.

Trying to be cute, he replied, "Oatmeal." Jimmy didn't respond and never asked the question again. But he didn't feel so weird that he thought about chocolate when he kissed Cindy. Jimmy fired a few more strikes at his father before they called it a day.

By late afternoon, the four boys had packed some sandwiches and cookies into a sack and made their way back out to the Cattank Furnace to check the progress on their fort. It was nearly done. Jake and two other men were at the site attaching the front door. It was made of thick wooden slats and hung by three large hinges. The handle was crescent-shaped and cut from similar wood.

The fort was done. All windows were in, the door was up, and the roof shingled. It was quite a sight for an eleven-year-old boy. Jimmy, Dave, Chad, and Kevin just stared at it in awe. Along each wall was a slot cut out about four inches high and two feet long. They were gun slots designed to protect the fort. None of the boys had actual guns to do battle with, but a stick would suffice, and every one of them was a pretty good shot with a stick.

After a few last-minutes touches, the men left the boys to be with their fort. Instantly, a battle ensued between an enemy of lesser matched skills and the boys. They quickly gunned the enemy down in a blaze of fiery battle.

"This is so cool," said Kevin. The others agreed. It was cool, and it seemed miles away from their little world of Walnut Creek. Jimmy reloaded his stick with a full clip of ammunition and set the hammer back. In his sights he laid out Dave, and silently and mutinously ended any question as to who led their brigade. Chad watched in horror. Dave shot him back.

"Got ya," Dave said.

"You can't shoot me. You're already dead," Jimmy argued. And within seconds a hail of gunfire riddled the cabin. All four boys battled it out. In their excitement, they barely heard the truck that was pulling up the dirt road. When they did, they scurried into a defensive position within the fort. Two men to each gun slot—the approaching stranger had no chance. The truck came to a skidding stop as dust kicked up and covered the area. The man got out of his truck in the dust cover and went around back.

When the man appeared out of the haze, he was carrying a large metal cage. It was the old man that spoke of the groundhog, but what was he carrying? He put the cage down and approached their door.

"Hold it right there, mister," a voice from an old western movie sang out. He froze with his arms up. "What you carrying?" said the voice again. Chad had seen a few westerns in his time.

"I got yer hole digger," the old man drew from his gravelly throat, and he gestured to the cage. In it was the fattest groundhog anybody had ever seen.

"Step away from the cage," Chad said in that same voice. The man obliged. The four boys, brandishing their weapons in caution, appeared from the fort.

"Check it out," Kevin said, completely forgetting the game. The others dropped all pretense to check out the varmint.

"What's your name, mister?" Jimmy asked.

"Otis Tillman. Yours?"

"I'm Jimmy."

"Kevin."

"Dave."

"Chad, sir," and Chad stuck out his hand, and Mr. Tillman shook it.

"How you boys like your fort?"

"We love it, sir, thank you for helping build it," Jimmy said.

"Well, here's your groundhog. Caught him last night near the chicken coop. He was digging a mighty fine hole at the time," he said. The boys were interested and eager.

"What's his name?" Chad asked. Otis looked at him oddly.

"He ain't no pet, he's a wild animal," Otis said. Kevin got a little too close, and the critter snarled at him, making Kevin jump back and land on his bum.

Jimmy and Dave began laughing at Kevin. Then Dave started jabbing it with his stick. The animal defended itself with a burst of fury, and Dave jumped. No one laughed after that.

"Let's call him Brian," Chad said.

Otis looked worried that these boys would try to make it a pet. He shrugged and said, "The best thing to do is to set him up in the open doorway and butt the cage in the way so it can't get out. One of ya get up on the cage and open the cage door. It'll scurry off and right into the fort. Close the fort door after him and wait. He'll dig himself right on out if he thinks he's trapped."

"Wow," Kevin said. The boys all thought that was such a grand idea, so well thought out it had to work.

"All right, Brian, you got some digging to do," Jimmy told the groundhog.

"Be careful, boys, and remember, he'll rip you apart if you back him into a corner," Otis said trying to instill in them, once again, that this animal was not a pet. "Just let him do his thing, and his thing is diggin'. Wonce he's done, you'll end up with a mighty fine tunnel," he added.

"Thank you, sir," Jimmy said. "Thank you for everything."

"Ah, it was nothin', boys, Brian jus—" The old man stopped with a flustered look having just called the groundhog Brian. "The groundhog just came around last night. It was some kind of fate. That it was. I'll see ya'll, boys." And Otis got in his truck and left.

The boys got right to business and pulled the cage up to the door. They opened the fort door and wedged it ajar with the cage. Everything was in place just like the old man had instructed. Even Brian seemed to know what to do as his snout was up against his cage in the direction of the fort. His snorting was stirring up dirt from the ground. Chad climbed on top of the cage.

"Open the cage," Jimmy hollered. Chad pulled the cord that opened the sliding door. The cage rattled a metallic tinny echo, but the animal couldn't go into the fort. That part of the cage was still intact. Brian circled within the cage and started towards the opening, an opening that led outwards into the wild.

"Close the door," Jimmy ordered. "It's facing the wrong way." Brian's neck was almost clear of the cage. He was advancing towards his freedom. Chad scrambled for the trigger to release the door back down. In a flurry, Jimmy and Dave used their sticks to beat back the beast. That didn't work, it only provoked Brian more, and with that, he advanced further out of the cage. Kevin took his stick and jabbed Brian in his back.

"Don't—" Jimmy said, thinking it would only push the varmint out further, but it didn't. Brian instead turned and started attacking Kevin's stick. It worked, and Brian led himself right back into the cage. Chad finally found the trigger for closing the door and down it came. The boys collapsed in relief, as Brian was once again a caged animal.

They turned the cage to face the correct way and tried again. Brian was less cooperative this time. He was curious, as all groundhogs get, but in no mood for the extra prodding that came with trying to get him to leave the cage. The boys waited patiently, and it paid off. Brian finally waddled his fat butt into the fort. Jimmy yanked the cage out of the way and slammed the door shut behind him. It was just a matter of waiting now for Brian to do his thing. Soon, the boys could hear snorting and clawing coming from inside the fort.

"How long do we wait?" Kevin asked, as if someone else knew the answer.

"I guess until we see him come out through a hole in the ground," Jimmy said. It was foolproof. The whole idea, for that matter, was brilliant. Otis was some sort of genius. They waited, more scurrying and scratching came from inside. It was driving them crazy not knowing what was going on inside. Then they heard a crash, like something fell over. They only had a small table and bench inside.

"What was that?" Chad asked. The boys rushed over to the gun slots to see if they could spot what was going on. The noise got louder through the opening but still no groundhog in sight. A metallic rattle resonated from inside.

"What was that?" Dave cried. They could make out the tail of the critter as it came in and out of sight.

"What's he doing?" Jimmy pushed forward for a better look, but there was no better vantage. The creature was scurrying about as if it were a monster with stealth-like abilities. They could hear it getting into something, but what, they did not know. The anxiety was dreadful. The gun slot was not large enough to really see into the fort. They must have been designed to fend off such intrusions.

"Can you see *anything*?" Kevin asked Jimmy, who was struggling the most for a good look.

"I'm goin' in," Jimmy said and barged his way to the door. Dave intercepted him.

"You can't," he said. "We have to wait, like Otis said." Jimmy became incensed, but he knew Dave was right. He had to wait, and so they continued to do just that, wait.

After some time had passed since they last heard anything from the groundhog, they decided it was time. Their growing impatience was too much. They couldn't wait for Brian to dig himself out of the fort. They needed to check his progress. He was obviously underground somewhere, or they would have heard him.

Jimmy, followed closely by Dave, Chad, and then Kevin, approached the door. They were apprehensive. Each one slightly crouched behind the other in a line. Jimmy put his hand on the door and slowly eased it ajar. There was no sign of the burrowing mammal. Jimmy eased the door open even more, still nothing. Finally, he pushed the door completely open. The boys scanned the fort.

"He must be underground," Chad said. They relaxed and started to enter the fort when from behind the door walked Brian. The boys startled, but the animal was not threatening. He merely waddled out of the fort. He had peanut butter and jelly all over his face, and in his mouth, he had a cookie.

CHAPTER FIFTEEN

-A TURTLE WITHOUT A SHELL-

By Wednesday, the weather could not have been better for a baseball game, and the Wildcats travelled to the town of Woodmore to take on the Gray Sox. Woodmore was close to Beaver Creek, but the wind must have been in their favor. If Jimmy were to stink the place up, it would be evident it was his pitching and not the cow pies.

The Wildcats jumped to an early lead with an onslaught of offensive prowess led by Dave's two-run home run in the top of the first. Kevin and Chad each added a hit as did Carl and Phil. By the time the teams switched places on the field, the Wildcats had put up five runs.

Adam took the hill first for the Wildcats. He was a second-year player, kind of scrawny but not a bad ballplayer at all. His pitching was spotty, much like Jimmy's or anybody on the Wildcats, really. He held the Gray Sox to three runs in three innings, which was good considering the Wildcats had added five more runs by that time for a 10-3 lead.

"Jimmy, go warm up," the coach ordered. Jimmy was up, warm, and ready in no time at all. He had been waiting to get the call all night. He felt good. His confidence from the last game was spilling over into the night. When the Wildcats took to the field, Jimmy darted to the mound. He would not waste any time here. He arranged the dirt just so and then took his warm-ups.

His first inning was good. His second was not so good. He gave it everything he had, but he just couldn't get anybody out. Five runs pushed across the plate before the coach went out and changed pitchers. A second-year player named Jason came in and mopped up that half of the inning. He had good stuff and shut the Gray Sox down, striking out two.

The Wildcats came up big again and answered with three more runs in the top of the sixth. It turned out they needed every one of those runs too as the Gray Sox scored four runs in the bottom of the inning to nearly tie it up. Jimmy made a spectacular diving catch in left field to stop the drive and end the game for the win. His teammates immediately mobbed him as he made his way in from the outfield. Even though his pitching had again been dismal, he was feeling pretty good. He was once again being celebrated as the hero, and that was something he could get used to.

The ride home was quiet, but it had a certain euphoria from the game that made it go by quickly. Jimmy said good night to his friends and the coach, and after making plans to go out to the Cattank tomorrow, he went inside his house.

•   •   •

"What'd your mom pack ya for lunch?" Kevin asked Jimmy as the two of them set off for Dave's house the next morning.

"The usual," Jimmy replied.

Kevin nodded. "Peanut butter and jelly sandwich and cookies. I don't think my mom knows how to make anything else."

"Yeah, mine neither," Jimmy sighed.

Chad was already at Dave's house when Kevin and Jimmy got there.

"What are you guys doing?" Kevin said. Chad was standing funny.

"Just check this out," Dave said with a grin. Chad poised his acute olfactory to the wind which just happened to be where Jimmy and Kevin had come from. "What did Jimmy have for breakfast?"

Chad went into a trance of some kind. "Blueberry pancakes," he said. Jimmy's mouth dropped open. Jimmy did have blueberry pancakes for breakfast.

"What did I have, what did I have?" Kevin asked, bouncing up and down. "Froot Loops," Chad replied. Kevin's eyes lit up.

"That's incredible," Kevin said. Jimmy looked at Kevin, rolled his eyes, and pulled a Froot Loop from the front of his shirt.

"Yeah, I could have told you he had Froot Loops, ya Froot Loop." Jimmy walked past Kevin, a little more agitated than a minute ago. Time was a wasting.

"How d'ya know Jimmy had pancakes?" Kevin said, slightly embarrassed about the Froot Loop stuck to his shirt. Chad pointed to his nose and smiled as if it were a superpower he possessed.

"Chad is really honing this nose thing. It may save our lives sometime," Dave said.

"From what?" Kevin asked.

"Can we just go to the fort?" Jimmy sighed, even though he was a little impressed with Chad. His nose powers were getting stronger. They marched on through the neighborhood until they reached a dense patch of woods off to the side. They cut a path into the woods and headed for the fort.

"How come we ain't using the Cattank road?" Kevin asked.

"Takes too long from here, we'd have to double back most of the way," Dave said.

"Don't worry, if you get separated from us, just head left in a circle," Jimmy said, but Kevin didn't seem satisfied.

"Left? Which way is left when you've gotten turned around in woods you don't know?" Kevin said nervously.

"It's like the one-armed man in the wheelchair. He goes to the left, and he eventually comes back around. You'll be fine," Dave said.

"Go west then," Jimmy said.

"I'm not a compass."

"Just don't get lost," Jimmy said.

"Chad, which way is west?" Dave asked.

Chad studied then inhaled deeply. "That way," and he pointed to his left.

The four boys marched on through the dense growth and made quick work of the woods, soon finding themselves on Cattank Road just shy of the fort.

"Hey, what's that up a head?" Kevin asked. There was a dark lump in the road. They continued towards it.

"Not sure," Jimmy said.

"Maybe its Brian. Maybe he's come back to finish the tunnel," Kevin said. A little hopeful, they walked. If it was Brian, he probably would have scurried off into the thicket by now. Then Jimmy realized who it was.

"Hi, Erwin," Jimmy said.

"Hey, Erwin," Dave said.

"Hey, Erwin," Chad said.

"Hey, fella, who are you?" Kevin said.

"That's Erwin, if you couldn't tell," Jimmy said. Kevin, investigating the reptile, presented the tip of a stick to Erwin's face. Erwin's neck stretched out and his jaws slammed hard and destroyed the end of Kevin's stick in a shower of splinters. Kevin more than flinched. He landed on his bum in the middle of Cattank road.

"Why d'ya do that," Jimmy asked. Kevin was still a little scared but began to get up.

"I don't know."

"That's Erwin. He's a snapping turtle. You don't want to mess with him. See his hooked nose. That will tear your arm off," Jimmy said.

"But you guys said hello like he's your friend."

"He's been in these woods since forever," Dave said. Kevin didn't get any closer but wanted to examine the creature. His nose was in the shape of a hook and he had black dots for eyes. He was creepy and prehistoric looking. Kevin wanted to see it destroy the stick again. He reached it out towards Erwin when suddenly they heard a low, rumbling noise approaching.

As Erwin crushed the end of the stick very much like the first time, the boys looked down the dirt road. The rumble was getting closer, and with it, a cloud of dust rose on down Cattank Road. Soon they realized a car was racing in their direction. The boys moved off to the side of the road. The car never slowed down. Erwin just tucked himself in his shell.

The thud, thud of running over a speed bump too quickly could be heard just as the car flattened the turtle. The car lurched, swerved a little and was gone, swallowed by the same dust that brought it there.

The boys all just stared on in disbelief. Erwin was nothing more than a broken shell with a tire track down his back. His remains had been squished out along the road and were no longer discernible. After the shock wore off, they stood over Erwin and lamented.

"Did you know turtles leave their shell when they outgrow them and look for a larger shell to move into?" Chad asked. There was silence.

"No," Kevin answered solemnly. Dave looked as if he was thinking. Jimmy poked at Erwin's remains with a stick.

"If that were the case, there would be one turtle, the largest turtle ever, walking around without a shell," Jimmy concluded. Silence followed as they walked off leaving Erwin to the flies.

CHAPTER SIXTEEN

-DIRE STRAITS-

The boys continued down the dirt road with less purpose than before as Erwin's demise was pressing on their minds. That was one less shell for the turtles to use in their cycle of shell swapping. Now it was possible that there were several turtles in dire straits.

"So, who was in that car?" Kevin asked.

"Don't know," Dave answered.

"Whada ya think they're doing back here?" Kevin asked.

"Don't know," Jimmy said. "Most of the older kids 'round here hang out at the walnut groves." To the east of town were several walnut grove farms, but many of those farms no longer farmed their walnuts. Some trees were sold off as lumber, but most remained untouched and left to grow wild.

"I hear that place is haunted," Dave said. Jimmy wanted to dispute the remark but didn't have the conviction to back it up, and he was sure Dave would call him out on it too.

"Hey, you guys smell smoke?" Chad asked. No one had. They figured maybe Chad smelled something burning at the dump.

As they reached the clearing at the end of the road, the boys saw the car that had killed Erwin. It was parked haphazardly just outside of *their* fort. The tire marks behind it showed the car had come to an abrupt stop.

Worry crept over Jimmy and his friends like never before. Eyes wide, Jimmy darted for the fort, his friends in tow. Smoke was billowing from the gun slots and laughter rang out from inside. Jimmy, Dave, Chad, and Kevin threw themselves against the fort's front wall and leered in through the smoke-filled opening.

"Can you see anything?" Dave asked frantically. Jimmy had the best shot at seeing anything, but he could not.

"No," he shot back and started coughing from the smoke.

"Is the fort on fire?" Kevin asked.

"I don't think so," Jimmy said. He struggled for a better look.

"What's all the smoke from then?" Kevin asked. They waved uselessly at the billows of smoke slowly pouring out. They couldn't see anything, but they could hear plenty, and they were hooting it up pretty good in there.

"If they are burning it down, I'm gonna kill 'em." Jimmy said, his anger rising.

"Maybe we can see better from the other side," Chad said, and so they quickly shifted to the side wall gun slot. It had a better vantage point, but it was still hard to make out what was going on inside.

Then, in the deepest and most manly voice he could muster, Dave hollered out, "Hey, you boys better get out of here before I call the fire department." Jimmy, Chad, and Kevin looked on, horror-struck, but then Chad nodded.

"You boys are trespassing and are in big trouble," Chad said with the same authority. The boys inside grew quiet except for some scuffling sounds. Peeking in through the gun slot, the boys could see they were scampering about. Then the door flung open with a crash. The four young boys peered around the corner to see the front of the fort.

A boy, about sixteen or seventeen, burst out of the open door, almost as if he had been pushed. He resembled a much older Kevin. Then another boy was hurled from the fort in the same manner. That one stumbled and fell to the ground. He was about the same age as the first boy and had long black hair, kind of like a girl. The two teens righted themselves and gaped around.

"You guys see anything?" said a voice from inside the fort. The two boys outside peered around more diligently. Jimmy and his friends ducked down just in the nick of time.

"I don't see nothin'," said the one boy. Two more boys exited the fort. They were about the same age as the first two, sixteen or so. One had a thick neck and looked mean. The other appeared collected and cool. He was obviously the leader.

"Well, somebody said that," the cool one said. Jimmy was certain he had seen those boys before. They were from Walnut Creek.

"Ain't nobody out here, Bobby," said the first boy who had been tossed from the fort.

"Shut up, Eric," said Bobby, and he punched him square in the arm. Eric retreated slightly to rub his wound.

"What a jerk," Jimmy thought of Bobby. The teenagers peered around the corner one more time.

"There," proclaimed the thick-necked boy. The others turned just as the four young boys ducked back behind the corner of the fort.

"Brad, Ralph, go that way," Jimmy heard. Then Jimmy, Dave, Chad, and Kevin heard footsteps rustling through leaves and dirt. They could make out that someone was coming around from behind them and someone was coming straight at them.

Then Jimmy did what no one ever expected. He stepped out in front of the oncoming teens, Brad and Ralph, to challenge them. It startled the older boys for a brief second until they realized they were looking at an eleven-year-old boy.

"What do we have here?" Bobby said with a slight chuckle in his voice. His cohorts joined in as they rounded on Jimmy and his friends from behind. Jimmy never wavered.

"Get the fuck out of our fort," Jimmy snarled. Chad and Kevin's eyes went wide. Dave stood a little taller. Bobby and Eric chuckled. Their friends, Brad and Ralph, were slow to the punchline. Brad and Ralph resembled an older form of Dave and Chad.

"Now, wait a minute, didn't I hear one of your daddies crying about the fire department?" Bobby said. This sent Jimmy into a fury. Everyone could hear his teeth grinding. What ensued no one would have believed.

Jimmy tucked himself down slightly as if he were getting ready to charge, and with ire he never imagined, he lashed out at Bobby. He kicked him sharply in the shin then attempted to punch him the best he could, his arms flailing. He landed several good shots before the bigger and stronger Bobby could get out from under Jimmy's wrath. When he had, Jimmy paid dearly.

Bobby punched Jimmy clean and hard in the eye. Jimmy buckled to the ground.

Brad leaned in towards Jimmy and pulled his arm back to pummel him again when Kevin somehow jumped onto his back. Brad swung around, trying to buck the new hitchhiker, but Kevin clung tightly to Brad's neck. As Brad twisted frantically, Kevin's feet swung out from behind him and coincidentally struck Ralph in the head. Ralph went down clutching the side of his face. The score was even. Startled by what just happened, Brad stopped and changed directions, inadvertently clubbing Eric with Kevin's feet and pushing Eric into Bobby.

Dave grabbed Bobby around the neck with everything he had, but Bobby was too strong. Unfortunately, Dave was about to pay for his aggression with a shot to his eye. Then Chad caught an elbow in the nose as Eric reared back to punch Jimmy, who had just stumbled to his feet. But the move cost Eric. Chad's nose must have connected with Eric's elbow in that spot they call the funny bone because he grasped his arm, writhing in pain. Chad cupped his nose as the blood gushed through his fingers.

What looked like the three stooges fighting the Marx brothers in a neighborhood brawl lasted about two or three minutes. Jimmy and his friends fought gallantly. They fought with honor. But in the end, they were the losers, and to the victors went the spoils.

Jimmy, Dave, Chad, and Kevin limped downtrodden and defeated down the dirt road in which they had come, a sniffle escaping here and there. They left the fort behind, the fort that was rightfully theirs but now taken from them. Chad could barely breathe through his blood-clogged nostrils and gasped repeatedly for air. Not a word was spoken. They all knew the same thing. The fort was gone. They walked past where Erwin lay, lamenting briefly before walking on.

When they reached the neighborhood, they kept walking. Where they were going was not clear, but what was clear was that they needed time to think this thing out and they needed a place to do that thinking. But that place was gone. Oh, the irony. They made it out to Main Street and walked along it for a while.

"The ball field," Jimmy said. "Let's go," and the four boys, war-torn and weary, headed to their new lair.

Jimmy pushed on the gate and heard the chain rattle. He had forgotten they locked up the field. His heart sank. He yanked on the chain and lock desperately. Nothing happened. Jimmy wanted to cry but knew he couldn't. Was there no place sacred for a boy to go where he could think about his troubles, sort his life? Jimmy was starting to think the only place he was safe to do those things was his room, which to that point in his life was where he was always sent as punishment and to read.

"Now what?" Dave said.

Jimmy looked around and had an idea. "I know," he said and walked away. Dave, Chad, and Kevin followed. "You guys hungry?"

"Yeah," was the consensus.

"You guys ever been to the diner?" Jimmy asked.

"Not without my parents," everyone replied.

"I ain't got no money," Kevin said.

"Me neither," Chad said. Jimmy reached into his pocket and pulled out an assortment of trinkets along with what looked like a few wadded-up dollar bills.

"We're good," Jimmy proclaimed and herded his friends back out onto Main Street in the direction of the diner.

"Where d'ya get that money?" Kevin asked.

"I stole it," Jimmy said. He thought that sounded cool, and his friends were impressed, but he did not steal that money. It was left over from his birthday money that his grandmother always gave him. That wasn't nearly as cool.

"Hey, there's a booth," Kevin said.

"Shut up. We ain't sittin' at no booth," Jimmy punched Kevin's arm.

"Ow, what was that for?" Kevin whined as he rubbed his shoulder.

"Just go sit at the counter," Jimmy said. They made their way to the counter and swiveled the old fashion stools around and put their butts down into their seats and turned back around to face the counter. Then, as if it were inevitable, the boys went into a frenzy of spinning and whirling their stools until a young woman dressed in a waitress's outfit approached them. She didn't seem to mind that the boys were being boys.

She was twenty something, very attractive with sandy blonde hair. Her skin was smooth and shiny, shiny from the thin layer of grease that covered everything in that diner. Her greasy hair was tied in a bun, except for those few strands that escaped the taut bundle and stood wildly out into the air around her.

"Hey, boys, what can I get you?" she said as she wiped the greasy counter with an even greasier rag. Then she paused. "You boys been fighting?"

"No, ma'am," they all replied. She glared with a roll of her eyes and never mentioned it again. She got Chad a cold, clean rag and a small bag of ice for his nose, however.

"Ma'am, I only got three dollars," Jimmy said. The waitress, Tammy according to her nametag, looked around and then back at Jimmy and smiled.

"That's okay. You boys play for the Wildcats, don't ya?" she said. They all looked up at her, surprised to meet anyone who recognized them as Wildcats. She was way too young to have children on the team. She would fit the mold of an older sister, maybe.

"Yeah," Jimmy said, nodding his head.

"I think we can take care of you," Tammy said. "How 'bout I get you boys four chocolate shakes?"

"Can you make mine strawberry?" Kevin asked. Jimmy would have but Dave was closest, so Dave punched Kevin in the arm.

"Strawberry," Jimmy mimicked.

"You want strawberry too?" Tammy asked Jimmy with a smile. Jimmy just looked at her with disappointed eyes.

"Okay, three chocolate shakes and one strawberry coming up," Tammy said, and she bounced down to the other end of the counter and began making the shakes.

Looking at Chad holding a bloody rag and ice on his face, Jimmy felt bad. "Can you even breathe through that thing?"

"All that matters is that he can still use it to fight crime," Dave said.

"What?" Jimmy said.

"The superpower thing," Dave explained. Chad chortled and ended with a cough, probably of blood.

"Here you go, boys, four shakes," Tammy said as she slid the shakes across the counter and in front of Jimmy, Dave, Chad, and Kevin. They dove in as the ambient sounds of diner life echoed around them. The first to pull up was Chad, only long enough so he could take a breath. Then Kevin took a breather, his chest and throat frozen from the ice cream.

Dave and Jimmy both had half their shake gone before they took a break. Each one came up red in the face from the cold and from trying to suck the countertop through their small straws. And then as if they were continuing a race, they went right back to their task, sucking for all they were worth.

Jimmy won and gloated some, but they all had a grand time with it, and in the end, they laughed until they belched.

"Oh my," said Tammy. Embarrassed, the boys laughed some more. As their laughter subsided, the day's troubles came back to them. They were still clueless about their dilemma.

"What are we gonna do?" Kevin asked. Jimmy stared into the empty glass in front of him. He did not have an answer. Dave and Chad both waited for Jimmy's lead, but it never came. He sunk deeper into that glass. Finally, Chad spoke up.

"We need someone to chase 'em off," he said. The others agreed, except for Jimmy.

"They need to want to leave, or they'll just come back," Jimmy said.

"We just need someone big enough to make them want to leave," Chad said in his defense.

Jimmy shook his head. "They'll just come back, I'm telling you," Jimmy said.

"It's better than nothing," Kevin said. Then Jimmy turned to face Kevin to remind him what came of their tangle with the teenagers and what would come again. Dave turned in too, also displaying his black eye. Chad wheezed a little. Kevin nodded. "Sorry, I guess I forgot."

Jimmy put one of his dollar bills on the counter and spun around on his chair one last time before hopping down. As they walked outside, it appeared Jimmy either had brain freeze or an idea.

"What is it, Jimmy?" Dave asked.

"It won't get us our fort back, but meet at the field in the morning and bring everybody."

CHAPTER SEVENTEEN
—BOLT CUTTERS AND FRILLY STUFF—

It was a cool damp morning before the sun went to work burning off the early morning dew that glistened on the grass of the baseball field. Dave, Chad, and Kevin, along with four or five other kids from Jimmy's baseball team, were already waiting at the field with a couple of their friends and a brother or two. Jimmy strode up holding a bag that looked very heavy. He sported a black eye.

"Your mom say anything about your face?" Dave said.

"You know she did," Jimmy said. They all laughed.

"Yeah, mine too," Dave, Chad, and Kevin, replied.

"I can't believe she let me out of the house today," Jimmy said.

Jimmy greeted everyone else and made his way over to the fence. He had every intention of being the hero that day. He reached into his bag and pulled out a large pair of cutters.

All the other boys oohed and aahed at the marvel.

"What is that?" a small boy asked. Jimmy zipped his bag back up and approached the fence along the right-field side. When he reached a spot near a bush and a light pole that was slightly inconspicuous, he stopped.

"They're bolt cutters," he said. Jimmy surveyed his surroundings, checking to make sure the coast was clear. When he spied no adults, he knelt at the fence. Snip. One link cut. The bolt cutters made easy work of the chain linked fence, and within minutes, Jimmy had a straight opening cut in the fence about three feet long.

"Can I try?" asked another young boy.

"No," was all Jimmy said.

The others watched as he continued his masterful work with the cutters. He snipped another section of links and gave the loose flap a yank. The hole was nearly big enough for any of them to squeeze through. Jimmy worked it some more. He left the opening as a flap so it would appear closed. All anybody needed to do to get in was push or pull the flap and crawl through. The task was admirable, and Jimmy's lore grew. He was not great at anything yet, but this hole was his distinction, and maybe the start of his legend in Walnut Creek.

"Play ball!" Jimmy said, as the hole was complete. The boys all stormed the fence and ran onto the field feeling liberated. When the elation subsided, they divvied up teams.

"Can I play?" Cindy asked. This took everyone by surprise. Where did she come from? Everybody looked on, kind of frozen.

"Yes," Jimmy said.

"No," Dave said, but they both said it at the same time so it wasn't clear if she was playing or not. "Okay, but she's on our team."

"Fine," Jimmy said. Dave knew it wasn't fine, for Jimmy anyway. Nobody else cared.

Jimmy and Kevin made their way out onto the field as teammates, as Dave and Chad and now Cindy joined their team in the dugout. They would kick first. The game started with an undeniable energy, as all sixteen kids came there to play. It was more than just a game of kickball to them. A certain mischief peppered the air. That was probably the most defiant any of them ever had been. And only by the chance Jimmy had a set of bolt cutters in his garage. That day, Jimmy gained notoriety.

Jimmy took to that role on the field too as he made one brilliant play after another and kicked solid line drives to the outfield every time up. One resulted in a triple and the other a home run. He was on fire.

"Why can't ya play baseball this good?" Dave said to Jimmy when they passed each other at the inning break.

Jimmy turned in a fury at Dave. "What? Shut up, man." Jimmy spit the words at Dave. Everyone oohed but didn't dare ah. Dave's eyes grew wide, and he backed off slightly only to find Jimmy advancing on him.

"It's cool, man," Dave said, throwing up his hands as he conceded. Jimmy stared him down a moment longer, then he continued to left field. No one else said a word until play resumed and the game was in full swing. Jimmy had never played like that before. Maybe it was his heroics with the bolt cutters, or maybe it was having Cindy around. Whatever it was, Jimmy was just reveling in the moment.

Dave was up first in their half of the inning and stood locked in on the ball as Kevin rolled the pitch in his direction. Dave sent the ball screaming into the gap in left center. Jimmy gave chase, trying to cut off the angle but had to turn and run after it.

When he reached the ball, his momentum sent him crashing into the fence. The resulting dust cloud from the warning track dirt momentarily obscured everyone's view. Jimmy somehow landed on the ball and was up with it in no time. He turned ready to heave the ball back in towards Dave but noticed he was way too far away to get it anywhere near the infield, so he drop-kicked it and sent it flying back through the air in which it came.

Dave had rounded second and was charging third rather quickly. No one moved as they watched the ball carry back into the infield. Dave was around third and nearly out of gas, but he wasn't stopping. He was going for home. The ball carried over the first infielder's head, then the next.

"Hey!" screamed a wily, old voice. A few boys turned, startled. The voice sounded familiar. It had a ping to it, maybe a clicking noise. "Hey! You ain't suppose ta be here," the voice continued. Dave never missed stride. Most everyone else was concentrating on the ball. "Hey!" screamed the voice again.

Finally, the ballplayers turned their attention to the voice screaming at them. It was the old man who locked up the baseball field after their baseball game. He was brittle and old and craggily looking. He had slipped inside the fence and was holding up the lock in accusation. Everyone stared at the old man like a deer in headlights.

"Get the hell off this field," he clattered. Dave hesitated slightly, but the ball didn't. Whack! The ball caromed off the top of his head and flew toward the old man. The old man was standing near the newly cut hole in the fence. None of the boys and Cindy knew what to do. Most of them were hoping for some kind of direction from Jimmy.

Dave staggered, but he didn't fall. His feet quickly righted underneath him. Chad ran towards the old man to retrieve the ball. The old man was hollering at the boys as he went for the locked gate. Still, everyone looked for Jimmy's lead.

To everyone's surprise, Jimmy ran straight at the old man, almost goading him to chase him. The old man gimped after him but knew it was useless. Jimmy continued provoking the old man long enough for everyone to get through the fence hole including Cindy. Then it was Jimmy's turn. Jimmy darted past the old man and ran like his life depended on it. He reached the hole he cut and dove through it. He landed on the other side of the bush and was gone from the old man's sight.

Jimmy spied back through the bush. The old man seemed frozen as if he didn't believe what he just saw because what it looked like was Jimmy ran right through the fence and disappeared. It didn't appear as if he ran through a hole in the fence at all. The old man stumbled across the field and found a seat in one of the dugouts. He looked like he had just seen a ghost.

Most of the kids were so scared of getting caught they never stopped running even after getting through the fence. The few who remained were out of breath and wildly excited about what just happened. They all agreed they would have to do it again soon. Dave, Chad, and Kevin were dusting themselves off, while Jimmy was looking at Cindy.

"Thanks for letting me play," Cindy said. Jimmy looked at her. She was dusty and sweaty and still pretty.

"Sure," Jimmy said. "You played well."

"Thanks, see ya," she said. Jimmy could sense his friends weren't quite as welcoming towards Cindy as he had hoped right then, but he understood. They still had a very important mission ahead of them.

When it was finally just Jimmy, Dave, Chad, and Kevin, they headed towards Main Street hoping for an answer. The reason for cutting the hole in the fence was to have somewhere to brood or mull over stuff, but it would be a few days before it was safe to try that again.

"Ya know, Cindy is quite a little ball player," Dave said.

"She was great out there, wasn't she?" Chad added.

"She could play on our Little League team," Jimmy said.

"Yeah, she could take your place," Dave said.

Jimmy looked like he wanted to fight but knew better. "You were out by the way," Jimmy said. He needed something on Dave. They continued walking.

"What?" Dave said.

"You were out," Jimmy repeated.

"Out what?"

"In the kickball game, the last play, you were out."

"Whatever," Dave shrugged, but Jimmy knew he was right and that Dave knew it too.

"Just saying...you were out." Jimmy wanted this one.

"You're gonna be out in a second," Dave said. The other two stayed out of the conversation.

"Fine, just so long as you know, you were out," Jimmy said. Things quieted down after that.

They traipsed back down along Main Street in search of an answer. It was a quiet walk, and they often paused at the many window fronts for a look inside. When they moved on, they left a nose print or four behind. The most interesting store had to be the old hardware store with its many old and unique tools on displayed. They even had a sled propped up as part of a backdrop. Still, nothing came to them.

They kept walking. At the corner of Main Street and Sycamore Avenue, they came across an old store. They stared peculiarly into the shop. It was one giant tea setting of doilies and lacy things. Two old biddies walked out.

"This is stupid," Dave said. Each reflection in the window nodded back at them in agreement. It was stupid.

"Who would shop in a store full of this cra... oh man," Jimmy said as he tried to duck.

"Oh man," they all chorused in line as they swung away from the window. The door to the shop jingled as it opened, and out came the twins, Jessica and Erica, with their mother.

"Hi, Jimmy," they sang gleefully in unison. The girls were very prim and proper in attitude and identical in dress. They were dressed just as ridiculously as the lace-clad storefront. That's how Jimmy saw it, anyway.

"Little Jimmy Hamilton," their mother said. Mrs. Parker was in her Sunday best as well. The theme was obvious. Her girls giggled. She greeted the other boys but with no mawkish endearment towards Dave, Chad, and Kevin.

"Hi, Mrs. Parker," all the boys said. Jimmy couldn't stop staring at the twins. He was less terrified of Erwin, rest his soul, than he was of these two girls. He wasn't sure why, but he knew if there had been just one of them, he would only be half as frightened.

"Were you looking to buy your mother something from the tea shop?" Mrs. Parker asked with a helpful tone. Jimmy was still in a trance, or maybe it was a spell. The other boys did not respond.

"Huh?—What?—No!" babbled Jimmy. Then he scowled at the shop window and wondered why he would want to do that.

"Well, if you change your mind, I'd be glad to help you pick out something pretty."

"Thanks," Jimmy replied. Was this lady stupid? Jimmy puzzled over something that registered in his mind from their exchange, all the while thinking how dumb they looked dressed like a matched table setting.

Jimmy moved on, and his friends followed. But Jimmy was distracted. He was onto something, something he was not yet ready to share, and until he figured it out, he was keeping silent. But his friends were growing anxious.

"Jimmy, whada ya got?" Dave asked. They found the confines of a dank ally between two shops suitable for thinking. Jimmy paced while his friends sat and watched. And with Otis-like wisdom, Jimmy had an idea.

"What would be the one thing that would make our fort so bad you wouldn't want to hang out in it," Jimmy asked.

"Your mom being there," Dave said. Jimmy opened his mouth in her defense but quickly realized Dave was on the right trail.

"Real funny," Jimmy said.

"I know, giant mosquitoes," Chad said.

"How giant?" Kevin asked.

Chad made a face then extended his arms out. "This big," he said. Jimmy sighed while Dave looked like he was trying to picture such a creature.

"What about giant moths?" Kevin asked.

"They'd be a mess, but mosquitoes bite. Giant mosquitoes would be much worse," Chad said.

"Could you imagine a frog eating a giant moth with its mothy wings," Kevin said.

"Probably like eating a powdered donut," Dave said.

Jimmy sat down and waited for them to finish. And they did. Jimmy put his face in his hands and pulled at the layers of skin as if they were too tight.

"Are any of you trying to figure out how we're going to get our fort back?" Jimmy asked. They looked at Jimmy shamefully.

"Sorry," was the general response.

"Would any of you guys be caught dead in that store? The one the twins were in," Jimmy asked. No one knew where Jimmy was going.

"The old biddy store?" Dave said.

Jimmy nodded. "Yeah, that one."

"No way," was the consensus.

"Exactly," Jimmy said. The others were starting to think perhaps Jimmy had lost his mind.

"What are you talking about?" Dave asked.

"Hear me out. What if we decorated the fort like that store window, with frilly curtains, and tablecloths, and tea cozies, the works? I mean all out, with pink pillows for the couch and bows on the..."

"Ooh, pillows would be nice," Kevin cooed. Jimmy pounced on Kevin and punched him so hard he nearly cried.

"Anybody else want some?" Jimmy asked. There were no takers.

"Why would we do that? We wouldn't want to hang out there," Chad said.

Jimmy shook his head. Frankly, they weren't getting it, none of them. "If we wouldn't want to hang around in a fort with all that shit in it, well, neither would they," Jimmy said, referring to the older boys. "Guys hate that crap, am I right?"

"So, what do we do?" Kevin asked. Jimmy thought about it for a moment.

"I know, why don't we get the girls who were at your party to decorate the fort?" Chad said. As horrifying as that sounded, it was a good idea. It had to work, and it would work. Jimmy was certain of it.

"That means someone's gotta talk to the twins," Dave informed everyone, though he directed it at Jimmy more than anyone else.

"I'll do it," Jimmy said, standing up straight. He would do it... for their cause, for their fort. He would talk to the twins.

CHAPTER EIGHTEEN

−A BOWL OF PEACHES−

The next two ball games the wildcats had on the schedule were rained out. It was a heavy and cold rain for summer, and it washed out everyone's plans. By the following Saturday, the skies had cleared, and baseball was once again on Jimmy's plate.

The team made the thirty-mile drive out to Dembrill, thinking the field would be in a playable condition. It was not, but the coaches from each team knew they needed to get this game in before too many rainouts backed up their schedules. They each had two rainouts already, a third would make it nearly impossible to reschedule.

The field was a muddy mess, but they played the game, anyway. It was the most fun those kids had all season. It was almost impossible to take the game too seriously as each team slopped around, sometimes in ankle deep mud. Each base had its own moat protecting it. And every inch of every child was covered in mud by the end. The more mud they had on them, the more fun they seemed to have had.

They played the game for as long as they could, but they ran out of dry baseballs by the third inning. At that point the game was 22-20 with the Wildcats ahead. It didn't really matter to anyone that they called the game early. Everybody had their fill of baseball, and everybody had more than their fill of fun.

Jimmy did not take the mound in that game. There just weren't enough innings for the coach to get him in to pitch. But Jimmy didn't seem to care one bit. He was covered in mud from head to toe. The only part of him that didn't have mud was his eyes. The Wildcats went home muddy and happy.

It was still a nice day when they all got home so Jimmy got cleaned up and set out to do what he knew he had to do, and he went alone. This was something he knew he had to fix himself. He wasn't even sure it would work or even if the girls would be willing to help, but he had to try. He had to get the fort back.

Jimmy was overlooking the one rule every boy's fort had: NO GIRLS ALLOWED. Was he crossing a boundary that he could not return from? He was grateful Cindy didn't take much heed in rules when she climbed up in his tree fort on his birthday. But this was different. It was for the greater good, or was it?

Jimmy approached the house where the twins lived, feeling sick to his stomach. He rang the bell, looking down at his feet, not sure he could face the task ahead. When he pulled his head back up, the twins were standing right in front of him.

Jimmy shrieked and ran off before saying a word. When he was around the corner and out of sight, he stopped. He was panting and sweating. Not willing to try that again, he headed home.

His father walked in on Jimmy as he brooded in the family room. He sat in the chair across from him with a bowl of peaches.

"What ya up to, son?" he asked.

"Nothin'," Jimmy muttered softly. At face value, he was doing nothin', but his father raised his eyebrows. He knew better.

"How was the game?" his father asked.

"Okay," Jimmy answered. His mind was certainly elsewhere. Jimmy played with his lip between his teeth.

"How's the fort?"

Jimmy tried not to react, but he was in trouble. "Okay," he said.

"I heard there was an incident," his father said. Jimmy knew the jig was up. He was about to give in, spill the beans. "Otis Tillman says he brought ya a groundhog to help ya dig a hole."

"Huh...what? —Oh yeah," Jimmy said. Then he started laughing. "That didn't work." His father joined in the laughter.

"Yeah—Otis, he ain't right," Jimmy's father said.

"Nope, he ain't," Jimmy agreed. When the laughter died, Jimmy's dad sat quietly, looking at Jimmy, waiting for more it seemed. Jimmy added the other lip to his dawdling. They sat quietly for a while before Jimmy spoke up.

"Dad, you ever had twins?" Jimmy asked. Jimmy's father started choking on his peaches. "You okay?" Jimmy added.

"Yeah," his father answered, wiping peach juice from his chin. "But what did you say?"

"Twins, you ever had twins around, while you were growing up or anything?"

"Are you asking me about the twins that were at your birthday party?"

"Yeah," Jimmy said, thinking he finally got through.

His father set down his bowl of peaches. "Twins, huh? They're a handful." Jimmy was thinking they were two handfuls. "Well, I would imagine if they both liked you, they would be okay with it. Twins think differently than most people. They play to be opposites, but there is some kind of power that connects them both." His father paused. "Twins huh?" He shook his head while an odd smile played on his lips.

Jimmy stared at his father. He did not know what he was talking about, and he thought his father didn't either, for that matter.

"Is Mom home?" Jimmy asked.

The question shook his dad wherever his thoughts had taken him. "Oh, um, no, she took Mrs. Wilshire to the pound to look for a new cat."

"Oh, okay," Jimmy said, and he headed off to his room while his father finished his peaches.

Jimmy sat up there for much of the afternoon trying to figure out how he was going to talk to those twins. Dave was the only one who could talk to girls. He could always get his help, but he really wanted to do this himself.

Then he thought of it. The one girl he could talk to was Cindy. She knew the twins well enough to talk to them. All three could be in on it.

Jimmy thought that was absolutely genius. Having decided, he put his plan into action immediately.

By late afternoon, his work was done. He had gotten Cindy to talk to the twins. The twins were more than happy to help and even invited another girl to come along. Her name was Corrine.

The next morning, the boys set out to escort the four young girls to the clubhouse. They took them down Cattank Road but not before blindfolding each girl. How they got the girls to agree to the blindfolds was anybody's guess, but they did, and it was a slow walk down the dirt path. Up ahead, the boys noticed some crows picking at the remaining carcass of Erwin. It was a shame. When they got nearer, the birds flew off in all directions. The birds then settled in the nearby trees waiting for the strangers to pass before resuming their early morning scavenger hunt.

It was a beautiful morning for a hike, but that was lost on the boys who were too focused on their purpose to care. The boys slowed their approach as they neared the road's end and hunkered down behind some brush with each girl. They hushed the nervous girls.

"Everybody wait here. I'll go check it out," Jimmy said, putting on a brave front. He hoped Cindy noticed. He moved out into the clearing.

"What's going on?" asked Jessica.

"It's okay. We're checking to make sure no one else is at the fort," Dave said, putting his arm around her for comfort. She relaxed.

Jimmy made it to the fort okay and peered into the gun slots. He listened. There was nothing. He went for the door and rushed inside. The fort was clear, and Jimmy waved everyone forward. They removed the blindfolds from the girls as they reached the fort. The girls looked around for the first time, smiling. Cindy looked back at the dirt road.

"Hey, ain't that Cattank Road?" she said.

"Dammit!" Jimmy grunted. The one thing they never counted on was that girls like to explore just as much as boys. The girls found the fort to be very comfortable, and it wasn't long before they put their mark on the clubhouse.

They all visited the fort daily, and the girls worked on it a little each time. And since Cindy knew exactly where they were, the girls even made trips out to the fort without the boys. By the end of the week, it was a girl's palace.

The boys hated it! They even began to wonder what in God's name they were thinking. The place was even creeping them out. They asked the girls if the older boys had been out that way yet, but the girls hadn't seen them.

"This is not good," Dave said looking around at all the pink and the bows and the lacy things that now occupied their fort.

Disgust was written on each boy's face. Kevin ran his hands over a soft blanket on one of the chairs, and Jimmy nearly punched him.

"Man, this place is somethin' else," Chad said. He held up a potholder with a chicken on it.

"You girls certainly did..." Jimmy said slowly, taking it all in.

"You're welcome!" Jessica said proudly. "It was fun." But Jimmy wasn't really leaning towards thanking anybody. He was still too flabbergasted, thunderstruck, mystified, and addled to know what to say. Jessica fluffed up a pillow as Erica adjusted a tea set on the table that stood where Jimmy had once shot a man.

"Yeah, this ain't good," Dave repeated. Then out of nowhere, a car could be heard coming down the dirt road. The girls didn't react, but the boys all froze for a split second before scurrying about in hopes of a secret passageway, perhaps that tunnel Brian was supposed to dig.

When they realized there was only one way in and one way out, they grabbed the girls and took off for the front door. When they didn't see the car coming down the road yet, they all ran from the fort and into the woods just to the rear of their haunt.

"Who's coming?" Erica asked. Jimmy peered out from the brush that obscured them from any on comers.

"Shhh," he insisted. The noise became louder as the car plowed down the dirt path. Jimmy was certain it was those same boys from before. He nodded to his friends, making sure they stayed concealed.

"I'm scared," Corrine said. Jimmy gave her a reassuring look. It would be okay.

The car emerged suddenly and came to a skidding halt in the middle of the clearing. It was the same car, and it was the same four boys—Bobby, Brad, Ralph, and Eric. They climbed out of the car, pulled a cooler from the trunk, and went inside.

"What the fuck is this?" Bobby said. The door closed behind them. "Ain't this just fucking cute," he added. Jimmy and his gang all ran to the rear of the fort and hid below the gun slots. Three of the girls were terrified, but Cindy was cool. Jimmy peered in.

"Can you see 'em?" Kevin asked.

Jimmy could just make them out. The boys inside were all looking disgusted, especially Bobby.

"Did you do this, you queer?" he asked. Eric looked around nervously after Bobby caught him smiling. Bobby slugged him in the arm. Eric flinched, and so did Kevin a little.

"I didn't do it," Eric whined. Brad and Ralph put the cooler down on a table. Bobby turned around and looked at Brad and Ralph.

"What the fuck ya doin? We ain't stayin' here." Bobby shoved a few of the pieces of a tea setting from the table. They shattered against the far wall. He gave the place one last look of disgust and stormed out. His thugs followed behind faithfully. Jimmy's gang sat back down against the rear wall of the fort and waited for the sound of the car to be swallowed by the thicket of trees along Cattank Road. They were gone, and Jimmy was reeling.

"It worked," Chad said. Jimmy knew. They all headed back inside. Jimmy watched curiously as the girls followed them in.

"What are you doing?" he asked them. They walked past and once again made themselves at home inside the fort. Jimmy just stared at them.

"Ooh, look what those terrible boys did?" Jessica said, and she began picking up broken pieces of a teacup as if nothing was unusual. Jimmy looked at Dave. Dave shrugged.

"Thanks," Jimmy said, meaning get the hell out.

"Oh, you're welcome," Jessica said, clearly meaning you're welcome.

Cindy moved towards the door. It appeared she understood what Jimmy was trying to convey and was ready to leave. The other girls were completely clueless.

"We don't need your help anymore," Jimmy said, politely meaning get the hell out.

"Nope, ya don't," Jessica said kind of comically. There was a pause, an awkward pause.

"GET OUT!" Jimmy screamed. His face began turning red.

"No," Jessica said calmly. She finished picking up the broken china from the tea setting. Jimmy was furious.

"This is our fort," he insisted. No one moved. "We didn't say you could stay when it was over."

Jessica walked over to Jimmy. "Then why would we have wanted to help you, silly boy."

"This ain't good," Dave kept repeating. Right then, everybody thought Jimmy was going to kill Jessica, he was so red with fury.

"Get out."

"No."

"Yes!" Jimmy screamed.

"No," she said.

Dave, Chad, and Kevin just looked on like helpless spectators. No one knew what to do. They had recaptured the fort from the older boys with a genius plan only to have it taken right back out from under them by a bunch of girls.

"Let's get out of here," Jimmy fumed, and as he walked out, more tea settings found the floor.

"You don't have to leave," Jessica said softly. Jimmy, madder than ever, left with his buds, which now included Cindy.

"That ain't cool," Chad said.

"I knew this wasn't a good idea," Dave said.

"You never said any such thing," Jimmy said. Kevin and Chad dropped back a step in fear of getting hit by an errant punch.

"It wouldn't have mattered. You don't listen to anybody when you get some foolhardy plan in your head," Dave said.

Jimmy balled his fists. "You agreed to this plan, just as Kevin and Chad did."

"Well, everybody knows girls aren't allowed in a guy's fort," Dave said. Just then, they realized there was a girl with them. They turned on her. She threw her hands up.

"Don't look at me. I did what Jimmy asked me to do," Cindy said, standing firm.

"Why are you even here?" Dave asked.

She gave him a dirty look. "I wasn't gonna stay there with them," Cindy said.

"Why not? You probably invited them to stay in the first place. And the only reason you aren't in there now is so Jimmy doesn't think you betrayed him," Dave said. Those were big words with harsh accusations, and nobody moved. Then Cindy looked at Jimmy, the betrayal she felt etched on her face. Jimmy said nothing in her defense. He didn't know what to say.

"Jimmy," Cindy cried softly. He looked down. He wouldn't face her, he couldn't. His friends seemed more important right then.

"I hate you," she said and punched him in the arm as she stormed past. He stood there rubbing it in the same fashion Kevin always did when Jimmy punched him. Cindy ran off down Cattank Road, never slowing as they watched her disappear.

"What's wrong with you, Dave?" Jimmy asked. Nobody took pleasure in what just happened, but it happened.

"Screw you," Dave said. It was as if the boys were now sailors on a weekend pass. Every other word out of their mouths was vulgar. They painted the horizon with freshly recited indelicacies. It was a magnificent display of bawdy for eleven-year-olds. One last time, Jimmy told Dave what he could do, and then the punches ensued.

Dave punched Jimmy on the side of his head. Jimmy, reeling, landed hard on the ground. Dust billowed. Jimmy's hand went straight to his face to cover the blow. He was crying behind his hand and stumbled trying to get up. He got to his knees but looked wobbly, so Dave took his foot and pushed him back down. Jimmy fell onto his face. Dave and Chad walked away. Kevin looked confused and didn't know whether to go on with Dave and Chad or tend to Jimmy.

"You motherfucker," Jimmy said to Dave. "When I get my fort back, you ain't gonna be allowed to use it." Jimmy looked up at Kevin, who was still indecisive. "Here, I'll make it easy for you." And Jimmy got up and ran past Kevin and then past Dave and Chad. Dave braced for a potential blow from Jimmy, but Jimmy just tore on by and never looked back.

CHAPTER NINETEEN

-PLUNK 'EM-

When Jimmy got home, he wiped the tears away and cleaned himself up a little before going inside. He could tell his mother knew immediately that something was afoul, but she did not pry.

Jimmy ate an early supper and put his baseball uniform on and then waited for his father to come home to take him to his game. He sat quietly while he waited.

The Beaver Creek Braves arrived all together on a big bus, not a school bus either. It was an old touring bus, the kind that would bring strangers into towns like Walnut Creek or take guys off to war. The Braves all piled off the bus and onto the field. A couple of adults lugged equipment bags from the cargo hold of the bus, and they too took to the field.

Baseball was in the air, and that bus left the vague taste of an old-time game of years past. The kind of game fought between small hick towns on the minor league circuit, with kids gritting it out for a chance at the big leagues. No one ever heard of a Little League team having a bus. Jimmy thought it was cool.

Jimmy sat on the end of the bench, mostly by himself. Dave seemed to avoid any kind of encounter with Jimmy. That left Chad and Kevin sort of in the middle. Kevin could muster a "Hey" from Jimmy, but that was about it.

Chad nodded. Jimmy looked for Cindy but saw no sign of her anywhere. He couldn't blame her for not wanting to come see him play.

With two outs, Walnut Creek pushed two runs across the plate in the bottom of the first off a double by Dave after Kevin and Todd each walked. Jimmy came up to bat next but struck out to end the threat by the Wildcats. It was a good start for the home team, and the two teams traded spots on the field.

"Way to go, Hamilton," Dave said as he walked past Jimmy in the dugout. Jimmy was defenseless and shied away from any kind of confrontation. "Yeah, I didn't think so," and Dave walked up the dugout steps and jogged out to his position at shortstop. Jimmy moped to right field. He was better than right field and knew it, but he went there anyway.

Alex was on the mound for the Wildcats. He was big for his size and not very bright. He would have made Yogi Berra proud. Alex never had much to say until he opened his mouth. Yeah, he would make Yogi very proud. Alex struck out the first batter of the inning. Then he gave up a double to the gap in left center. The next batter hit a screaming line drive, sure to score a run, but Dave dove to his right and came up with the ball for an out. The runner on second base dove back to the bag just under Dave's tag. Two outs. Alex walked the next hitter and plunked the next. The crowd moaned when they heard the thud of the hit batter. They were definitely into the game. The batter took his base. The bases were now loaded.

After a quick conference at the mound, the game resumed. "Say shooter," Dave hollered encouragement.

"Strike!" the half blind umpire bellowed.

"Two more now, just two more," the crowd yelled. Alex went into his windup. A long fly ball came off the bat and everybody's eyes followed as it screamed towards Jimmy in right field. He had his head raised and glove out to catch the flight. The ball glistened from the intense light of the halogen bulbs high above the field. Jimmy never moved except for his head. The ball darted downward, straight for Jimmy. His glove went up. The crack of leather on leather broke the silence, and the crowd erupted.

Jimmy came in off the field with the ball still in his glove. Everybody gathered around him and patted him on the back, everyone but Dave.

"Nice catch, Hamilton," Dave smirked. It was hard to read how he really felt. Jimmy's coach took the ball from Jimmy's glove and tossed it back out to the Braves' pitcher so he could warm up.

By the fifth inning, the score was still 2-0. Alex had pitched a brilliant game but his arm was sore, so he sat out the rest of the game. Todd pitched the fifth inning, but he wasn't sharp. He only gave up one run, but when the Wildcats took the field in the sixth inning, Jimmy stood on the mound.

He took some extra time to rearrange the dirt around the rubber so it was just right, then he took his warm-ups. The first pitch hit the umpire who scooted a few more feet out of the way for the next pitch. That pitch only hit the backstop. Jimmy glimpsed Cindy sitting in the bleachers. A charge of adrenaline ran through his veins like ice water. He was on. That unmistakable pop of leather let Jimmy know, he was warmed up and ready.

His first live pitch sent everybody ducking, ball one. The next pitch sent only the batter ducking, ball two. No, wait, the ball tipped the bat, strike one. A murmur of laughter and oohs filled the crowd. Jimmy fixed the dirt around the mound again. Kevin almost caught Jimmy's next pitch, but it made its way to the backstop, ball two. Thunk. "Dead ball, batter take your base," called the umpire after Jimmy beaned the batter. The boy was on the ground reeling from the blow and wasn't taking the free base as his coaches poured out of the dugout in concern.

After a brief moment, the boy got to his feet and was applauded on his way to first. The coach of the other team glared at Jimmy as he made his way to the dugout steps.

"You be careful, son," the opposing coach told Jimmy. Jimmy's coach heard it and was up the steps and out of his dugout before the man took another step.

"Hey!" Jimmy's coach said as he confronted the man. Face to face with the other coach, he said. "Don't you ever say anything to my players, you hear me. You got a problem, you talk to me." His players couldn't believe their eyes, clearly enjoying the show. They knew their coach was balls to the wall tough, but that was cool. It gave them all a charge.

"All right, everybody calm down," the umpire said. "You go back to your dugout." And he nodded at Jimmy's coach.

"I mean it," Jimmy's coach warned with a pointed finger. Jimmy's coach took the umpire's coaxing and walked back to the top of his dugout where he stood waiting for another crack from the opposing coach. Thunk!

"Oh, come on!" shouted the Beaver Creek man.

"Take your base," the umpire said as if nothing was unusual. Jimmy was quickly becoming unraveled. Dave hissed at him. Jimmy didn't hear him. His coach went out to talk to him. Jimmy didn't hear him either. He was in his own world, and at the moment it wasn't where he wanted to be.

Jimmy tossed the next pitch almost as if he was aiming it. The outcome was not good. The ball screamed past Dave at short. Dave gave it his best shot but came up without the ball. The team lined up the proper cutoffs and got the ball in before anybody scored, but the bases were now loaded.

The next batter looked like a grown man. He was very tall. Jimmy cowered at the sight of him. When Jimmy let the next pitch go, he prayed. It didn't help. It was quickly 5-2 in favor of the Braves. The very large boy had just hit a grand slam.

Jimmy was devastated. He kicked at the dirt in frustration. Kevin, who was catching, went out to calm him down. Jimmy was fighting back tears.

"Don't let the coach see that," Kevin said crowding Jimmy. Jimmy sniffled. Kevin looked back over his shoulder and into their dugout. No sign of the coach yet.

"Let's go boys," bellowed the umpire.

"Pull it together, Jimmy," Kevin said. Jimmy only sniffled more. The opposing coach was whooping it up a little too much with his players. Jimmy's coach was about to have issues with that, or about to cause an issue. He was furious.

"Coach looks pissed," Jimmy noticed. Kevin looked back again.

"He ain't mad at you, he's about had it with that other coach, I think," Kevin said. Dave walked to the mound to buy some more time before the umpire insisted they resume the game. Jimmy wasn't in the mood for whatever Dave was about to say until Dave opened his mouth.

"Bean this next guy."

Jimmy's eyes widened.

"What?" Kevin said.

"They can't be dancing around on our field like that," Dave explained. "Plunk 'em, and make him feel it."

So Jimmy did just that, fastball high and tight. PLUNK! The batter went down in a hurried heap. He was screaming from the pain. Coaches poured out of each dugout. The man whooping it up earlier was at the top of his steps yelling at Jimmy. Jimmy's coach was across the field before the man reached the infield grass.

Punches flew, kids cheered, and the umpire went home. The game was called. No one knew the outcome of the game, but technically if the game was called in the top of an inning, that inning would not count. So, if the score reverted back to the last full inning played, the Wildcats won the game 2-1. No one really cared. The hoopla that led to the game being canceled was all that anyone talked about.

"Man, did coach kick that guy's ass or what?" Kevin said. Jimmy, Dave, and Chad all agreed as they slurped on their frozen iced drinks after the game.

"That guy was twice the size of coach," Chad said.

"Yeah, but when coach grabbed that other guy and clunked his head against the dugout, I almost died," Dave said.

"He never let go of the first guy either," Jimmy added.

"Why d'ya think he went crazy like that?" Kevin asked.

"'Cause he is crazy," Chad said. They all laughed as brain freeze crept in. Kevin started rubbing his forehead, but nothing happened.

"He ain't crazy, he's cool," Jimmy said.

"It was pretty cool," Dave added.

"The Braves' coach was pretty mad at you, Jimmy," Kevin said.

"It was Dave's fault. He told me to plunk the next batter. You heard him."

"And why d'ya do that?" Chad asked Dave.

"Same reason the coach went nuts, respect."

"What?" Kevin said, slurping his freezing soda too fast.

"The coach stood up for us today, especially Jimmy. I told Jimmy to hit the next kid because they did not respect our team or our field. And by taking no shit from them and plunking that kid, well that was Jimmy's way of standing up for Walnut Creek," Dave said. They sat quietly and contemplated Dave's words. It seemed as if things were getting back to normal. The boys were laughing again, even though they each now suffered greatly from *sphenopalatine ganglioneuralgia*, better known as brain freeze.

"Man, that hurts," Kevin said, but no one paid him any mind.

"Yeah, I guess he did." Jimmy began to feel a little proud.

"He did," Chad said. Jimmy felt pretty good about things. They finished their frozen drinks and walked back out to the warm evening air, which did little to thaw their heads.

"You guys want to do something tomorrow?" Jimmy asked, as if things were all good once again.

"Yeah, like what?" Dave said. "You want to go to the fort and hang out?" Jimmy was crushed.

"Yeah, let's do that," Kevin said.

"We can't... remember, Jimmy gave the fort to a bunch of girls," and Dave proceeded to slug Jimmy hard in the arm as he walked off and away from his friends.

Jimmy watched him go, tears forming in his eyes. He thought things were good again, but they were not.

CHAPTER TWENTY

-PATCH-

The next morning, after Jimmy finished breakfast, he went right back up to his bedroom. He stayed there brooding and contemplating his dilemma. Jimmy did not know what to do. He had achieved what he originally set out to do before the end of the summer, and that was kiss Cindy and get a new fort after his father cut down the tree fort.

He hadn't thought for a minute those two things would be mere shatters of a memory, and so soon. The feeling that had settled in the pit of his stomach was awful. He was only eleven, but he was suffering from full-blown adolescence. He had no fort and no Cindy.

"Jimmy," his mother hollered up the stairs. "You've got baseball early tomorrow, so get your books ready to return to the library. We're going today."

"I haven't read the ones I got the last time," Jimmy hollered back. He quickly realized that was not what she wanted to hear. The door to his room flung open.

"Well, the cat's out of the bag now, isn't it?" and his mother turned and swept down the hallway and out of sight. Jimmy moped about, collected his books, and met his mother downstairs.

The car ride to the library was a quiet one as Jimmy pressed his nose into one of his books, *A Groundhog in The City*. It was a silly little tale of a wayward groundhog who inadvertently wound up in the city and couldn't find his way home because there was nowhere for him to dig. The entire city was cemented over, and he couldn't get a hole started anywhere. It reminded him a little of Brian, so he read on. Or did it remind him of himself?

Jimmy's mom pulled over to the curb on Main Street and parked the car. He got out with his books, never finishing the story of the stupid groundhog. Jimmy figured the groundhog somehow made it safely home to his family, but he thought a better ending would have the groundhog getting run over by a car on his long journey home. Jimmy was sour.

Jimmy's mother took her son's hand, and they walked the half a block to the library. Walking up the library steps with his head down, Jimmy happened upon a gray lump blocking his path. It looked like tree bark and old, wet newspapers and dirty clothes in a pile. He wasn't sure if he had ever seen that before, but he thought it looked familiar. He was so engrossed by the lumpy mass he never detected the twins, Erica and Jessica, as they walked out of the library and down the steps right at him.

As the girls drew close to the gray matter, it stirred. Then it moaned. The girls shrieked and jumped back. Jimmy noticed that. The pile rose up from the steps and growled at the disturbance. The girls screamed and ran down the steps, not even saying hello to Jimmy.

The pile of grayness finished rising, and within the dirtiness was a man's face. Its color was dirty gray, matching the color of his clothes. The whites of his eyes and yellow of his teeth stood out from the grunge. His hair was so matted it looked like an old hat.

"Don't stare," Jimmy's mother said, and she whisked him away and into the library. Jimmy couldn't help but look back at the poor man. The man settled back down and practically disappeared in the lumpy disguise of his clothes.

Once inside the library, Jimmy escaped the clutches of his mother and went straight to the gardening section of the library. He read aloud any pertinent words in the titles of books he perused.

"Insects, insecticide, pest control, weasels, varmints... there, *Rid Your Yard and Garden of All Nasty Varmints.*" He pulled the book from the shelf, sat down, and gave it a look. There was nothing in it about girls. Dang. He put the book back and kept looking.

But he couldn't get that old man out of his head. Did he live in Walnut Creek? Who was he? Why did he look like that? Then a light bulb went off in his head, and Jimmy ran out of the library and stood in front of the gray bark-like lump. It stirred again and made that same grumbling noise. Jimmy stood perfectly still. He was not afraid. The bum growled, but Jimmy did not move. Then the bum waved his arms around like a monster, but Jimmy stood his ground.

"What ya want kid?" the man grunted, but Jimmy could tell he didn't really want to know. Jimmy looked at the vagrant with an eager expression. He knew what he wanted from the old man, but he wasn't sure just how to go about asking for it.

"What's your name, mister?"

"Grrrrr, beat it, kid." the old man said. He had a gravelly voice, but Jimmy could understand him perfectly. Jimmy didn't think he was actually as mean as he sounded.

"I need something," Jimmy said.

"Well, I ain't got it. Now get out of here," and the bum swiped his arm at Jimmy's legs.

"You live here, mister?"

"No, I'm just visiting your library," the man said with an acid tone. He grunted some and then looked up at Jimmy. "You don't hear well, do ya, kid?"

"What?"

"I said get out of here," and the old man rose slightly from his stupor to scare Jimmy off.

Without moving, Jimmy said, "I need your help." Just then a sweet and innocent voice sang out.

"Hi, Jimmy," and Cindy swept by like a cool summer breeze. The interruption startled Jimmy, but it was a welcoming voice.

"Hi, Cindy," Jimmy replied, and she was gone. Jimmy wasn't sure why she said hello. He thought she hated him. Maybe she had forgotten all about it, or maybe it was seeing him talk to this stranger. He thought that he probably looked pretty cool talking to this guy, not being afraid or anything.

"That your wife?" the gravelly voice asked, this time a bit more friendly.

"Nooo." Jimmy chuckled. The old man kind of grinned, but it was masked with a troubling look, and he turned away again slightly, hiding the bit of color he possessed. When he was merely a gray mass, he gave off a sense of macabre. Jimmy didn't really like it much. He felt sorry for the man.

"Why you still here?" grunted the gray mass. Jimmy didn't say a word. "I told ya to beat it, kid."

"I need your help," Jimmy blurted out. The old man turned to face Jimmy. He had no expression, just the whites of his eyes. Jimmy felt as if he had just imposed. The old man looked at Jimmy with cold hard eyes. His lip was curled, exposing the yellow teeth. His skin was so cracked and gnarled it looked like tree bark.

"Go on," the man said. Jimmy nervously began to explain what he needed. Jimmy told the old man about Erwin and about the teenagers. He told the old man about his brilliant plan to rid the clubhouse of the older boys. And he described how his plan worked but then backfired on him and his friends. Then Jimmy told the man about his friends.

"I meant, go on, get," the man said as he shooed Jimmy away.

"He's got blond worms for hair, always smelling stuff..." Jimmy went on but stopped abruptly when he saw Kevin and Kevin's mother walking up the steps of the library. Kevin looked at Jimmy and gaped. Kevin's mother whisked Kevin along. Jimmy was almost certain he heard her tell Kevin not to stare.

"So, you want me to scare a bunch of girls for you?" asked the old man.

"Yeah," Jimmy said, nodding.

The old man shifted slightly. He finally got it.

"I don't do that kind of thing. I don't like scaring people," the bum said. He looked away.

"Everybody's scared of ya. Don't ya see how they all scurry by?" Jimmy said.

The bum gave him an exasperated look. "But not you," he said.

Jimmy was proud of that fact—nope, not him. Jimmy smiled, but a terrible thought hit him. What was the likelihood his mother would have gotten word from Kevin's mom that he was out here speaking to a stranger, and a bum at that. He better hurry and get this over with.

"What's your name?" Jimmy asked.

"I'm nobody," the old man grunted.

"You gotta have a name, mister," Jimmy said. "Mine's Jimmy."

"Patch Palmer," the man replied. Jimmy held out his hand. Patch looked at it, and the expression on his face softened. Patch took his hand.

"I really should get back in the library. My mom will be looking for me," Jimmy told the man.

"Okay," Patch agreed.

"So, will you do it?"

"I don't know, kid," he grunted again. Jimmy looked disheartened. "I tell ya what, meet me here same time tomorrow, and we'll talk about it."

"Okay," and Jimmy smiled at the poor man.

"And bring some food," Patch blurted. Just then, the library door opened. Jimmy and Patch were both blinded by the whites of Mrs. Hamilton's eyes. Jimmy lifted the arm she always used like a leash and off he went.

"What did I tell you about talking to strangers?" she scolded.

"But mom, he's my friend," Jimmy said as the library doors swallowed them up.

Jimmy picked out three books, two on pest control, neither of which would help him, and a book titled, *Denny the Drifter*. He got the book because Denny was wearing the same old bark-like jacket that Patch had on. When Jimmy finished checking out his books, he and his mother left the library together. She kept a close reign on Jimmy, but she needn't have bothered, Patch was gone. Jimmy looked everywhere for the man as his mother ushered him to their car, but he didn't see Patch anywhere. It was almost as if he had never been there.

CHAPTER TWENTY-ONE
—FIVE MEN AND A BAT—

Nobody came calling on Jimmy the rest of the day, so he became an expert on removing moles from a garden and what to do when swarms of Japanese beetles are destroying your rose bushes. He'd rarely hit such levels of boredom.

Saturday couldn't come soon enough, but when it did, it was a great day for a game, and Jimmy had a good feeling it was going to be just that. He was up and dressed to play before he even had breakfast. His mother discouraged him from eating with his uniform on, but he insisted. So when he left the house, he sported a blueberry stain on his chest about the size of a baseball. It started out as the size of a blueberry, but just got smeared more and more until it was as big as that baseball.

"Just wonderful," his mother said, rolling her eyes. Jimmy finished messing with the stain and got out of there fast.

Mr. Spencer drove all four boys to their game. The entire ride over to the field, Kevin looked to be bursting at the seams to talk to Jimmy, but he did not. It was a cardinal rule of boys; you don't talk about big stuff in front of anyone's father.

The second they were all out of the car and out of earshot of Kevin's dad, Kevin burst out, "Dude, who was that guy you were talking to yesterday in front of the library?" Jimmy looked nonchalant.

"Just a friend," Jimmy said. Dave and Chad suddenly became interested in the conversation. Dave said nothing but nodded for Chad to inquire further.

"Who ya talkin' 'bout?"

"Nobody," Jimmy replied.

"Nobody. Are you kidding?" Kevin said excitedly. "Jimmy was talkin' to that old man who sits on the steps in front of the library." Jimmy looked oddly at Kevin. As many times as Jimmy had been to that library, how come he had never seen the guy before?

"Yeah, my dad says he's a bum," Dave said.

"He ain't no bum," Jimmy said.

"He is a bum. He sleeps in a cardboard box," Dave said.

"No, he's not," Jimmy said again.

"He does live in a box," Chad said. "So, I think that does make him a bum."

"You guys don't know nothin'," Jimmy said, and he stormed off and into the dugout. After they put their gear in the dugout, Jimmy looked around to see if he could sneak away for a few minutes without being noticed.

Kevin, Dave, and Chad all saw him sneak off, but none of them said a word. They took the field and tossed a ball around in a mock attempt to loosen up, but they were more interested in Jimmy's whereabouts than baseball right about then.

"Hey, Patch," Jimmy said. Patch was startled by the greeting, but he relaxed when he saw who it was.

"Hey, boy," he said. Jimmy smiled. He looked at Jimmy's uniform. "You got a game today?"

"Yeah," Jimmy replied. Jimmy looked back over his shoulder at the ball field.

"Who ya play?"

"I think we play Rockville."

Patch thought for a moment. "The Rockville Nine?"

"Yeah," Jimmy said, surprised.

"They any good this year?" Patch said scratching his chin.

Jimmy paused. "Don't rightly know. We played them before in the mud."

"Well, good luck to ya."

Jimmy felt out of place in his uniform in front of the hobo. "Would you like to come watch us play?"

"Yeah, maybe, kid," Patch replied. Jimmy smiled. He wanted so badly to ask Patch if he had changed his mind about helping him with his problem.

"I would like it if you did," Jimmy said.

The old man smiled. "Okay, kid," Patch said with a half chuckle. "You got anything to eat?" Patch added with a vulnerable look in his eye. He was starving.

Jimmy reached into his back pants pocket and pulled out some sunflower seeds. "Here."

"No, no, no, I can't take them," Patch said. "They're for your game."

"Take some," and Jimmy poured out a small handful into Patch's outreached hand. He took them and cherished them. His hands were as old and dirty looking as his face. "I should get back for warm-ups. I'll see ya later." Jimmy tore off while Patch settled back down on the steps and ate his sunflower seeds.

Jimmy started the game playing second base. He played okay, but he was preoccupied until he saw Patch lingering near an old maple tree that stood several yards off the left field foul line. Patch paced back and forth nervously. He seemed timid near the crowd and the atmosphere buzzing around the field, but Jimmy knew Patch came to watch him, and it was time to shine. And shine he did.

Jimmy made one brilliant play after another, diving to his right, then diving to his left. Nothing got past the boy. He was a human vacuum machine. At the plate, Jimmy drove in three runs with two crushing doubles that made it to the outfield fence. His coach wasn't sure if this was the same kid, so he put him in to pitch with the Wildcats winning 7-5.

Jimmy gunned down the first two batters with strikeouts. Then he walked the next batter, but then he composed himself enough to get the last batter out on a routine ground ball. Jimmy was sharp again, and both teams swapped places on the field.

"Man, you're on fire today. What's gotten into you?" Kevin said with great enthusiasm.

Jimmy only had a smile for Kevin. He didn't know what had gotten into him any more than Kevin did. Jimmy began rifling through his baseball bag.

"Hey, when are you up?" he asked Kevin.

"I was the last out," Kevin said, meaning he wouldn't be up until everyone else got to bat. "Why?"

"Go get me two hot dogs from the concession stand." Jimmy handed Kevin two dollars.

"Ketchup, mustard?"

"Um? I don't know... Ketchup, I guess," Jimmy said, and he urged Kevin to hurry. Jimmy crushed another double down the right field foul line. He thought of going to third but remembered the golden rule, never make the first or last out at third. He stood at second with nobody out. Then Dave belted a letter-high fastball to the fence, and Jimmy scored, being mobbed as he made it to the dugout. Jimmy smiled at Patch, who nodded in acknowledgment.

Kevin soon returned with the two hot dogs, and when the dust settled, he gave them to Jimmy. Jimmy took the two foil-wrapped hot dogs and ducked out of the dugout. Most of his teammates thought nothing of it; the coach hated when the kids ate during games.

It was hard for Jimmy to be inconspicuous as he made his way from the dugout. He felt as if he was on a stealth mission, but he was clearly visible, and a lot of parents took notice when he stopped under the maple tree and offered the hot dogs to Patch. Patch pulled back slightly in shame, but he was hungry and took the wrappers from the boy. Jimmy smiled. Then he began walking back to the dugout.

"Nice hit, kid," Patch shouted. Jimmy turned around feeling proud. By that time, the entire crowd from Walnut Creek was abuzz with Jimmy's exploits, especially his mother.

•   •   •

Patch, on the other hand, was unaware of the commotion he was causing and so, settled down against the tree and ate his hot dogs. Pickled condiments or not, Patch relished the dogs.

"Hey, mister," a voice shouted. Patch looked up, hoping it was more food, but it wasn't. It was one of the men from town, and he was accompanied by several other men from town. Patch grunted something and then rolled himself around so he was on the opposite side of the tree. The men rounded on the bum. Patch crouched down, protecting what was his, which was really nothing more than a modicum of pride.

"You need to leave, mister," one of the other men said. They had him circled with the tree to his back.

"I ain't gotta go nowhere," he mumbled. One of the men nudged him with his foot. Patch growled and swung his arm wildly at the man's leg. The man leapt back as if Patch was a poisonous snake.

"Let's go, mister," yelled the first man. Patch grunted, and again they kicked at him. By then, half of Walnut Creek was watching, and most of the kids playing baseball had stopped to observe the entanglement. The umpire tried to continue the game, but no one was paying him any attention.

Jimmy watched in horror. He didn't know what to do. It was his fault it was happening.

"Hey, leave him alone," Jimmy finally yelled out and ran to Patch's aid.

"This doesn't concern you, boy," said one of the men as he pushed Jimmy away.

"Get your hands off me," Jimmy insisted and tugged his arm free of the man's grasp.

"Let's get a move on, old man," said the first man. Patch again merely grunted. Then the second man wielded a wooden bat for Patch to see. Jimmy grabbed the stick and held on for his life.

One of the other men peeled Jimmy off the bat and ushered him away. Jimmy could see the man with the bat move in closer, and he was standing directly above Patch. First, he prodded Patch with the weapon. Then he drew it back in a threatening stance and lurched at Patch.

"Go ahead," Patch said.

"I will, mister."

"No," Jimmy cried. Patch did not flinch. Instead, he snatched the bat from the man and swept himself upward. All five men took a step back. Their eyes widened, never leaving Patch with his new bat.

"Yeah, that's what I thought," and Patch lurched forward with the bat as the first man had. All five men flinched. "Pussies," Patched slurred. Then Patch dropped the bat and walked away. The men stood there, mouths agape. Patch was gone.

•   •   •

"Yeah, pussies," Jimmy repeated with a righteous tone. The men looked at each other and hung their heads. Jimmy smiled. Five men needed a bat, he thought, and still did nothing.

"Play ball," the umpire shouted a moment later. With the commotion over, the game resumed. A hush and a few murmurs still floated about, but things soon settled down, and baseball was once again at the forefront.

Jimmy took the mound in the top of the sixth inning with an eight-run lead. He dug his cleats at the ground as if he were mad at it. The soil was hard and worn unevenly. When he was done, he was still mad. He took his warm-ups. The coach should have seen it then, but he didn't and so left Jimmy in to pitch.

Things turned ugly quickly for Jimmy. He hit three batters, walked four, and gave up two doubles and a home run. When he was done, the score was tied. Jimmy never found his earlier form and fought back tears as his coach came to take him from the game.

"Get 'em next time, son," the coach said. The coach shielded Jimmy somewhat from the crowd and motioned for Dave to come in to pitch. He took the ball from Jimmy and nodded towards shortstop.

Jimmy couldn't believe it, shortstop. The coach wanted him to play shortstop. Shortstop was for the elite players. He bolted for his spot.

Dave pitched a couple strikes and got ahead in the count with his first batter. Then he drilled the boy right in his ribs. That loaded the bases with nobody out. Dave struck out the next batter for the first out of the inning, but the bases were still loaded. The next batter swaggered to the plate. He was looking to put his team ahead with one swing of the bat, but Dave was going to have something to say about that.

Dave let go of a fastball about belt high, not where he wanted the pitch. The batter's eyes widened with anticipation as he swung. A crack sounded as the bat splintered into pieces. No one saw the ball leave the bat, their attention focused on all the wooden projectiles whirling into the air. The ball skimmed through the Bermuda grass infield right at Jimmy. He saw it and made a play for the ball. The crowd held its breath. As wood chips landed around him, Jimmy came up with the ball and gunned it home. That made two outs. The town went wild. Jimmy smiled.

The next boy was looking to hit his second home run of the inning. Dave was poised to stop him. Dave rocked back and sent his first pitch up and in on the boy. The boy dusted himself off and Dave sat him back down with another pitch at his head.

"Say shooter!" a voice from the crowd rang. Dave grooved a strike at the boy's knees. The batter dug back in and challenged Dave. Dave kicked a little dirt around and was set. Dave rocketed another fastball. The ball shot off the bat and headed for Jimmy once again. He put his glove to the ground, but it was too late, and the ball went right between his legs. Two runs scored. Jimmy was crushed. His teammates were crushed. They still had a chance to tie it up in the bottom of the inning, or even better, they could win it. All they needed was two to tie and three to win.

It was quickly over. The Wildcats went three up, three down in the bottom of the sixth and lost the game 15-13. Dave just glared at Jimmy. Some of the boys consoled Jimmy with a, "Good game, get 'em next time," but Dave's expression said it all, and that was all Jimmy cared about.

CHAPTER TWENTY-TWO
-THREE FRIGHTENED GIRLS-

"You'll get 'em next time, son," Jimmy's father assured his boy as he tussled his son's hair. Jimmy put his cap back on in hopes of his father not doing that again.

"It's just a game, Jimmy," his mother said. Jimmy scowled at her. What did she know about it?

Jimmy wanted to hang out in town and maybe look for Patch, but he knew if he didn't come up with something good for an excuse, he was going home with his parents. His mother would never believe the library as an excuse. He needed something. He had nothing.

"Hi, Jimmy," Cindy cooed. Jimmy turned around and smiled. She was dreamy. Even better, she was a great excuse.

"Hi," Jimmy said nonchalantly. He was the cool of cool.

"Sorry 'bout your game," she said. He nodded like Humphrey Bogart might. "You played really good in the beginning," she said, adding insult to injury. He forced a smile that faded quickly. She needed to shut up.

"Would you kids like to go for ice cream at the diner?" his mother asked.

"Are you coming?" Jimmy asked his mother. His mother made a face. Cindy giggled, but for once it didn't bother Jimmy. He liked her laugh, and it felt warming.

"Are you going to drive Cindy home after your date?" his mother asked in a playful but retaliatory fashion. Jimmy's eyes widened. He didn't have a car, and worse this wasn't a date. What was she thinking?

"Mo'om," he said.

"Honey, give the kids some money for ice cream," she told her husband. "We'll leave you kids be." Jimmy's dad handed Jimmy a few dollar bills. He went to tussle the boy's hair once more, but Jimmy ducked down and then past his father.

"Thank goodness you came along," Jimmy told Cindy. Cindy added a bounce to her step then a smile to match.

"Are you really gonna take me for ice cream?" she asked. Jimmy looked at her oddly. They kept walking.

"Don't you want ice cream?" he said.

"Sure, I do," she said. They went into the half-crowded diner and found two empty stools at the counter. Tammy came right over and took their order.

"I want..." but this was going to take a while. Cindy's legs dangled from her stool, and the more she thought the more they swung. "A strawberry shake," she finally ordered. Tammy looked at Jimmy.

"Me too," he said.

Tammy smiled. "I know your favorite is chocolate," she whispered in his ear. He couldn't help the guilty look on his face.

"So, where are your friends?" Cindy asked.

"I don't have any friends. At least not after today."

"Oh, it wasn't so bad," Cindy said. Jimmy looked at her and wondered how it was she was so cool.

"I'm really sorry about that time at the fort," Jimmy told her. She smiled. Jimmy didn't really know it, but those words were the very best thing he could have said.

"It's okay," she said. It seemed like it was taking Tammy forever to stir up two strawberry shakes.

"Thanks," was about all he knew to say. After all, he was still Jimmy. Still no shakes, Jimmy noticed.

"So, who was that guy you were trying to protect from those men at the game?" she asked.

"That's Patch," Jimmy was happy to answer.

"Was he the same guy at the library?"

"Yep," Jimmy said.

"Who is he?" she asked.

"Just a friend," Jimmy said.

"He's your friend?" she asked, surprised.

"Here you two go," Tammy interrupted as she slid two large strawberry shakes in front of the kids. Tammy walked away, and both Jimmy and Cindy began their descent to the bottom of their glasses.

"You're gonna get brain freeze." She giggled.

Jimmy stopped sucking and made a face. "Too late," he said, grimacing. They both laughed. The regular crowd began to bustle their way in, and the diner was quickly full. Jimmy and Cindy hadn't noticed a thing.

"So, how do you know Patch?"

"I just got to talking to him. He's not as mean as people think," Jimmy said.

"He looks it."

"Did you see him fight off those men?" Jimmy asked.

"I did. It was impressive," Cindy said. "What was that about?"

"People don't like him much, I guess." Jimmy said.

"Where's he from?"

"I don't know." Jimmy shrugged and went back to another round of brain freeze.

"You gonna see him again?"

"Actually, I was gonna go looking for him after we're done," Jimmy said. "You wanna come?"

Cindy looked surprised. "Oh no," she said instantly and shook her head. Jimmy watched as her hair flowed in a way that made him forget all his problems. He snapped out of it like he was just awakened.

"Okay," Jimmy said before slurping mostly air from his shake to let everyone know he was finished. Cindy followed suit, but a little quieter. Jimmy's head was frozen.

"I think I have brain freeze too." Cindy giggled.

Jimmy sat upright, bold and pretentious. "I don't get brain freeze," he said. She giggled some more. He couldn't hold the look on his face and grabbed for his forehead, laughing too.

"Should we go?" she asked. He looked at her. She was cute. He really liked her.

"Yeah." Once again, Tammy didn't charge him for the shakes. Jimmy left a dollar on the counter, and the two walked out.

"Thanks for the shake," Cindy said.

Jimmy nodded coolly. "No problem." Then there was a pause that neither of them had experienced before.

"See ya," she said, turning to leave.

"You sure you don't want to meet Patch?" he tossed out one more time.

"That's okay," she said and whisked away with her dark hair rippling in the soft gentle air. Jimmy stood watching her, oblivious to everything. When he realized he had lost himself in the sea of Cindy's hair again, he quickly righted the ship and went searching the town for Patch.

Jimmy walked down Main Street, passing the ball field, and headed in the direction Patch was going when he was ousted from the park. He didn't see his wayfarer friend. Jimmy tried to think as Patch would, but he knew nothing of the transient lifestyle until just a day or two before. Jimmy stumbled down one dirt path, two alleyways, a wooded lot, and soon found himself right back on Main Street. He wasn't sure where to go next and decided on walking Main Street for a while. When Jimmy got to the library, he saw Patch sitting in his lump of a pile on the library steps. Jimmy was pretty sure that Patch wasn't there earlier when he walked by.

"Patch," Jimmy called out. The lump stirred. It looked more like a gust of wind sent a pile of trash in an upheaval. Jimmy could make out the whites of his eyes. That's how he knew he was looking at him.

"Hey, boy," Patch grunted as he got himself upright. He dusted the ever-present dirt from his jacket. A cloud formed, then it quickly settled right back in.

"Where you been?" Jimmy asked him.

"Nowhere," he grunted. Jimmy noticed a yellow mustard stain on his dull gray clothes. It stood out like a splash of color in a black-and-white photograph. Kevin was told ketchup. Then something moved amongst the pile that was part of Patch. Jimmy saw two eyes that belonged to a mangy-looking critter. It raised its head from the heap of gray. It was a dog. Jimmy studied it close, and it yapped at him. Patch shushed it and then reached over and patted it on its head. The dog nudged back. He was a puppy.

"Is that your dog?" Jimmy asked. Patched looked back at the dog.

"Naw, he's not my dog. He's his own dog," Patch said quietly. Jimmy was confused. The dog looked like Patch, had the same color gray to him as Patch, and the dog sat right next to Patch as if Patch was his master.

"Whose is he?" Jimmy asked. Jimmy looked at the dog again. It had to be Patch's dog.

"He's nobody's dog. He does what he wants and comes and goes as he wants," Patch said. Jimmy cocked his head. It made no sense.

"What's his name?"

"Rufus," Patch answered.

"Who named him that?" Jimmy said, trying to uncover the mystery.

Patch never missed a beat. "I don't know," he replied. Jimmy looked at Patch, disconcerted. "It's the dog's name, kid. I don't know."

"Let's call him Charlie," Jimmy said, figuring it wouldn't matter to Patch what they called him. Patch looked at Jimmy oddly.

"Go ahead, kid, call him whatever you like," Patch said.

"Charlie!" Jimmy said. "Charlie!" he called again. Rufus never looked up. Patch turned to the dog.

"Rufus, the kid's talking to ya." Rufus looked at Patch, then to Jimmy. Jimmy looked suspiciously at them both.

"He's your dog," Jimmy said with a slight chuckle.

Patch snorted, or maybe he hiccupped. Jimmy couldn't tell the difference. Rufus crawled out from behind Patch and put his paw out for Jimmy. Jimmy shook Rufus' paw. That kind of sealed it for Patch. Jimmy was okay in his book.

The three walked down the steps and headed down Main Street three wide as Jimmy explained to Patch just how he got to be in this predicament.

He told Patch of his first tree fort and Mrs. Whilshire's cat. Patch got a good laugh from that. He didn't care much for cats. Then Jimmy detailed his new fort, including the tale of Brian and the peanut butter and jelly sandwiches. Patch again had a good laugh. Apparently, he liked peanut butter and jelly sandwiches, too. Finally, Jimmy explained how he lost his three best friends and his new fort all in the same day.

Patch stopped walking and looked Jimmy in the eye. "Let's go get your fort back, kid, and your friends," Patch said. Jimmy nodded. He was up for both. The three drew plenty of impolite stares and a little gossip as they walked, but no one stopped them. In fact, no one said a word to them.

When they reached the neighborhood, they took to Cattank Road and walked the dirt path that led to the fort. Jimmy played with every stick and rock along the way. He and Rufus had a good exchange of fetch going on, as Patch just seemed to be enjoying the company.

"Got anything to eat?" Patch asked Jimmy. Jimmy reached into his pocket and pulled out a wad of kid stuff, including a collection of lint that had to be as old as the pants themselves.

"I've got some gum," Jimmy pointed out. Patch took the gum from Jimmy's outstretched hand.

"Thanks," he replied.

"Don't eat it, it's gum," Jimmy said.

"I know what gum is, kid," Patch said.

Just then, Rufus came from nowhere and slammed his two oversized paws hard against Jimmy's waist. Jimmy fell back onto the ground as Rufus put his snout into everything that Jimmy had once had in his hand. Rufus sneezed when he got a good muzzle of lint. Patch corralled him and patted his head. "He's hungry," Patch said.

"There's food at the fort," Jimmy said. "No dog food, though."

"That's okay, he don't need dog food," Patch said. "A nice cat would do," Patch added.

Jimmy looked up to see if Patch was serious or not. Patch made a silly face and shook his head no. Mrs. Whilshire would be happy to know that. Jimmy collected his remains from the ground, and they pressed on.

"You ever play ball?" Jimmy said, then took a rock and aimed it at a tree as if it was a strike zone. He missed by three feet.

"I played a little ball," Patch said casually. Then he took a rock and pelted the same tree Jimmy had just missed. Jimmy was impressed. Jimmy threw at it again, and again, he missed by three feet. Patch pelted it once more before striding on.

"Did you play pro ball?"

"You ask too many questions, kid," and Patch quickened his pace.

Jimmy sped up to catch him. "Did you play for Walnut Creek?" Jimmy asked.

Patched grumbled to himself. "Yeah, kid. I was a Wildcat many years ago."

Jimmy thought that was so cool. He had a million more questions for him. "Then where d'ya play?"

"Around, boy," he said, but with an edge to his voice, letting it be known he was getting irritated.

Jimmy wanted nothing more than to hear that Patch played in the big leagues, but he was pretty sure even if Patch did play in the bigs, he wasn't going to say so. "Can you teach me to pitch?" Jimmy asked with the same enthusiasm he asked all the other questions.

"Maybe, kid... maybe."

They reached Erwin's resting grounds in the middle of the road. Erwin's remains were nothing but a shell. It had been picked clean by the buzzards. The tire tracks were nearly washed away by the rain, but it was still clear how the old boy died. Patch didn't even notice and spun the shell as he clipped it with his shoe while walking past. Rufus gave it a snort, but nothing more. Jimmy thought it was a shame about Erwin.

The clearing was up ahead, and Jimmy instructed Patch to hang back until he assessed the situation. Jimmy darted forward stealthily. He did not reach the fort before he heard girl's voices. They were giggling and enjoying themselves inside his fort. He started to fume. His first instinct was to just barge in screaming and yelling, but then why did he bring Patch with him?

Jimmy doubled back and reported his findings to Patch. "They're in there all right. They're carrying on laughing and giggling just like girls do," he said, out of breath.

"Okay," Patch said as if he knew the drill. Patch stepped forward.

"Make 'em cry," Jimmy said.

Patch looked back at the boy. "I'm here to help you get your fort back, not to make little girls cry," Patch said. Jimmy was a little disappointed but thankful all the same for Patch's help. He had just gotten a little too carried away, that's all. Patch walked forward like a swamp monster in a movie. His large silhouette was backdropped by the fort with the sun bleeding through the tree limbs off to his left.

Jimmy ducked down behind some branches to stay out of sight. He was sure the girls would go straight to their mothers and tell them what he had done. He was shaking with excitement. Patch reached the door with his faithful companion by his side. Rufus strutted like some horrible K-9 experiment gone wrong looking for leftover flesh to eat. Jimmy loved it. He couldn't wait to see the horror on those girl's faces.

Patch pulled on the door, and the door swung open. He hesitated for a second as if taken aback some, then growled like Frankenstein's monster for an added effect as he entered the building. Then his body disappeared through the doorframe.

Jimmy heard three distinct sounds—the monster Patch, the girls screaming, and stuff breaking. Jimmy imagined the terror to be fierce and relentless. He did not feel bad at all. He knew these girls had it coming.

The horror continued, and from the sound of things, the inside of the fort would be trashed, and those girls would be scarred forever. He giggled. The screams never stopped coming through the gun slots. Yet no one emerged from the chaos. Blurs of images darted past the doorframe, but nothing Jimmy could make out. He watched eagerly for a face to emerge, a face twisted with pain. Still nothing.

Then a body burst out of the door as if it were flung from the wreckage. It was Kevin. Jimmy was confused. What was Kevin doing in the fort? Then another body darted out. It was Chad. Both of their faces were covered with tears. The screams became deafening, and they were coming Jimmy's way. He ducked down a bit. Then Dave emerged. He had tears all over his face as well. The last body to exit the fort was Patch.

Jimmy watched his three friends run past him and down the dirt path like three frightened girls. Jimmy took a moment to sort out what he had just witnessed. When he realized those girls, he thought were inside were actually his friends, he burst out laughing and could not stop.

Patch stood out in front of the fort with a look of satisfaction on his gray face. Jimmy rolled on the ground in laughter. He had tears running down his face from laughing so hard. He could hear Rufus getting into something inside the fort, but paid it no mind.

"I can see you're pleased," Patch said.

"Did you see the looks on their faces?" Jimmy asked. Patch choked on his attempt to laugh. They went inside to check the damage.

The fort was a disaster. Everything had been turned upside down. Rufus had found an open can of fruit that had spilled. They left him to it. Jimmy did not touch anything. He just observed the wreckage. Patch picked up a chair and then a table and righted them. The table was one of those large wooden cable spools. It was upright, which made it roll. Patch put it down on its side and pushed the chair up to it. Some order was restored. Jimmy plopped down on an old, worn out, blanket covered couch that had recently been added to the fort. Patch took the chair he had set right and leaned back comfortably.

Neither said a word for some time. They just looked around at the mess. The frilly things looked like rags on the dirt floor. All the fine china was broken and ground into the dirt. Jimmy chuckled again, thinking of the three faces he saw run from the fort.

"I thought you weren't gonna make 'em cry," Jimmy said.

"I thought you said they were girls," Patch said. Jimmy grinned some more. Rufus scoured every inch of the fort for food. Come to think of it, Patch may have been doing the same. So Jimmy got up and found some unopened cans. He had two cans of beans, baked and waxed. He wasn't sure how the waxed beans got there.

"Hey, want some beans?" Jimmy asked, holding up the can. "You want them heated up?"

Patch looked at him, puzzled. "You got electricity out here?" he said, scanning for wires.

"Nah, we can make a fire outside, though," Jimmy said.

Patch looked at Jimmy hungrily. "Maybe next time," he said and reached for the can, grunting a thank you and taking it outside. Jimmy never saw where Patch came up with the can opener, but he was halfway around the lid and licking his chops by the time Jimmy joined him outside. Rufus sat attentively at Patch's feet.

The old man slopped up half the beans with indifference to what anybody would think of him, then tossed the other half along with the can on the ground. Jimmy was shocked.

He didn't understand why Patch threw the beans out. Then Patch nodded at Rufus, and the dog tore into the other half with the same indifference. Jimmy didn't think any less of his new friends.

"There's more food if you want," Jimmy said. Patch looked interested, but Rufus was too immersed in the beans to care. Patch followed Jimmy back inside, and they scoured the mess for more food. The old man ate until he was full, Jimmy figured, probably for the first time in some time. Rufus cleaned himself like a respectable dog would after his belly was full. Occasionally, Jimmy would just smile, basking in his victory.

"So, those boys were your friends?" Patch asked, raising his eyebrows.

"They were," Jimmy said, concluding he had no friends after sending Patch into the fort. Patch chuckled, and Rufus yapped. Jimmy's face dropped as he thought of the consequences of today's plot. He would have more trouble, but for now, he was home, and he was happy.

Rufus' head popped up, then his ears stood up on alert.

"You hear that?" Patch asked. His head was up. It appeared to Jimmy that those two were always a little cautious about people approaching. They quickly scrambled to investigate. Rufus, on guard and ready to attack, sat at the door while Patch peered out the gun slot.

"Who is it?" Jimmy asked, on edge too.

"Girrrrls," said the old man. The fort was under attack. Jimmy scrambled about, not knowing what to do. Fake guns out the gun slots wouldn't deter those girls. Patch turned and grabbed Jimmy to calm him. "Out the back, boy," he told him. Jimmy gave him a side eye. That was enough for Patch to remember. "Right... Brian."

Patch thought for a moment. "Hide," he instructed. Jimmy darted his head back and forth, finally settling on a spot that was littered with trash. Jimmy lay still amongst the debris. He blended in some, but he was still the only thing on the floor with eyes, and they were wide open.

Patch ushered Rufus from the door and then took a seat on the couch. Jimmy didn't move an inch except for his eyes, which trailed Patch over to the couch. The voices were right up to the door now.

Jimmy froze, wide-eyed. The door creaked open very slowly. Three girls peered in, real girls, not Dave, Chad, and Kevin. It was Jessica, Erica, and their friend, Corrine. They gave a gasp, followed by a look of shock. All their time and effort in decorating their teahouse was for naught. Just the thought of this being a teahouse made Jimmy cringe. At the least, they could have the decency to call it a clubhouse.

The girls looked around without entering. There was nothing left of the fancy, frilly girls' touch they worked so hard to achieve. Jimmy watched without moving. A chair leg obscured his view slightly, but it also kept him concealed in amongst the trash.

"Go in," one of them urged. They leaned in a little. Not noticing a threat, they all stepped forward and entered Jimmy's fort. They stopped just inside the doorway and continued to look around. Erica, or Jessica, Jimmy wasn't sure which, met his eyes through the chair leg. Her eyes flew open and her mouth moved a little, but no sound came out. She grabbed her sister and ducked behind her. Patch saw this as his cue and began stirring as if he'd been asleep on the couch. He moaned out loud, and that got their attention.

Three high-pitched screams pierced Jimmy's ears. They weren't nearly as piercing as the three screams Jimmy had witnessed earlier. The girls wasted no time, and not unlike Dave, Chad, and Kevin, they ran straight out of the fort and down Cattank Road.

Jimmy had his fort back. He felt triumphant. He also felt a little bad about the girls being so scared, but not so much about Dave, Chad, and Kevin. And if he was being honest, he was kind of glad Patch took it easy on the girls.

CHAPTER TWENTY-THREE

-JIMMY'S SECRET REVEALED-

Patch was soon asleep on the couch, and he and Rufus made the same sounds as they slept. Jimmy straightened up a little, but not too much. He mostly got rid of the frilly remains and the broken and unbroken pieces of china. He left most of the mess. After all, he was a boy.

Quickly and without warning, Jimmy found the fort under attack by hundreds of Indians. Luckily, he had his rifle loaded and ready. The first wave was simply no match for Jimmy's imagination. The second onslaught he deemed more worthy, but still no match for an eleven-year-old boy. It was quite a battle, and Jimmy was nothing short of heroic. Patch and Rufus slept through the whole thing.

It was widely known that the Indians pull their dead from the battlefield, so Jimmy had nothing to show Patch when he woke. Everything was as he saw it before he napped. Jimmy told him the entire tale, however, feeling a little foolish by the time he was done.

"I've heard that of the Indians," Patch said. "Apache or Iroquois?"

Jimmy shrugged. "They were mean," he said. Jimmy wasn't aware that mean was not a kind of Indian.

"Probably Apache," Patch said.

"Yeah, probably." Jimmy paused. "Can you teach me how to pitch now?"

Patch thought it over. "Well, I don't see why not." And he rubbed his full belly with a satisfied smile. "Do you have a glove or a ball or anything?" Patch asked, looking through the mess.

"There's a ball around here somewhere, but my glove is in my mom's car."

"That's okay, the ball will do," Patch said. Rufus followed them out of the fort and settled down to watch.

The two went back and forth. First Patch gave him some pointers then Jimmy would throw to Patch. As hard as Jimmy could throw, Patch caught the ball with his bare hands. His hands were hard and dirty, much like an old leather mitt.

Jimmy was wild at first, and he would chase down anything that Patch couldn't catch, each time running past Patch and then by him again the other way to find the spot he was using as a mound. Patch gave him more instruction, and soon Jimmy was throwing it right to Patch. He was really doing well, and now that Jimmy was hitting his mark more often, Patch's hand got a little sore.

"I think that will do for today," Patch told him.

Those words excited Jimmy. "That will do for today," meant there would be more another day. Jimmy had found himself a pitching coach.

"Cool," Jimmy said. "I'm already better, I can tell."

Patch chuckled a little. "You sure are kid... you sure are," Patch said.

Rufus had lain quietly wanting nothing more than to fetch that ball, but he never moved. Patch tossed the ball and jerked his head to indicate to Rufus it was okay to fetch it, and Rufus tore off. Jimmy tossed it several times himself, and Rufus was in heaven. He fetched until he was plum exhausted.

Patch scratched his head, watching. "This dog hasn't had much fetchin' in his short life. Mostly all he knows how to do is scavenge. He seems in heaven."

The trio ducked back inside the fort when they were done. Patch got comfortable on the couch again. Rufus licked himself some more and lay on the floor. Jimmy was beginning to wonder if the two were making his fort their new home.

He was sure he had not given Patch the impression they could. This was his fort after all, and Patch was only there to help Jimmy clear out those girls. There just wasn't any sign that they intended to leave, and that was troubling Jimmy. Jimmy knew he didn't have the nerve to say anything, and he wasn't sure he should even if he had the nerve. They both started snoring again. Jimmy watched Patch as he thought about what he would do.

After a while, Jimmy began picking up some of the mess again. He was deliberate in making as much noise as he could. They stirred a little, but it was a while before Patch was awake again.

"Hey, we should get going, it's getting late and my mom's gonna want me home for supper," Jimmy said. Patch looked up a little confused but got the message and collected himself to leave. Rufus, on the other hand, wanted to stay. He jumped up on the couch panting and wagging his tail. Patch shot Rufus a look, and he jumped down only to jump right back up with the same fervor.

"Come on, boy," Patch said, kind of like he talked to Jimmy. They all left down the dirt path of Cattank Road.

"See ya, Patch." Jimmy bent down to tussle Rufus once more before they parted. "See ya, boy," he added to the dog.

"Keep working on those mechanics," Patch told Jimmy as he made a pitching motion in midair. Jimmy grinned.

"I will. Thanks, Patch."

Patch walked on with Rufus in tow. Jimmy felt kind of good about his pitching prospects but had a slightly sick feeling that he didn't do Patch right by not letting him stay in the fort.

•   •   •

The following morning, Jimmy woke with a good feeling inside him. He had his fort back for one, he was sure he was a better pitcher already, and Cindy was cool with him again. What a difference a day makes in only twenty-four hours. Jimmy too had a little Yogi Berra in him—most guys do. Girls just think guys are stupid—it's a fine line.

Breakfast was quick and painless. Church on the other hand was grueling. It never lasted more than an hour, and Jimmy could endure that. He saw Kevin and waved to him. Kevin mustered a forced wave back, but it seemed a daunting task. Did Kevin know what Jimmy had done? It wasn't against Kevin. When mass was over, Jimmy went right over to Kevin, but Kevin seemed withdrawn.

"Hey, dude," Jimmy said.

"Hey, Jimmy," Kevin mustered.

Jimmy sensed something, but it was unclear what. "I got our fort back," Jimmy informed him with a sense of great achievement.

Kevin paled and shook his head. "I don't think so," he mumbled.

Jimmy was confused. "What are you talking about?"

Kevin looked ashamed. "We had the fort back yesterday—me, Chad, and Dave. We were there ready to scare away those girls and reclaim our fort..." and Kevin paused.

"And?"

"And... we gave it up before those girls ever got there," he finished.

"Why?" Jimmy asked, cautiously, knowing more than he wanted to let on.

"We got chased off by that old man who looks like driftwood," Kevin said.

"Who?"

"That old guy you gave a hot dog to at the baseball game yesterday," Kevin said then tipped his head looking at Jimmy sideways.

"Patch?" Jimmy asked innocently. He was busted.

"Yeah, Patch. How'd he know about the fort?" Kevin stared Jimmy down.

Jimmy hesitated, torn about telling the truth. He spoke then hesitated again. This was harder for Jimmy than he had thought it would be. He was sure he would lose his friend once again as soon as he told him what he'd done.

"I got Patch to scare the girls away for us," Jimmy started, and then he waited for Kevin's reaction. There was none. "We went out to the fort yesterday."

"You were there yesterday?" Kevin's eyes grew big.

Jimmy was developing a knot in his belly. "Yeah, I was there," Jimmy confessed.

And then it hit Kevin like a ton of bricks. He started laughing. "Oh my god, did you see us?"

"Yeah."

"Where were you?" Kevin asked, still laughing.

"I was hiding on the side of Cattank Road. Just before the clearing. What happened to you guys?" Jimmy asked.

"You don't know? Man... Dude... it was crazy. We were inside, taking down all that girlie crap when the door slammed open," he said. "All we could see was the silhouette of what we thought was a monster, and next to him was some kind of crazed beast, drooling and champing at the bit. We thought for sure we were all dead, it was just a matter of whether we were eaten alive or killed first then eaten."

Kevin had a crazed look on his face as he relived the trauma. Jimmy said nothing, but the laughing was contagious. It turned out, Kevin wasn't mad at all. That's not what Jimmy had imagined.

"I saw you guys run by," Jimmy said. "It was so fast, I didn't know who it was, though," he fibbed.

"It was us," Kevin chuckled. "I hit the door first and was gone. I figured, all I had to do was outrun Chad, so I never looked back."

"Dude, I had no idea. I sent Patch in to get rid of those girls. I didn't know you were in there."

"I think Chad wet himself, he was so scared," Kevin giggled.

"Well, I know one thing for sure," Jimmy said.

"What's that?"

"The fort is ours again," Jimmy said.

"What a relief," Kevin sighed. "Do you know what this means?"

"No, what?"

"We are no longer the top turtle," Kevin said. Jimmy cocked his head slightly. Was Kevin turning into Chad?

Later that day, Jimmy arranged to go back out to Cattank with his three friends. He still wasn't sure how Dave would react to the whole situation, but Jimmy was hoping he would take it much the way Kevin did. With peanut butter and jelly sandwiches in tow, he and Kevin set out to meet Dave and Chad.

"Hey, dude," Dave said, his voice a little tentative.

"What's up?" Jimmy greeted both Chad and Dave.

"I hear you got the fort back?" Dave said.

Jimmy puffed up with pride. "I did."

Chad and Kevin were both elated, but the other two still needed sorting.

"You know it nearly got us killed," Dave said, staring down Jimmy.

"All you had to do was outrun Kevin," Jimmy said. All four boys started laughing. Everything was just fine.

They made their way down Cattank Road doing the usual boy stuff like throwing rocks at targets as a competition. Jimmy was unbelievably accurate, and the others noticed quickly.

"What's got into you?" Dave asked, suspicious. Jimmy just shrugged as he pelted yet another target dead on. Chad and Kevin roared at his uncanny marksmanship.

"I bet you can't hit that guy's face growing out of that tree."

Nothing else had to be said. All four boys turned on a dime, screaming for their life. Patch stepped out from the trees and stood in the middle of the dirt road in the cloud of dirt the boys kicked up with their tennis shoes. They were down that path in a hurry.

"Is it safe?" panted Chad, still running at full speed.

Dave gave a quick glance behind them. "I don't think so."

Jimmy slowed down, realizing something was not right. It couldn't have been a tree monster. Even Kevin thought Patch looked a bit like driftwood. It had to have been him.

"Guys... wait," and he came to a stop. The others didn't come to a halt until they were close to thirty feet past Jimmy.

"What is it?"

"It was Patch back there," Jimmy said.

"The guy that was going to kill us?" Chad said.

"Why was he hiding in the trees?" Dave asked. Kevin and Chad turned to Jimmy for an explanation.

"Yeah, that was creepy," Kevin added.

"He was probably just hiding," Jimmy said in Patch's defense.

"From what?"

"People from town, I guess," Jimmy said.

"We're 'people from town I guess,'" Dave snapped.

"I mean people who don't like Patch."

"We don't like Patch," Dave said.

"You don't like Patch? How come?" Jimmy said.

"Because he made me damn near wet myself... twice now," Dave cried. Chad and Kevin nodded their agreement.

"He's all right. You just got to get to know him," Jimmy said.

"I have to agree with Dave," Chad said. Kevin sort of nodded, and Jimmy soon realized he was alone on the matter, a matter that could easily tear them apart once again.

"Just come out and meet him," Jimmy pleaded. No one said a word. Chad, Dave, and Kevin exchanged glances with one another as Jimmy looked on.

"I don't think so," Dave finally said, shaking his head. Jimmy's heart sank as did his head into his chest. He was not going to win this battle. He didn't want to choose between his friends and Patch, but in the end, inevitably, he would choose his friends. His heart sunk even further.

"The guy gives me the willies," Chad added, breaking the stony silence. Jimmy just turned and looked at Chad. He had nothing to add.

Kevin appeared to waver like he wanted to take Jimmy's side for once, but he too was terrified of the man in the woods.

They gathered themselves, caught their breath, and continued back to the neighborhood without realizing where they were going. They weren't heading back, that was for certain. Jimmy glimpsed back down the trail from which they came, hoping for a sign, maybe of Patch walking their way.

"You guys wanna go to the park and play some ball?" Kevin asked. Dave and Chad were game, but Jimmy wasn't even paying attention.

"Huh?" Jimmy turned back, preoccupied. "Nah, you guys go ahead." Jimmy looked down the trail as if he had seen something.

Chad, Dave, and Kevin exchanged glances. "I'm not waiting around for Patch to show," Dave whispered. The three boys bolted, leaving Jimmy just standing there looking back. That was fine with Jimmy, but instead of heading back down Cattank Road, he continued into the neighborhood.

CHAPTER TWENTY-FOUR
—A FRONT ROW SEAT—

When Jimmy emerged from his garage sporting his baseball glove along with an old mitt, his dad used to use, it may have appeared he was going to the park to meet with his friends after all. The can of beans, two bags of rolls and a package of deli meat told a different story. He looked up and down his street for possible onlookers. When he saw no one, he headed off in a hurry, stealthily but still in a hurry.

Patch wasn't around when Jimmy first got to the fort, so he put the food inside and took his glove and ball and went back outside to toss the ball up to himself. He did that several times before he heard the panting of Rufus and rustling of brush as Patch appeared from the thicket behind the fort.

"Hey, Patch!"

"Hey, boy," Patch replied with his usual gruff voice.

Even Rufus yapped an enthusiastic hello to Jimmy. Jimmy grabbed the extra mitt he had brought for Patch. Patch was hoping it was food and so was Rufus by the looks on their faces. They played catch instead.

Jimmy was getting better with every throw and every pointer Patch gave him. He couldn't help but beam with confidence. Patch was quite the teacher and Jimmy quite the pupil. Jimmy would have thrown his arm ragged that day if Patch hadn't stopped him. Jimmy moaned a little, but Patch sat him down and explained the nuances of his new craft. He no longer just threw the baseball, Jimmy was now a pitcher, and he needed to learn about more than just how to pitch. Patch explained to him about arm strength, conditioning, mental awareness and toughness. All of that seemed a bit advanced for an eleven-year-old, but Jimmy hung on every word Patch said.

"Can you come to my next game?"

Patch just looked at Jimmy. Jimmy's heart dropped. He knew Patch would most likely run into the same trouble he did at the last game. It was probably something he dealt with most of his transient life.

"Yeah, kid," and Patch nodded as if he would be proud to go to Jimmy's game, trouble or not. But Jimmy sensed some uneasiness.

"Maybe you should stand in amongst the trees near the outfield," Jimmy said trying to be helpful. Patch was not insulted, instead appearing to consider it.

"I'll find a spot."

"You hungry?" Jimmy said, changing the subject.

Patch and Rufus perked up. "Yeah," Patch said, "we are." Rufus panted with his eyes on Jimmy.

They ate the ham first, one slice at a time. Patch would swallow down a slice then sling one to Rufus. They did that until it was gone. Then Patch opened the beans, and he offered some to Jimmy who declined, not because Jimmy was too good to eat with them, but because they were much hungrier than Jimmy had ever been in his life. Patch slopped up most of the beans and the thick syrup they were in with the rolls. Rufus waited his turn. Finally, Patch got up and tossed the remaining beans out the door for Rufus to scavenge, and he did. A good nap ensued. Jimmy cleaned up a little while the two slept. It wasn't that he was a clean kid. His room at home was a mess. It was more out of consideration for his guests than anything.

Then Jimmy heard a commotion outside. It started out as nothing more than a little rustling in the bush, and Jimmy was sure it was his friends, so he burst out of the cabin to greet them.

The rustling turned to scuffling, and that turned to growling. Jimmy turned in a panic to see what was making the noise. He stopped dead in his tracks, with his back hunched in mid stride, arms hung awkwardly out to his sides like a cartoon character. He stared ahead at two very large skunks with tails drawn in a duel for the remaining baked beans Rufus left in that small can.

With a front-row seat, Jimmy watched in horror at what could amount to a Gallagher comedy show, except there was no large wooden sledgehammer. No, this show was two skunks, which may or may not have been eating baked beans. Whatever the outcome, it was going to be messy, and Jimmy was far too close to the show.

Each skunk jostled for position on the other. Jimmy didn't know the gastrointestinal effects of baked beans on skunks, so he remained riveted while slowly backing away. What if one just happened to fart because of the beans? The retribution from his rival would be fierce. Jimmy laughed at their predicament. The skunks were startled by Jimmy's snort. They began turning, tail end out, at each other and at Jimmy.

He ducked inside and waited. He would know soon enough. Jimmy thought of how this would probably kill Chad with his keen sense of smell. He heard nothing, but more importantly, he smelled nothing. He peered out the gun slot and could make out a tail. Then he caught a movement out of the side of his eye.

"Rufus, no!"

"Huh? wha'?" Patch muttered.

Jimmy lunged for Rufus and grabbed him just before he got to the door.

"What are ya doin' to my dog?" grunted a groggy Patch.

"Your dog?" Jimmy stared at him, raising his eyebrows. Patch looked a little guilty. Then he rubbed the sleep out of his eyes and grunted some. Jimmy guessed it was a response.

Patch's dog or not, Rufus squirmed under Jimmy's grasp, worked his way loose, and scurried for the door. He was out. Jimmy jumped to the gun slot to watch.

"Whada ya getting at boy?"

Jimmy just watched what little he could see. He saw two black and white tails poised high and moving back and forth like a synchronized puppet show. Then a terrible hiss followed, and the pup whimpered, scampering off out of sight.

"Whoa, boy, that you?" Patch asked.

"Nope," Jimmy said. He giggled a bit as the funk entered the fort. Patch collected himself off the couch with great effort and made his way towards the door. He was very agitated but did not yell at Jimmy or even give him a cross look. Instead, he went straight outside to check on the matter.

The dog yelped then could be heard running off into the woods. The smell got steadily worse as it continued to creep into the fort.

Patch seemed indifferent and walked back inside. "Skunk done ran off."

"There were two skunks, and they were eating beans." Jimmy said.

"Nothin' we can do," Patch said.

"Should we go look for Rufus?" Jimmy asked.

"Nah, he'll be fine," Patch mumbled.

"He's gonna stink something awful when he gets back," Jimmy said.

"He didn't smell right to begin with," Patch said. Jimmy giggled to himself as the smell continued to waft through the air.

Rufus never returned to the fort, at least not before Jimmy headed home. Patch stayed behind, which Jimmy didn't mind. The dog would find Patch eventually, but he would most likely return to the fort first, and there was no reason for Patch not to stay.

The air was still funky with the aroma of skunk, and Jimmy couldn't wait to get back to the neighborhood, or at least far enough away to escape the stench. When he thought he was in the clear, he wasn't. The smell had etched itself just enough into Jimmy's nose that it would stay with him for a while. Jimmy turned the corner into the neighborhood still rubbing his nose, still wondering why the smell wouldn't go away.

"Jimmy," hollered Kevin. Jimmy looked up to see Kevin walking towards him with Chad and Dave in tow.

"What's up, guys?"

"Not much," was the usual response. Chad began looking ill, like he just had a bug fly up his nose.

"He all right?" Jimmy asked gesturing to Chad. Then Dave and Kevin got a whiff and quickly had the same look as Chad. Dave leaned in slightly for a closer opinion.

"You stink, dude."

Jimmy didn't know what to say. He pointed behind him and was going to explain, but then he stopped himself. He wasn't sure his friends wanted to hear any tales of him and his new friend Patch.

"I do, don't I?" he said as he got a good whiff when he turned to look back behind him and down Cattank Road.

"Tomato soup," Chad said with watery eyes. "You're gonna need tomato soup."

"You smell like skunk," Kevin informed him, a little slow on the uptake. Chad gagged a little. Dave thought it was funny.

"So, what happened to you? Were you practicing your pitching, that why you stink so much?" Dave asked.

Jimmy wanted nothing more than to tell them, so he did. His tale included the skunks and their battle for the last of the beans. Jimmy was riveting, and his friends hung on his every word. It was a story of all stories, and Jimmy shone with each moment.

When Jimmy was done, they were all a bit closer. Patch didn't seem quite so scary as before, and his dog was just comical. They weren't sure about going back out there just yet, but they seemed to be warming up to the idea, something Jimmy really wished for.

"So, let me get this right, the bum now thinks the fort is his home, and his dog who didn't smell right to begin with and now smells worse 'cause of the skunks is also making the fort his home?" Dave said, sorting everything out.

"Yep," Jimmy said without hesitation. Then he noticed that was not the answer his friends wanted to hear. They wanted that fort for themselves. They did not want to share the fort with anyone, not even an eccentric old ragamuffin of a man and his ratty old goofy dog.

"Dude, the bum has to go," Dave demanded. Jimmy was shocked. Chad and Kevin's expressions said they sided with Dave.

"How come?"

"Well, first of all, 'cause he's scary, and his dog's got fleas," Kevin said.

Jimmy's heart sank. "Can't we share it with him? He's got nowhere else to go," Jimmy said.

"No, we can't. He'll find a new home, anyway. That's what they do," Dave said with a wicked glint in his eye. Dave was visibly looking to punch Jimmy. Jimmy looked to Kevin and Chad, but they clearly were with Dave.

"He's pretty scary," Chad reluctantly admitted.

Jimmy knew in his heart that this was it, the last time they were going to have this conversation. He was going to have to choose.

CHAPTER TWENTY-FIVE

—STINKY CHEESE—

"GUYS," Chad said. He had his sights down Cattank Road. "What are those?"

"SKUNK!" And all four boys turned and ran as fast as they could. Both skunks were waddling their way down the path like they had no place to go. Skunks are usually nocturnal but possibly not when hopped up on baked beans. The four boys were well into the neighborhood before any of them slowed down.

"I can still smell them," Chad said.

"That's Jimmy, remember," Dave said. It was Jimmy. He had a lingering scent of skunk, and it was following him into the neighborhood. The boys tried to outrun the smell but Jimmy kept up so they weren't getting away from it. They reached the park without even realizing they were headed that way.

The boys snuck through the opening Jimmy cut in the fence just a few days before and took refuge in one of the dugouts. Each one took a seat next to the other on the bench but left a few feet between themselves and Jimmy, probably because he stunk.

"Ya think it's safe here?" Kevin asked, thinking of the old man who had chased them off the field during their kickball game.

"If that old geezer doesn't see us in here, we're okay," Jimmy assured his friends. They were satisfied and began to relax in their new digs. Jimmy could appreciate just what it meant to have such a place, even a makeshift citadel as this.

"So how do ya reckon we get rid of this homeless guy?" Chad asked Dave. Dave thought hard on the question but said nothing. Kevin looked more like he was waiting for an answer than trying to help with a solution. Jimmy was still hurt.

"What if we chase off that dog?" Dave finally answered. "Do ya think the old man would go after it?"

"No, that dog is no more his than these trees belong to the forest," Jimmy said. Everyone looked at Jimmy. He wasn't even sure what that meant, but he knew that dog belonged to no one, especially Patch. "Plus, that dog is meaner than it smells." He knew that wasn't true, but he hoped it might hold his friends back.

"It looks like an overgrown rat," Kevin said. Chad snorted.

"It just needs a bath," Jimmy said. Defending those two was not getting Jimmy anywhere, and he knew it. He needed to come up with an idea that showed his friends he was with them. It was hard, as Patch was a good friend and Jimmy's new pitching coach. If only his friends could see that part of Patch. Jimmy mulled things over.

"That old guy wouldn't go off looking for his dog if it didn't show up for several days?" Dave asked.

"I don't think so," Jimmy replied. "It ran off when it got sprayed with skunk juice, and he didn't think twice about going after it."

"That's odd," Chad said. It was odd, but Jimmy could not explain it any better than that.

"The old man probably didn't go chasing after that mangy mutt because he stunk so bad," Dave said.

"The dog or the bum?" Chad said. Jimmy looked at Chad, focusing on his acute olfactory.

"We could stink the old man out of the fort," Jimmy said. If it were Chad, that might work.

"That'd be good, but what smells worse than a bum and that ratty dog?" Dave asked.

"Skunks for sure," Chad said.

"What smells worse than skunk?" Jimmy pondered.

"Your pitching," Dave said. Jimmy glared at him.

"I've come across some pretty smelly cheese that my parents like to eat," Chad said.

"How bad could it smell if they're willing to eat it?" Dave asked.

"Oh, trust me, pretty bad," Chad said. The look on his face was very convincing. "They get the giggles and act like we would when they eat it."

"Why would you want to eat anything that smells really bad?" Kevin asked.

"Don't rightly know," Jimmy said.

"Do you know what kind of cheese it is?" Dave asked. He had a sense of urgency that drove the group.

"I'd know it when I smell it," Chad said.

"I think we'd all be able to do that," Dave said.

"So, we are going to stink him out?" Jimmy asked trying to prove his solidarity.

"I say that tomorrow we get together and go find this cheese Chad speaks of," Dave said.

"Where?"

"I don't know, a cheese store, I guess," Dave replied.

"We have baseball tomorrow night," Jimmy informed them.

"We'll do the stinky cheese in the morning and be back in plenty of time for baseball," Dave said.

"Who do we play?" Kevin asked.

"I think the Ravens," Jimmy said. "Clarksburg?"

"Yeah," Dave said.

"We lost to them," Jimmy said.

"Not tomorrow," Kevin replied.

"All right, tomorrow then," Dave said, and they all went their separate ways. As Jimmy walked home, he pondered his decisions for the day and their consequences. He wanted none of it, but at the same time he wanted all of it. Tomorrow would bring more answers. Tomorrow would possibly be his reckoning. Jimmy just wished he could explain to his friends what

Patch was like, how he had helped him with his pitching, and how they got along.

"The game," Jimmy said aloud. "I'll show them at the game, and they'll see how good I've gotten as a pitcher, and..." Then Jimmy realized the game would be some time after the eviction. His heart sank.

•   •   •

The next morning, Jimmy woke with an immediate burden pressing on his chest. He did not want to face what was coming, but he also didn't want to miss it either. If he wasn't there, he might miss out running interference and thereby saving his little world. Maybe there was still a slight chance Dave, Chad, and Kevin could be persuaded to change their minds. When he met up with his friends, he had the usual packed in his sack, peanut butter and jelly.

He hadn't asked for an extra sandwich, but he didn't think with the way the day was to unfold that he would have a chance to get it to Patch, anyway. If it turned out that he could, he'd be happy to share the one sandwich he had with him. His friends were goofing around as usual. There was no urgency attached to today's adventure, an adventure that would require stinky cheese. Or maybe they were frightened.

"So, we need to find some stinky cheese," Dave said.

"Yep," Jimmy said.

"We're gonna use Chad's nose to find us the cheese store," Dave said.

"Which way then?" Jimmy asked. They looked both ways, a little confused. They never needed a cheese store, so why would they know where it was?

"This way." Chad pointed after some time of sampling the air. They all followed Chad like a bloodhound heavy on the scent.

"He's incredible," Kevin said. "We should rent him out to the police."

"And birthday parties," Dave said sarcastically. Chad pointed ahead.

"There it is, Katzen's Deli and Cheese Shop," Chad said.

"Amazing," Dave said.

They went inside. "It stinks in here. You gonna be able to tell which cheese it is that stinks the most?" Jimmy asked him.

"Yeah," Chad said, nodding. They looked around and noticed everybody was holding a little piece of paper with a number on it, so they looked around for a number dispenser.

"Here," Kevin said, pulling a small slip of paper from a plastic holder. He held up the ticket to display the number twenty-seven.

"What number are we on?"

"Eighteeeeen," called a portly fellow from behind the counter.

"Eighteen," Kevin said. Jimmy looked at him as if he should be punched.

"Let's look around at the cheeses. Maybe Chad can pick one out before they get to our number," Jimmy said. They perused the glass display case and all the smaller refrigerated compartments in the middle of the store. Chad was overwhelmed by the aroma, but he was having a go at it just the same.

"We should ask somebody," Chad finally conceded. "Everything stinks in here." Several numbers had been called while they looked around, and they had drawn the attention of many of the patrons, as well as the deli workers.

"Number twenty-seven!"

"Hey, that's us," Dave said holding up Kevin's hand with the number in it.

"What can I do for you boys?" The boys looked up at the portly man wearing a greasy white apron. He looked jovial.

"We want to buy some cheese," Dave said, taking command.

"What kind of cheese would you boys like?" he replied. "We have many to choose from. There's American, Swiss, Cheddar, Gouda, bleu..." he paused. The boys looked confused. They needed to hear stinky.

"Hey, how we gonna pay for this?" Kevin whispered under his breath.

"I got money," Jimmy said.

Turning back to the portly man, Chad said, "We want some really stinky cheese."

The man looked surprised. "Well, that will narrow it down slightly. We have Limburger, Taleggio, Epoisses, Camembert. Those are all very pungent cheeses."

"Which one is the stinkiest?" Kevin asked. The man looked even more surprised. Jimmy nudged Kevin to cool it. He figured the man might think they were up to no good.

"Well, they're all very stinky cheeses, as you say. Camembert is very pungent. It comes from France and is ripe, rich, and a very creamy cheese. Epoisses is also from France and also a creamy cheese. It is first washed in brine then cured in humid cellars before being rinsed with a liqueur. I'd say it's probably the most aromatic of the cheeses. Limburger is the most noted of the stinky cheeses. It was originally made by Belgian Trappist monks and adopted by the Germans. It's tangy and has a creamy texture. This cheese goes nicely with a slice of raw onion and rye bread," the man went on and on. The boys hung on every word, though they hadn't a clue what he was saying. They just got excited when the portly man finally said stinky.

"Can we smell them?" Dave asked. This drew an even more curious look from the fat man.

"What exactly do you want this cheese for?" he asked.

Three blank looks like deer in headlights peered up across the deli case then Jimmy blurted out, "It's for a friend. He likes cheese, and he says he can eat just about anything." This was not a lie either.

"So, this is a bit of a dare?" asked the old man.

"Yeah," Jimmy said coolly.

"Okay then. There's also Taleggio. It's from Italy, but since this is a dare, I'm sure you don't really care where it's from, do you? You just want the stinkiest cheese we have."

"Yep," Jimmy said.

"Epoisses has to be the stinkiest," he said. Now he was getting it. "It is very expensive, though. I would gamble to say that Limburger would do the trick just as well as the Epoisses would and for a lot less money."

"Okay, let's get a whiff of this Limburger," Dave said. They bellied up to the deli case with Chad as the lead nose. The fat man barely had the cheese from its wrapper when Chad took ill and his friends began to cringe as well. The man laughed.

The smell of aged feet stained the nostrils of everyone in the deli. The boys laughed through their pinched nostrils. It was an uncontrollable laugh, like when one of them farted on the school bus. This was much fouler.

"That'll do nicely," Dave said all nasally, still pinching his nose. He gestured for the man to wrap the stench back up.

"So that's not even the smelliest cheese you have?" Kevin said almost as a dare to bring out the Epoisses. The fat man grinned.

"I think this will do," he said as he watched Chad nearly gag on the smell.

"I think it will," Dave said. The portly man wrapped up a wedge of cheese without even asking them how much they wanted and handed it to Dave.

"There you are, boys," he said with a tone that matched the jovial look he had.

"Thank you, sir," Dave said. He waited for the man to tell him how much he owed them. The man gestured for them to be on their way. The boys understood, thanked the man, and turned to leave.

"Good luck," he chuckled as they left the store.

The boys were beside themselves. The first stage of their operation was already a success. With stinky cheese in hand, they made their way to the Cattank Road path. Dave held the prize wrapped tightly in its plastic wrapper. He could still make out the pungent odor. Chad was in tow, and by the looks of it, he could still make out the smell too.

"Why would anybody eat something that smells like feet, and not just any feet, nasty, rotted, and very old feet?" Kevin asked.

"Beats me," Dave said. He looked at his prize once more.

"Did anybody bring crackers?" Jimmy joked. Dave slowed down for Chad to catch up.

"We got 'em right here," and Dave helped Chad pull a box of crackers from his pack. The box looked a bit tattered. Dave shook the box, and its contents sounded intact.

"So how are we gonna do this again?" Kevin asked. They nearly stopped walking. They hadn't thought that through yet.

"Patch is very keen to his surroundings," Jimmy noted. "He'll be suspicious right from the start."

"But it's food, and he's a bum. He eats out of trash cans," Dave said. Jimmy wanted to defend Patch but chose not to. He just made a face instead.

"He's not supposed to eat it, is he? He's just gonna get a whiff of it and want to leave," Chad said. "At least that's what I thought was the plan."

"Then why'd we bring crackers?" Kevin asked. They all wondered that for a moment.

"I thought we were gonna just chuck it inside with him in there," Jimmy said.

"But then he'll know we're up to something," Dave said. That was true, and Jimmy didn't want that.

"Go with the crackers," Jimmy said. "He might not notice anything odd except the smell. If he's not there, when he returns, he may think that someone else left the cheese and crackers there."

"Crackers, no crackers, either way the smell will drive him away," Kevin said. This was unfolding nicely. They were pleased.

"What if he's there?" Chad asked.

"We can wait him out," Dave said.

"Most likely he'll be sound asleep," Jimmy said.

"The only problem then would be that ratty dog," Dave said.

"If the dog ever returned," Jimmy replied.

The boys made it to the clearing just before the fort in no time at all. They clung to the edges of the trees for cover. Sitting and listening, they heard absolutely nothing.

Just who had the nerve besides Jimmy to go up to the fort was soon coming to be known. It seemed no one did. Dave had the most to lose by not stepping up. After all, he was so adamant about getting rid of the bum in the first place. Jimmy sensed his weakness, but he never let on. Instead, he stepped up to play the hero and take care of the matter.

"Damn that shit stinks," Chad said as they unwrapped the cheese, placed it on a plate with several crackers and handed it to Jimmy.

"Damn, you guys thought of everything," Jimmy said.

"You mean the plate?" Chad asked. "Thank you."

"Are you good?" Chad checked with Jimmy, clearly hoping Jimmy had this by himself.

"Yeah, I'll be fine," he said gallantly, as if he were staring death in the face. His friends looked at him as if he were braver than they were, hoping this wasn't the last time they would see him alive. Jimmy marched out into the clearing and faced his charge.

He got to the fort without incident and tried to peer into the gun slots for a glance at Patch. If he was in there, he was not on the couch. He didn't hear a sound and, with that, concluded Patch must not be in there.

Jimmy took a moment to collect himself. He wasn't sure which smelled worse, the cheese or the residual skunk musk. He knew the mix of the two was awful. Jimmy thought he might be sick. He braced himself against the fort and gathered his senses.

•   •   •

Watching from a distance, Chad knew the look. Jimmy got up and just walked into the fort with the plate of cheese outstretched in his arm. He disappeared into the cabin.

"He really likes that guy, doesn't he?" Dave asked his friends.

"I think he does," Chad said. They watched the cabin as a creeping sense of the horrific loomed.

"Come on," Dave said impatiently. Jimmy was taking too long. Kevin shrugged in response.

"I think he's fine. He walked into the fort like he was visiting an old friend. There was nothing suspicious about that. He even brought food. I think he knew exactly what he was doing. If the old man is in there, Jimmy just came a calling," Chad concluded.

He was right, except the old man wasn't in there. Neither was the dog, which became clear when both came rustling out of the woods just behind the cabin.

"Oh shit," Dave blurted out.

•   •   •

Jimmy heard Patch and Rufus coming, so he put the cheese plate down, peered quickly out the gun slot, then slid out the fort door. He looked over to his friends for guidance. Jimmy threw his hands back and forth as if to say which way should I go? Chad caught on and pointed to his left. Jimmy didn't know if that meant he should go left or if Patch was coming from the left. He had a fifty-fifty shot at getting it right. If he didn't run, he knew he could act as if he came to visit, but if he ran, it was all or nothing. If Patch caught him, that would be the end of his friendship with the vagrant. It was probably over anyway.

Jimmy turned to run in the direction Chad had pointed. It was the correct direction. Jimmy was safely in the woods hiding by the time Patch made it from the other side to the front of the fort. Rufus was on alert but didn't sense an enemy, so he quickly gave way to any pursuit. The dog turned back and followed Patch into the fort. Stage two of the mission was behind them. Jimmy was happy Rufus had returned.

Having a slightly better vantage point to sneak up on the fort again, Jimmy motioned for his friends to join him. One by one, they made their way over to him. Running hunched over seemed the most popular approach. Chad added a serpentine jaunt to his style.

"Dude, we thought for sure you were busted," Dave said, greeting his friend with praise as if they had never been quarreling.

"So did I," Jimmy admitted.

"Did you get the cheese set up," Kevin asked.

"Do you mean, did I put the cheese down and run like hell—yeah."

"Wow, that was close," Chad added. Jimmy just shook his head.

After they settled down some and the adrenaline had calmed, they peered out, looking for a chance to advance on the fort. They were dying to see what would transpire from their plan, each one now brimming with a renewed sense of adventure.

Again, one by one, they covertly made their way up to the fort wall, each using the serpentine and hunched over method Chad had looked so good doing earlier.

They were quiet and didn't move, waiting for Jimmy to take the lead. He did. He popped up like a meerkat on its hind legs and looked inside through the gun slot. Those things were handy for looking in or out. Patch walked by the slot oblivious to his visitors.

"Damn, you need a bath, boy," he said to the ratty dog. "You smell like shit," and he patted Rufus' behind. Jimmy's eyes lit up, and so did his friends' when they heard that. The plan was too easy, and it did smell like shit in there. Rufus whimpered a little. Rufus smelled, but it wasn't all him.

Patch walked back across the cabin in the other direction, but before he passed the gun slot, he stopped and looked back. He saw the stinky cheese sitting on the plate with the crackers.

"Ooh—stinky cheese."

Jimmy looked at his friends. They rolled their eyes and tried not to laugh but were busting at the seams. They quickly and wisely withdrew their position and headed into the woods.

"Well, I guess that plan didn't work," Chad said. He was glad to be done with it now that he could breathe again.

"We'll need another plan, I guess," Dave said.

"Yep," Jimmy said, quite relieved because Patch was still his friend, and he knew where he could find him if he needed him. "At least Patc... the bum got something to eat," he added.

"Yeah, if you enjoy eating feet," Kevin said. They all laughed, even Chad who looked ill just thinking about it. He shuddered.

"You guys want to take the long way home or go to the road?" Jimmy asked. They shrugged.

"We aren't in any hurry. Baseball ain't for several hours," Dave said. They took to the woods.

"So how come you like that bum so much," Dave blurted out.

"Huh?"

"That Patch guy, how come you like him?" Dave repeated. Jimmy heard him the first time but wasn't sure what to say 'cause it caught him off guard. He walked through the woods, deep in thought. Jimmy wondered if this was the time to sell Patch to his friends. It didn't feel right, so he waited.

CHAPTER TWENTY-SIX

-THE NO NO-

Dusk was settling in on Walnut Creek that Monday evening as the Wildcats played host to the Clarksburg Ravens. Both teams had already arrived for the night's game and were going through their pregame warm-ups. Much of the season was riding on tonight's game for the Wildcats. A loss would put them in fourth place and almost assure them of missing the playoffs that year.

A win, on the other hand, would keep the hopes of the season alive. With four more games left after that one, it was a must win atmosphere in the sleepy little town.

There was the usual bustling about as the crowd gathered. It was a pretty good turnout for the night's game. Several of the volunteer parents were setting up the concession stand as others waited for their family meal of hot dogs and cola.

When the groundskeeper had finished lining the field and preparing the pitcher's mound, he went over to the power box and threw the switch to the on position, and the hum of electricity began to energize the lights. It had a wonderful effect on the entire town, a Norman Rockwell moment for certain.

Once the lights were warmed up, it was close to dark, and the bugs made their way to the light and could be made out as little tiny light reflections dancing about their sun. It was game time.

Jimmy got the nod to start tonight's game, and he was excited. It would be the first chance he really got to use what Patch had been teaching him. The Wildcats took the field, and a low roar from the crowd boosted them up. Everybody felt good, and they all looked very sharp.

The crowd was noisy and full of commotion. Amid it all, Jimmy heard one distinct voice call out from a distance.

"Whada ya say there, boy."

Jimmy knew immediately that Patch was somewhere near the field. As he rearranged the dirt around the mound, he scoured the crowd, but Patch wouldn't be there. He would not be welcome. Jimmy took a little extra time with his gardening to look along each foul line. Jimmy caught a glimmer of Patch's face amongst the trees beyond right field. The rest of him blended right into the tree bark, gray and craggily. In the daylight he could probably go unnoticed in there as well.

Jimmy's heart felt good, but more importantly, his confidence was high. He was absolutely brimming with it and couldn't wait to show it off. His warm-up pitches showed just how confident he was. He threw hard, and he threw strikes. Kevin was shocked as he caught for Jimmy. Between every pitch Jimmy glanced over to where he knew Patch was. It was like a shot of adrenaline each time he did.

"Batter up!" hollered the umpire. He was a portly man and waddled a little when he walked. Jimmy was pretty sure he had had this umpire once before. Remembering one thing Patch told him, Jimmy tried to recall where the umpire liked to call strikes. Advanced learning for an eleven-year-old, but it was a very valuable detail to know. But Jimmy couldn't remember how the umpire liked his strikes, so he was going to find out.

"Strike one," the umpire rang out. His calls were drawn out and exaggerated, and as Jimmy worked the first two batters, his calls favored low strikes. Jimmy struck out the next batter to end the top half of the first inning—no walks, no hits, with two strikeouts. Everyone seemed impressed.

The Wildcats tallied a run off a double by Dave, which scored Kevin all the way from first. Two more hits followed but did not produce another run. It did, however, rattle the opposing pitcher some. The teams changed places on the field.

Jimmy walked up the slight incline that made it a mound, redistributed the dirt back to his liking, and went to work. He pitched another scoreless inning, another hitless inning for the Ravens. Jimmy walked off the hill with confidence. He looked over to where Patch was and tipped his hat. He could make out his faint image. Patch nodded.

Jimmy's teammates were all fired up after Jimmy's second inning of work and greeted him so. Jimmy just took it all in and stayed focused with a smile he could not lose.

The Wildcats pounded out three more runs, one on Chad's single up the middle and two more on a double down the right field line by Jimmy. The crowd was going crazy with renewed excitement for their Wildcats. That was the team and kind of play they always knew those players were capable of. For Jimmy, it was the game of his life.

His confidence was dawning a whole new attitude for the entire team, and still it was only the third inning. Jimmy did his gardening ritual, looked for Patch, and again went to work. Three batters, three strikeouts was how the score book read when it was done. Jimmy walked off the mound again with a tip of his cap in Patch's direction. This drew the attention of some of the crowd, but as they gazed over and into the darkness, Patch slipped inconspicuously into the night.

Two more runs were pushed across in the bottom of the third by hits from the first five batters. Then the Ravens changed pitchers. Their new hurler was good and managed to get them out of the inning but not before they pushed across one more run for a 7-0 lead after three innings.

Jimmy was ready to match anybody they brought to the hill, even though none of them knew how to keep the grounds proper. Jimmy had to clean up after each one. When the dirt was just right, he was ready. The Ravens tagged Jimmy hard in the fourth inning, but the defense behind him was on some kind of mission and made two spectacular diving plays in the infield and one great lunge to snag a ball that was practically inches from the ground. Shoeless Joe himself would have been impressed.

So, after four innings, the Ravens still did not have a hit. This seemed to be the topic of discussion in the Wildcats' dugout until the coach taught the boys a little lesson about superstitions.

"You never want to step on the foul line when coming on or off the field, and you never want to chew more than three wads of gum per game." The kids giggled. "You never want to shave after a post season win." They looked at each other and then giggled even more. "And you never want to talk about a no-no until the game is over or the no-no is broken up," the coach finished.

"What's a no-no?" one of Jimmy's teammates asked. The coach looked frustrated; he would have to say it.

"When the other team has not gotten a hit," he answered.

"Are there any other, you know, rules?" Jimmy asked.

"Well, Babe Ruth only had one—touch all the bases after you hit a home run."

"Ah cool," many of them said. Did the coach know Babe Ruth?

"I'm gonna do that one," Dave bragged. His teammates razzed him a bit, and then they all settled down, trying hard not to mention the no-no!

"There is another one I've heard of," the coach started up again.

"Yeah, what's that?" Jimmy asked, very interested.

"When one of your batters is hit by a pitch, you are supposed to say don't rub it."

"Don't rub it?" Jimmy repeated.

"Yeah, I think it's less superstition than it is about being tough," the coach said. Jimmy liked that. He could have gone on all day with the coach, but it was time to play ball. Dave walked up to the plate with a shit-eating grin on his face and the biggest bat the team had in its equipment bag. He glared out at the opposing pitcher, dug his feet in, and gave the first pitch he saw a mighty swing. Strike one. The bat was as big as he was, but he could somehow get around on it. The next pitch he timed better and ended up hitting a towering shot over the center field fence. And Dave touched them all, the bases, just like he said he was going to.

Jimmy took the mound after the Wildcats put up two more runs. He was still in command of his game, and his fielders behind him were all gunning for Jimmy to get that no-no. The Wildcats needed just six more outs. Jimmy was masterful, striking out the first batter with merely three pitches.

Patch had told him to never waste pitches but to never give a batter something to hit with an 0-2 count. Jimmy did neither. Instead, he blew a high fastball right by the kid. There was one out.

It was unclear whether Jimmy had it in him to finish the game. Every other time on the mound he would hit a wall at some point and have a meltdown of sorts. The energy in every nook of the park said otherwise. Jimmy was going to finish this and finish this right. The next batter dug in. He knew what was at stake. Jimmy sent a fastball just under his chin, a message of sorts.

"Dance to that," Patch would say to any kind of chin music. The batter got back to his feet, dusted himself off, and dug right back in.

"Ball two," the umpire called out. Jimmy had let a fastball tail out of the strike zone. Jimmy showed a little frustration as he snatched the ball from midair with his glove on the throw back from Kevin.

"Focus, boy," Jimmy heard from the darkness. Patch was still there. Jimmy knew not to show emotion, something Patch had briefly touched on. Jimmy collected himself and scratched at the dirt. He hurled the next pitch to the plate. The batter fouled it off. Jimmy had to challenge him, and he did. The batter drilled the next pitch deep to center field. Eddie, clearly the fastest kid on the team, gave chase. The whole town gasped as they stood on the edge of the cold metal bleacher seats. Eddie left his feet for a last-ditch attempt at catching the ball. He caught it, and the town went berserk. That made two outs.

Jimmy smiled slightly and went back to work. Kevin encouraged him from behind his mask and gave the sign for a fastball. Jimmy didn't have any other pitches, but it was fun for them to pretend.

Jimmy glared at the next batter then hurled the first pitch belt high and a little too over the plate. The no-no was over that quick as the batter stood on second base pumping his fist in triumph with a two-out double. The town sighed. Then they all stood up and applauded. Jimmy was fighting back tears, both good and bad.

He glanced over to see Patch walk out from under the darkness and into a canopy of light. Patch was clapping with pride. He then motioned for Jimmy to tip his cap to the crowd and Jimmy did. Some of the crowd crooked their necks to where Patch was, but he had ducked back into the darkness. Jimmy dug about at the dirt.

Jimmy was then facing his biggest challenge. Could he overcome the momentum stopper as the air was let out of the tires? Even the finest ball players struggled to get out of that situation. A meltdown was in order, but dammed if Jimmy was going to let that happen. He had come too far to revert to his old ways.

"Think of what Patch would do," Jimmy muttered to himself. He looked for Patch, but the darkness was not forgiving. Had Patch left? Jimmy's answer to that would be no. The battle was always more important than the conquer, and Patch would think that was the defining moment in the game, not any bid for a no-no.

Jimmy let the next pitch fly, and into the leg of the batter it went. The batter bent over writhing in pain.

"Don't rub it," Jimmy told the batter. That drew harsh criticism from the opposing team. But Jimmy was still quite focused. He was helping the young boy. Later, his coach had to explain to him why you only say it to your own teammates.

Jimmy went back to work and answered with three fastballs that the next batter swung for but never had a chance at. Jimmy stormed off the field mightier than he ever felt before in his life.

The Wildcats now knew the only important thing was to preserve the win and so drove in two more runs as insurance. When Jimmy took the hill for the last inning, they had a substantial lead, and the game was theirs to win, and win they did.

Jimmy was again spectacular, and when it was over, he was absolutely mobbed by the entire team and coaching staff before he even got out of the infield grass. That lasted for some time, and the dust never really settled before they turned the lights out for the night. Jimmy was slightly somber in the car ride home, staring into the darkness for his friend, a friend he was endeared to. A friend he owed the game to.

"Dude, what got into you tonight?" Dave said as he, Kevin, and Chad squirmed around the backseat of Jimmy's father's car with the adrenaline left over from the game. Jimmy turned to look at his friends.

"Patch," he whispered.

"Patch!" Kevin blurted abruptly. Jimmy's parents did a quick head turn into the backseat. Jimmy rolled his eyes at his friends having forgotten the cardinal rule.

"Yeah," he said with that same quiet tone. "He's been working with me every chance I get. He knows everything about baseball. I think he played pro ball," Jimmy said.

"No way! If he played pro ball, he wouldn't be a bum now," Dave said in protest.

"It's possible. Patch is old. He could have had some hard times over the years," Chad said. The boys wondered how hard it had to be for a man to be without a home or family, to be hungry and live on the steps of a library.

"I guess," Dave said. He was skeptical. The joy of victory remained, and the ride home was short and filled with energy.

By the time the first of the boys was dropped off at his home, an accord was reached among them, an accord that would finally bring Jimmy's friends together with Patch. Jimmy was elated. They would pack a hefty lunch and set out in the morning for an all-day sojourn at the fort.

CHAPTER TWENTY-SEVEN
-RUFUS' LIFE GETS HARD-

Peanut butter and jelly seemed the consensus among their mothers, and with baseball gloves and bats in tow, into the woods the boys ventured. They took the long way for some reason. It needed to seem adventurous, a journey, not just a short hike down an old dusty road that once wielded horse-drawn carriages bringing cannon balls to the war. They wanted to feel the wrath of those cannon balls.

They stopped along the way several times, sometimes just for a snack, other times to battle dragons with fake swords. It was no ordinary passage through the woods. They made the most of their crossing. It seemed a little odd. The boys had a purpose in front of them, but they didn't let it deter them from enjoying the journey. They meandered, they strayed, and they played. Maybe it was because they were still a little scared of Patch.

It was as if they had nowhere to go. Jimmy urged them a few times to hurry it along, but he was happy slaying thirty-foot monsters as much as anyone. After the last of the giant beasts were dead, they could make out the edge of the forest as light trickled through the dense canopy. They knew those woods as well as the back of their hands, and they knew they were close to the fort. The waft of skunk was still in the air, and that was a dead giveaway too.

"So, how come Patch likes to live on the library steps?" Kevin asked. This brought the group back to reality as the clearing drew closer and closer.

"I'd camp in the woods myself," Dave said.

"He doesn't have a tent," Jimmy said.

"And the library's got a bathroom," Chad said. "I don't think I'd give up running water for a campfire."

"You would in the winter," Jimmy said with a certain surety.

"You could have both if the woods were close to the library," Kevin added. That made sense, but nobody was sure what to say next, so they walked silently for a short bit.

"He's got it made now, doesn't he?" Dave said, a little put out and disgruntled by the inconvenience of it all.

"The fort is his turtle shell," Chad said.

"Okay, Chad," the rest of them said. In a way, the fort *was* Patch's turtle shell. They hit the clearing just down from the fort and took a minute for their eyes to adjust to the rush of light. Chad was also fighting the stench of death from entering his nose. The skunk's foul-smelling odor was very prevalent and had only gotten worse the closer they got.

There was no sign of Patch anywhere in the clearing, and things seemed eerily quiet until they came up on the fort. Their presence suddenly sent Rufus into a barking frenzy. It sounded as if he was in the fort. Still no Patch as they approached.

"Patch," Jimmy called out, not wanting to sneak up on the old man. Rufus' howling might not have given it away yet. They all looked around for the man, but he did not appear. Jimmy studied the woods around the fort carefully, since Patch was an expert at camouflage. Chad was pale, but still helping.

"Maybe he's in the bathroom," Kevin said, sort of trying out a new joke.

"Maybe he's hiding until we go inside, where he jumps out and slaughters us all in cold blood," Chad blurted out. The rest of them got worried looks on their faces, all but Jimmy, even though he reserved the right to be afraid later.

"He's probably at the library checking out *Moby Dick*," Jimmy said and paused. It never got old. They all started laughing. "Let's go inside. Rufus might just be hungry."

They swung the door open and walked in. Jimmy immediately saw Patch lying on the beat-up old couch against the wall. Rufus was standing on Patch's body in a guarding posture, still barking like mad.

"Patch!" Jimmy hollered. "Patch!" But there was no response from Patch. Rufus continued barking.

"What the hell's going on?" Dave asked Jimmy.

"Patch!" Jimmy yelled. Jimmy did not look good, but Patch looked worse as he lay there motionless. They all slowly moved in closer, much like a scrum. Rufus became more protective.

"Is he dead?" Dave said.

"Chad, what do ya think? You smell death?" Jimmy asked.

Chad's eyes were watering, and he did not have a good look on his face. "It's hard to tell, but I think he's dead."

"You can smell that?" Kevin asked.

Chad looked at Kevin. "No, he looks dead, and he's not moving. You're an idiot."

Jimmy approached Patch. Rufus barked, but allowed Jimmy to inspect the situation. "Patch," Jimmy called more subdued and gave Patch a nudge. Patch did not move except for where Jimmy nudged him. Patch was cold and white like a ghost. His face was gaunt, but worse than normal. Patch was dead.

The boys all stood there staring, not knowing what to do or what to say. Jimmy had just lost a good friend, a great pitching coach, and the person responsible for Jimmy getting back his fort. Jimmy began to cry.

His friends had not formed a bond with the old man and continued to stare in disbelief. It was pretty creepy, as Patch appeared to decompose before their eyes, but he was really just worn thin to the bone, and it showed more than ever.

"What should we do?" Chad asked. Jimmy turned quickly at those words but had no response.

Kevin's eyes were wide, and he looked pale. Dave couldn't look away, but fidgeted uncontrollably. None of them had ever seen a dead body before.

"Are we sure he's dead?" Jimmy asked. Expert advice from another eleven-year-old would have been fine. His friends looked in closer at Patch, but did not actually advance their position.

"I think he's really dead," Dave said and sat in a chair behind him.

"This is so bad," Jimmy said like a grown-up would. His friends nodded in silent agreement, and then they all sat in chairs. Rufus even took a seat, but was still on top of Patch.

"What are we gonna do?" Kevin said desperately. They looked at Jimmy for leadership. He was working on it, but he was getting nowhere.

"Should we move the body?" Chad asked. No one had an answer.

"Don't know if we could, even if the dog wasn't there," Jimmy said.

"He ain't much there, but I don't think I want to be touchin' him," Dave said. They agreed. Jimmy wasn't sure why, but he also agreed.

"We can't just leave him there, can we?" Kevin said.

"I reckon not," Jimmy said. "He'll get to smellin' something awful in a day or two."

"He stinks something awful now," Dave said. Chad rubbed his nose in agreement.

"I know," Jimmy said, beginning to cry again.

"The town will likely wallop our hides for takin' him in, ya know," Chad said.

"I know," Jimmy said. His heart was pounding, and his eyes continued to leak.

"Probably lose the fort," Dave informed them.

"I know," and Jimmy's heart couldn't sink any further.

"What will happen to Rufus?" Kevin asked. They all looked at the dog that stood atop Patch. Rufus was as dirty as his owner, stunk just as bad, if not worse, and had less than a stellar disposition.

"Patch said he never owned that dog, that he was as free as any man was," Jimmy mumbled. Jimmy had a hard time saying anything right about then.

"He'll end up in the pound, ya know," Dave said.

"Who would want him?" Chad asked.

"He's free, like Patch said," Jimmy said stubbornly, with a bit of anger forming in his tone.

"Why don't you take him home, Jimmy?" Kevin suggested. Jimmy didn't say a word, just sat on Kevin's words.

After a bit, they all got up and leaned in for one last inspection, hoping maybe the old man was just sleeping, a tired sleep.

"We should go," Chad said. They all grieved one last time, for different reasons, most likely. The loss hit Jimmy the hardest. Then they left. Rufus stayed behind. They walked the path that led back to the neighborhood, but it was a mournful march with their heads bent low.

"Hey, remember Erwin," Jimmy said as they got to the spot where the poor turtle met his demise. There weren't any remnants of his spoiled body in the dirt, just his shell. They took a moment to reflect.

"He was all right," the other three said. Seems Erwin had more of an impact on the other three than Patch did.

"A lot of dying has been going around because of my fort. It started with Mrs. Wilshire's cat, the snake, then that deer we found dead, then Erwin, and now Patch. This summer ain't been so great, ya know," Jimmy said with a sigh.

The other three looked at Jimmy and wondered how he could say that. Their baseball team was close to making the playoffs and had Jimmy so quickly forgotten he had a girlfriend at age eleven? It had been quite an adventurous summer for them, and none of them had kissed Cindy. They trudged on.

Not much else was said. It seemed like they poked and examined everything they saw if it needed it or not. Their feet were soaked from the swampy water they hiked through and from top to bottom they were covered in dirt. It was a somber walk through the woods.

"I'll see ya guys later," Jimmy mumbled as they got past the clearing and to where Jimmy would normally turn to go home. Kevin followed.

"Wait, Jimmy, what are we gonna say about Patch?" Dave asked. Jimmy just stared at the ground for a moment. He sniffed back a flood of tears.

"I don't know, we'll figure it out tomorrow," and the flood of tears came pouring back out. Jimmy turned without raising his head and walked the rest of the way home.

CHAPTER TWENTY-EIGHT

—CAN I GET A DOG?—

Jimmy sulked most of the day somewhat undetected, but it would be quite the challenge to keep anything from his mother for an entire day.

"Jimmy, suppertime," she hollered up to his room. He heard it loud and clear.

"Ugh," he blurted out, somewhat startled, as his mother's voice rang up the stairs and then down his spine. Jimmy trudged down what seemed like the longest set of stairs in his life. He kept going over in his head that he must remain cool and not show any feelings. He wasn't sure how he would ever get this one past his mom though. She read him like a book, and his eyes were red and dry.

Jimmy needed a plan. He needed something to keep his mind preoccupied, something that would make for a great veil. He turned the last corner and abruptly entered the dining room.

"Mo'om, can I get a dog?" he spilled. He thought, "What genius!" coming up with that. She'd never see through him.

"No, now what's bothering you? You've been moping around all day." His mother asked. She didn't even need reading glasses.

"Nothing..." Jimmy lied.

"So why do you want a dog? And what kind of dog? Even though you aren't getting a dog. You couldn't take care of a dog..." She was cool like Jimmy wanted to be. She fired those lines like she was throwing knives at a human target, just missing her mark but with great precision. She was artful. Jimmy was doomed.

He tried clamming up, but it wasn't working.

"Let's get a dog!" Jimmy's father said. "I like the idea."

"Shut up, honey... now, Jimmy, you tell your mother what is bothering you."

"Is that meatloaf?" he gushed, as if he couldn't recognize dreaded meatloaf. He hated meatloaf. Jimmy slumped. He knew it was over. He lasted all of four minutes and two of those minutes had been walking down the stairs.

"Do you remember Patch?" Jimmy said through the tears he could no longer hold back.

"I already told you we are not getting a dog," his mother said. Jimmy was confused.

"Patch is a cool name for a dog," Jimmy's father said. His mother turned her head and shot him such a look that quieted that thought once and for all.

"No, Patch was my friend," Jimmy said.

"Was?" his dad said.

"I don't know of any Patch that lives in this town," his mother said. She looked at Jimmy's father. "Do you know this Patch fella?"

"Nope, can't say I do."

Jimmy wanted so badly to tell the story from the very day they met, to the games of catch, to scaring Dave, Chad, and Kevin like little girls, but Jimmy did not know how to start. He was pretty sure the mention of the bum on the library steps would kill the opportunity to finish his story. Jimmy wanted them to accept his friendship with the old vagrant. He wanted them to understand and make things a little better. He was certain that would not happen no matter how he told it. So, he just blurted it all out just as fast as he could.

"Patch was on the library steps that one day, Mom, do you remember? He helped me rid my fort of the girls who took it over. They had first got rid of the teenagers for us. Then he taught me how to pitch. He moved into the fort we have in the woods. He scared Dave, Chad, and Kevin once pretty good. He had nowhere else to live, Mom. He's my friend, Mom... well... not so much anymore 'cause he's dead. He's dead, Mom! He's dead..." and Jimmy broke down once again in sobs.

His parents just looked aghast. They stared at their son. His mother hugged him and let him cry. And Jimmy did just that, he cried. She rocked Jimmy in such a comforting motherly way. Jimmy felt safe. He got it all out, and it seemed as if his parents were okay with it. Jimmy sniffled.

"Where is this Patch fella now?" his mother asked calmly. Jimmy sniffed one last time, ran the back of his hand across his nose, and tried to address his mother's question.

"He's at... at the... at the fort, Mom." And the tears started over. She wasn't supposed to know about the fort.

"It's okay, Jimmy," his mother said. His father even reached over and rubbed Jimmy's back a little, and his mother and father exchanged sympathetic glances.

"Are you sure he's dead, Jimmy?" his father asked. Jimmy nodded, wiped his nose with the back of his hand again, and fought back the remaining tears. His father slumped back into his chair and really pondered the magnitude of the situation.

"Will I go to jail?" Jimmy asked.

"Nooo, oh noooo, honey," his mother said with a pat on his head and an extra firm hug for her son. "You will not go to jail, honey."

•   •   •

Soon after the emotions had simmered down a bit. Jimmy was ushered to his bedroom while the grownups figured out what to do next. A phone call to the local authority, one sheriff Earl Hicks, was in order. Earl was young and spry, relatively new to the force and quite eager to keep order and peace in this small town. A call like that could easily wake him from his afternoon nap. Jimmy's father hung up the phone with the sheriff and turned to his wife. "Well, that's done."

"What are they planning on doing?" Jimmy's mom asked.

"Me and a couple of the boys are going to meet Earl down at the station then all head over together to inspect the body."

"Did you even have a clue that Jimmy was friends with some old town vagrant?" she asked her husband.

"Not a clue. It sounds as if they've been friends most of the summer," he replied.

"The things that boy gets into, I swear," she said. "Are you taking Jimmy?"

"No, just some of the guys, probably Tommy and Fred, maybe Sam. I don't think the kids should be there."

"I think that's a good idea. Jimmy's been through too much as it is. I still can't believe he's been able to keep this from us all this time."

"I know, I know," Jimmy's father said, letting out an exasperated sigh.

"Are you going out there tonight?"

"No, I think we'll head out first thing in the morning. Those woods can be strange enough in the daylight, ya know. Yeah, we'll wait until daybreak, get up there early, and figure this thing out."

Jimmy's father paused again and then got a stupid, silly look on his face that only Jimmy's mother knew.

"We are not getting a dog!" she said.

CHAPTER TWENTY-NINE

-PATCH'S REMAINS-

Jimmy cried himself to sleep that night. It was no surprise that it was going to be a long night, a lonely night, and no matter what Jimmy did, he could not shake the feeling of pain and even guilt that he had. He blamed the entire summer on himself. He was pretty sure it was the worst summer of his life, and considering he had only a few he could actually remember, he was right.

It was indeed the only summer he lost a good friend. But he hadn't stopped to consider any of the good things that happened to him that summer. He made two friends, but it was hard to contemplate that when one of them had died. Jimmy lost his fort three times during the summer but did eventually get to stake claim to it, at least he had. He wasn't sure how the adults would react to this latest predicament. Then it occurred to him, his mother didn't bat an eye when he mentioned the fort. So, did she know all along? Jimmy could only assume she had. He was pretty sure that fort was as good as gone. His baseball career was just beginning to take off, but without his new pitching coach, who knew what would happen. He would probably go back to playing in right field.

Jimmy was so exhausted from crying all night that he slept clear through daybreak. That turned out to be a good thing, giving his father and the other adults a chance to put some daylight between them and the boys if the boys had decided to venture out that way. And apparently, that was exactly what Jimmy was thinking when he woke.

His thoughts were hectic the moment he opened his eyes. He was groggy and his eyes bloodshot from all the crying, but he quickly made his way downstairs with a daypack stuffed for whatever the day would bring. He was looking for his dad, fearing that once again he would be left behind because he was only a kid.

"Mo'om!" Jimmy hollered. He rounded the hallway into the kitchen where he found his mother in the middle of baking something wonderful smelling.

"Good morning, sweetie," That took Jimmy by surprise. He was immediately suspicious. His mom was being a little too sweet, and she was baking cookies. Something was not right. His mom's eyes settled on the pack Jimmy was toting, but she said nothing. She placed a warm batch of chocolate chip cookies on a rack to cool.

Jimmy eyed them closely. He considered reaching out and just snatching one off the rack and stuffing it into his mouth before his mother even knew what happened. Then he looked up and into his mother's eyes, and he stopped himself.

It most certainly was a trap, a good one too. She moved more cookies onto the cooling rack. She had a coy expression, one that would have given Jimmy the false impression he could get away with eating cookies for breakfast. Jimmy was onto her, but the draw of fresh baked anything from that woman was hard to pass up.

"What's for breakfast?" he asked. And just as soon as he blurted that out, he remembered he did not have time for breakfast. He needed to gather Kevin, Dave, and Chad as soon as possible and get down to the fort. Those cookies were blurring his thoughts.

He had overheard enough of the discussion before to know his father was headed to the fort with some other men. Using a truck, they would certainly get there way ahead of Jimmy. He was at a loss. He needed to go.

"How does blueberry pancakes sound, honey?" his mother said. Jimmy was abruptly brought back to the food.

"Mom, I need to go to the fort. And I need to go now," he said.

"You'll have your breakfast first, then I'm going to take you out there a bit later," his mother explained. Jimmy cocked his head to the side. He was certain of what he just heard. He couldn't believe it, but he was certain he heard it. "Kevin is coming along too. Chad and Dave will meet you there," she said.

Jimmy was confused well beyond all eleven years. He thought of running off. He eyed those cookies then moved his eyes to the door. His mother had busied herself with the pancake making. She was scooping out pancake flour with a tin measuring cup then leveling the top with a knife-edge for an exact measure, all as if nothing was wrong. Her back was to the door and the cookies. Jimmy slunk down at the table totally confused.

"When are we going? Is Dad coming with us? Can we go now?" Jimmy was just blurting out everything that came to him.

"Relax and have a cookie," his mother said. She was playing this way too cool. Jimmy's suspicion was correct, and he thought those cookies were most likely poisonous or at least laced with something that would stop him from leaving the house. His mother walked over to the cookies, filled a plate full, and placed them in front of Jimmy. Jimmy sat back and stared down at his plate full of cookies. Jimmy did not eat a cookie. In fact, Jimmy barely moved.

"Honey, it's ok," his mom said as she noticed his reaction. She grabbed a cookie and took a bite. "See, they're ok. Have a cookie."

Who was this woman, and what had she done with Jimmy's mother? He took a cookie. How did she know? He took a bite. He watched his mother's reaction. He wondered if his mother had it in her to poison her only son. She patted him on the head, turned back to the stove, and poured out the batter to make pancakes. Okay, maybe she wasn't capable of that. He finished the cookie. Then he ate another before attacking a stack of pancakes.

"Can we go now, Mom?" he asked politely. She turned to her son and wiped her hands on her apron.

"Go up and clean your room."

"What?" he screamed. "You tricked..."

"Jimmy! Go up and clean your room. We'll be heading out right before lunch, I promise," she said. "But until then, I want you to clean your room."

He heard everything she said. He was very much aware of her stall tactics, and he wasn't too pleased about it either.

"Mo'om."

"Go now, or we won't be going out to your fort. You hear me? Now off you go." He felt betrayed. He stomped up the stairs as if he was counting each one of them for his mother to hear. Then he slammed the door to his room shut. Jimmy slumped to the floor waiting for the poison to kill him. He was not about to clean his room, especially if he was going to die. That woman was not clever enough for him. He would be dead soon, he thought, and from cookie poisoning. She could clean his room after he was gone. That would show her.

When the time came and Jimmy's mother finally came calling for him to go, he darted out of his room, down the stairs, and to the front door of the house to leave. He had his pack in tow, jacket half pulled on, one shoe trailing laces as he ran.

"Tie your shoe..."

"Come on, Mo'om," he said and quickly dropped to tie his shoe. "Where's Kevin?"

The doorbell rang that very moment, and it startled Jimmy a little. He hopped up, shoe tied and all, and swung open the door. Kevin and his mother stood quietly at the door.

"Hey, Jimmy," Kevin said. He didn't seem as eager to get to the fort as Jimmy, but Jimmy was glad just the same that he was going with him. He could do without all the mothers though.

"Hi, Janet," Jimmy's mom said as she gave her hair a last-second primping before reaching out to shake her hand. "I'm so glad you could come."

"No problem. It's just terrible what happened," Janet said. Jimmy and Kevin shot each other a glance. Kevin's mom didn't even know Patch. Jimmy was certain she wouldn't have approved of him either.

"It is. It's just horrible," Jimmy's mom replied. Jimmy shot Kevin another look. "Did Mr. Spencer make it out this morning with the others?"

"Yes, he did. We are so thankful you included us. We had no idea of this whole situation until you called us." Janet said. They piled into the Hamilton's station wagon and headed out.

"Chad and Dave coming?" Kevin whispered to Jimmy in the back seat.

"Yeah, I think. Mom, Chad and Dave are coming, right? You said…"

"Yes, dear, they're on their way. I spoke to their mothers earlier," Jimmy's mom replied. Jimmy glanced at Kevin and shrugged. Why everybody's mother needed to be involved Jimmy wasn't sure. They must be part of some kind of club, too.

Their moms gossiped quietly in the front seat. Jimmy tried to listen for information on Patch, but their tone came and went. Jimmy knew moms had a type of listening device implanted where they could whisper so softly that only another mom could hear it. He wanted that kind of stuff for his club, but that was neither here nor there 'cause he was pretty sure his club was no longer.

Jimmy tried to whisper top-secret stuff to Kevin, but every time he did, he noticed his mother shot him a look in the rearview mirror. It was hopeless, so he just sulked out the rest of the short drive to the fort. When they turned down the dirt road, it was quite apparent that it was not any kind of town secret. People were hiking in along the dirt road, and at least one car was up ahead of them. It was more like some sort of town gathering. As they neared the fort, it seemed nearly everyone from town was there. The sheriff and his deputy were there. The fire department even had a truck and several firemen there. And the coroner was there. Such a crowd had gathered in front of the fort. Jimmy couldn't see the fort from the car. He was aghast. That was his fort, and Patch was his friend. None of these people should be there.

When the car came to a stop, Jimmy jumped out so fast you couldn't see him in the dust trail he made. He ran to get to the front of the crowd. He wanted to see Patch. Jimmy knew he was still dead, but he wanted to say goodbye, and wanted to thank him for being a friend, and thank him for teaching him how to pitch. Jimmy wanted to give him the game ball he had gotten from the day he nearly pitched that no-no. He wanted to see Rufus and try to pet him.

He pushed through the crowd with Kevin following close behind. Dave and Chad caught Jimmy rushing by, and all four made a beeline for the fort. The last row of spectators to clear proved a little harder to pass, but they got through. They stopped dead in their tracks with the fort directly in front of them.

The firemen had roped the area off, and the deputy and a few other men were keeping people back. Jimmy tried desperately to break the barrier to get into the fort but was stopped cold by a fireman. Jimmy's father appeared from the fort's door followed by the fire chief, another fireman, and the sheriff.

Jimmy's father and the other three approached another man in plain clothes. The man's jacket had a small tag on it. It read County Coroner. Jimmy listened in the best he could.

"We could just leave him in there," the sheriff said.

"I agree," said the coroner, who seemed very disinterested.

"Be more trouble than it's worth not to, plus the guy will get one hell of a sendoff. I mean look at all these people." Jimmy's dad motioned towards the sizeable crowd gathered by.

"All right then," said the sheriff.

"Any sign of a dog around," Jimmy's dad asked.

"Nobody's seen one, sir," the firemen said. Jimmy eyed the woods for two beady eyes maybe watching all the craziness. He saw nothing. Rufus blended into the trees the same as Patch did, so he would not see him. That poor dog would probably be a scavenger the rest of his life. He was in for a rough go.

"Let's get these people moved back a bit," the fire chief said. The firemen spread themselves out, making a perimeter around the fort, moving the bystanders back.

"OKAY BURN IT DOWN!" the sheriff hollered. Two more firemen appeared with contraptions that shot fire. They took their flamethrowers to the fort. It caught quickly and went up in a blaze. Jimmy broke from the crowd just briefly before his father caught him and held him tightly while trying to console and explain. Jimmy knew Patch was still in the fort.

In no time, the fort was completely engulfed in flames. Jimmy broke down, and his hand, which had been clutching that game ball, let go. He wept like he had never wept before. The ball bounced off the dirt and rolled a few feet from the crowd towards the fort and came to a stop.

The entire town just stared on in wonder. Patch had only one true friend in that town, but everyone from Walnut Creek came to see his funeral. The townsmen working around the fort scurried about keeping the fire from spreading to the nearby brush.

Jimmy, Kevin, Chad, and Dave watched from the front row of the crowd. It was intense, the heat and sounds of fire were almost overwhelming. Jimmy continued to cry. Everything he knew, everything about this summer was now on fire. He felt alone, even standing next to his friends. He eyed the baseball that was too close to the fire to retrieve when, suddenly, a cool, comforting hand slid into his. It was small like his, and it felt good. He turned in that direction. It was Cindy. She smiled in a comforting way and squeezed his hand just a little bit more. Jimmy looked down at his hand in Cindy's and knew right then that things would be all right. They would never be the same, but they would be all right.

THE END

ACKNOWLEDGMENT

A journey is seldom taken alone. Those you encounter along the way can have a significant influence on the person you become. A special thank you needs to go out to those who have crossed my path. At a young age I had a baseball coach, Coach Will. He taught me so much about the game of baseball, how to respect it, and most importantly how to enjoy it. The baseball description may not have had the same impact without that. To the many teachers who encouraged me to succeed, I would say it's possible that I finally deserve that most improved award.

I would like to recognize and thank most of all, my wife, Marcia. She has been there for me through every typed word and every page read to her. She has supported me and encouraged me to go beyond where I would have stopped.

And a special thank you goes out to my editor, Mary Ellen. She helped a good story become better.

ABOUT THE AUTHOR

Paul Jantzen grew up in what would be described as typical Americana, and from an early age, he was fascinated with the art of storytelling. He loves captivating his audiences with his imagination and sense of humor. He took up filmmaking in college and his first short film, *The Leopard Frog*, debuted on the USA network in 1991. Though he does enjoy a good novel here and there, he was never big on reading, so he decided to write a book instead. *Sour Apples* is his debut novel. He currently resides in Frederick, MD and enjoys the outdoors.

NOTE FROM PAUL JANTZEN

Word-of-mouth is crucial for any author to succeed. If you enjoyed *Sour Apples*, please leave a review online—anywhere you are able. Even if it's just a sentence or two. It would make all the difference and would be very much appreciated.

Thanks!
Paul Jantzen

We hope you enjoyed reading this title from:

BLACK ROSE
writing™

www.blackrosewriting.com

Subscribe to our mailing list – *The Rosevine* – and receive **FREE** books, daily deals, and stay current with news about upcoming releases and our hottest authors.
Scan the QR code below to sign up.

Already a subscriber? Please accept a sincere thank you for being a fan of Black Rose Writing authors.

View other Black Rose Writing titles at
www.blackrosewriting.com/books and use promo code
PRINT to receive a **20% discount** when purchasing.

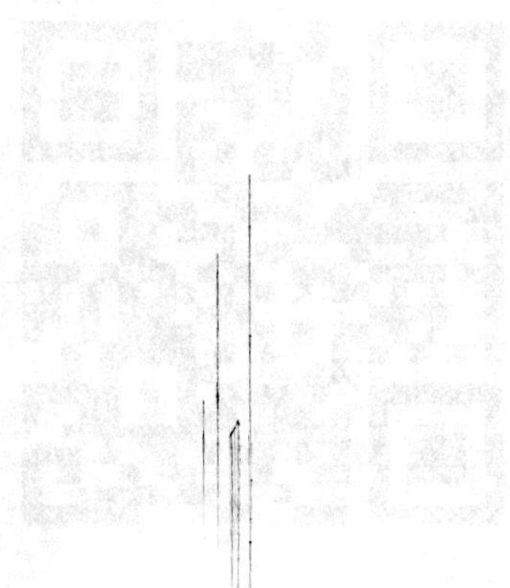